Murder at Tapestry Court

by Amy Barkman

Murder at Tapestry Court

© 2012, 2016 by Amy Barkman

Published by Voice of Joy Publications. www.voiceofjoy.com

All Scripture quotations are from the King James Version.

Cover design by Nick Delliskave.

Endorsements

"*Murder at Tapestry Court* is exactly the kind of mystery I enjoy most—engaging characters, charming setting, an intriguing mystery, and just the right amount of romance. I couldn't put it down."

~ Virginia Smith, author of *Dangerous Impostor* and *Bullseye*

"The heinous murder in the beautiful setting of Tapestry Court hides a dark secret—and an even darker proclivity. Amy Barkman's *Murder at Tapestry Court* is an old-fashioned whodunnit with an interesting cast of characters, an idyllic setting, and great description. This cozy mystery is contains all the elements for a fun read and the guessing game that goes along with every mystery."

~ A.K. Arenz, 2010 Carol Award Winner, *The Case of the Mystified M.D.*, Book 2 of The Bouncing Grandma Mystery Series

Murder at Tapestry Court is a place you want to visit and never leave. This cozy mystery has multiple characters and clues to keep you reading in an attempt to piece it all together before the heroine does. All wrapped up in a spiritual message of letting God speak to us and heal our souls.

~ Rose Allen McCauley, author of "Nick's Christmas Carol" in *Christmas Belles of Georgia*

Amy Barkman writes about life with wisdom, wit, and knowledge of the soul. The mystery in *Murder at Tapestry Court* kept me guessing to the end, and the characters charmed me from the beginning. Fun. Lively. Poignant. That's how I'd describe this delightful cozy mystery.

~ Victoria Bylin, 2010 Carol Award nominee

Tapestry Court is a divided community of secrets and hidden truths. Ms. Barkman plants Elizabeth Daily in their midst to cleverly weave the characters together with prayer and love revealing the beautiful picture tapestry of the Divine Creator and His desire for true community.

~ Jan Sullivan, author of *Forever Family*, *Never Alone*, and *Stand Strong*, Christian fiction for teens.

Amy Barkman surprises throughout. *Tapestry Court* seems an ordinary gated community until the warped underside begins to poke through the weft. New arrival Elizabeth, herself damaged by self-doubt and a pressing decision is the unwelcome tool that threatens to unrravel the secret of Tapestry Court. While exposing the mysteries of the past, she brings healing and restoration not only to the damaged tapestry, but also to herself. An excellent read.

~ Jim Cook, author of *The Third Hand*

Dedication

This book is dedicated to cozy mystery lovers everywhere, especially Agatha Christie fans. Murder at Tapestry Court began as my attempt to recreate an English village atmosphere in central Kentucky where I live. It grew into a desire to show real people overcoming emotional weaknesses and trauma by the powerful mercy of God through our Lord Jesus Christ. I'm grateful to all the American Christian Fiction Writer's critique group and Gail Louis who helped me make my first edits. Special thank-you's go to Virginia Patrick Smith, Susie Patrick Smith, and Jacque Lea who believed in the story and believed in me.

Tapestry Court
Drawn by Chuck Tate

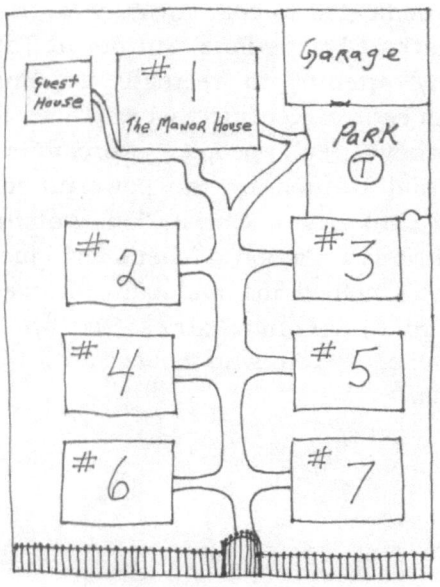

The Residents of Tapestry Court

Number 1. The Manor House has stood empty for the decade since the murder of its builder, Colonel Guy Tapestry. But now Elizabeth Daily has taken up residence for a year's sabbatical. Her friend, Galen Delaney, becomes a regular visitor to the guest house as the two of them try to decipher the Colonel's will. Somebody doesn't like their meddling - at all!

Number 2. Emily Caine devoted her life to Colonel Tapestry and has occupied this house, closest in proximity to the Manor House, since it was built. She resents the intrusion of outsiders in the Court. Her housekeeper Hattie Griffin has served Tapestry Court residents since she was a teen. She raised both George Tate and Charles Simmons. Hattie would do anything for her boys.

Number 3. Jenny Anderson received her home as a gift from the Colonel when her parents, long time employees of Tapestry Industries, died in a car wreck during her teen years. She and Joel have lived there since their marriage. But Jenny doesn't act grateful for her home. And why does she avoid the Manor House?

Number 4. George and Linda Tate along with their children, Reggie and Chuck, love their house. George grew up there as the orphaned nephew of Emily Caine, along with another orphan, Charles Simmons. Hattie is the closest thing to a parent either of them have ever known. Lately Linda fears her husband's distraction is shaking the foundations of their happy home.

Number 5. Directly across the courtyard from where he grew up, Charles Simmons lives with his beautiful wife, Mindy. What a shame he doesn't seem to appreciate her as much as their neighbor Bill Sinclair does. Has he even noticed? Everyone else has.

Number 6. Bill Sinclair is the only "new" resident at the Court. He came to Tapestry Industries as a salesman and was kept on as a trusted employee. Is he the unknown son and heir referred to in the Colonel's will?

Number 7. Harold Fowler, retired pastor and missionary, lives out his retirement there with his wife, Lucy Tapestry Fowler, the Colonel's sister. Bored with the retirement he so longed for, he is unashamedly glad to help Elizabeth sort out her emotions and make decisions. Why, then, doesn't he encourage his wife to expose her painful secrets - even in the interest of truth?

Chapter One

Chuck Tate refused to budge from the stoop in front of Number Four, Tapestry Court, despite admonitions from his mother concerning homework, or the temptation of freshly baked chocolate chip cookies whose fragrance at any other time would draw him like a magnet. The cookies would keep. His sixteen year old sister was on a diet and his parents never ate sweets anyway. Today was a big day and he didn't want to miss his chance.

Pink and white trees stood between him and the gate that guarded the entrance of the private community in which he lived. He strained to see through the branches, watching for any sign of movement. He had it all planned. If the woman rang the bell, he'd be the first to answer it. If she didn't, he'd introduce himself during her walk from the first gate to the one that led into the lawn of Number One, the Manor House. If she had a bag, he'd offer to carry it for her. Most of her stuff came last night by parcel service but Dad wouldn't let him go with the men to put the boxes and trunks in the house. He hoped she'd be carrying a suitcase so he could make a good impression right from the start. The mysterious Manor House had stood empty as long as he could remember. He wanted to be invited inside. Wanted it so bad his teeth gritted all by themselves when he thought about it. The whole place was off limits by order of everyone, especially his Great Aunt Emily. But he slipped into the grounds any time he thought he could escape the watchful eyes of the Court residents.

Chuck didn't like his great aunt and suspected that his father didn't either. George Tate told Chuck to treat her with kindness and respect because she had taken over the task of raising George when he was orphaned shortly after birth. But even while Dad was listing the reasons why they should feel grateful, Chuck could sense that he understood.

Chuck often grumbled about the restrictions concerning the manor property. "You'd think it was *her* house."

"She had a lot to do with designing and decorating it," was his father's response. "She wants to make sure it stays in perfect shape."

"All I want to do is look." But neither pleading nor reasoning had any effect. So, his furtive explorations were always brief and doomed to end in frustration. He'd discovered and named the "secret garden" which was actually no secret, but the brick wall enclosing it and the deserted fishpond within created a mysterious atmosphere which demanded the name. As much as he tried, Chuck could discover no hidden access to the house.

Now someone was coming to live there after all these years - ten years, his father said. The house had been empty since Chuck was only one year old. He hoped the new resident was not grouchy like Great Aunt Emily. But even if she was, he determined to make her like him in order to gain entrance to the house.

The Reverend Harold Fowler, retired, watched with amusement as his wife diligently dusted each piece of bric-a-brac in the front room of Number Seven, Tapestry Court. Her gaze strayed repeatedly through the window toward the front gate.

"Poor lady," he remarked, directing his comment to the oriental carpet.

His wife turned from her careful inspection of a jade figurine on the table in front of the window.

"What are you talking about, Harold?" she asked with an air of innocence that her husband recognized. It appeared when she suspected he was seeing through her.

"First night in her new home and half of the Court will descend to inspect her belongings and the lady herself."

"Well, I certainly won't." Lucy Fowler drew her little body upright with dignity. "I shall give her at least two days to settle in...before calling to welcome her."

No one but her husband of fifty five years would have suspected the effort with which she hastily revised her plans in acquiescence to his subtle reminder of the dictates of genteel behavior. He knew that during her years as a pastor's wife, before coming to live at Tapestry Court, she had considered it her duty to call on new arrivals in the community at the earliest possible moment. Now, as she sighed, he knew she was realizing that here she had no official standing . . . or excuse.

"Unless, of course, as Guy's only relative here, you think I should . . ."

"No, my dear. I don't think that is necessary." Harold Fowler picked up the paper from his lap and returned to his perusal of it. He had fulfilled his duty.

Next door at Number Five, Mindy Simmons heard the clock chime the half hour. She wiped the excess body lotion from her hands onto a tissue and slipped her black shorts on over the pink panties that looked so nice against her newly acquired tan. The matching bra was then covered by an aqua sleeveless pullover. She hoped Charles would notice the tan. She hoped he would notice the new lingerie. Mindy spent a lot of time hoping her husband would notice things.

Bill noticed things. And maybe that was natural, but surely her husband should too. Had she and Bill made a mistake at the time she married Charles Simmons? It was a question continually on her mind lately.

Mindy went down the steps and into the kitchen to begin the process of preparing Charles' dinner. She left partially chopped vegetables a few times to peer out the front window.

At Number Three, between the Simmons' house and Tapestry Court Park, Jenny Anderson paused the DVD just as Daryl Hannah, having had her true identity as a mermaid exposed to the world, threw a desperate look at Tom Hanks for help. "Splash" was one of Jenny's favorite movies but since she had seen it dozens of times, it did not seem irreverent to leave the heroine frozen in the poignant moment. Not when something new was actually happening in the Court.

The walk was still empty; no sign of Number One's new tenant. Of course it would take a few minutes to get here from town. Jenny hoped Miss Daily would be nice. Not that Jenny wanted to visit her in that house. The thought sent a slight shudder through her frame, and she quickly turned back to the remote control. Movies kept her from being alone with her thoughts.

She hoped she would be able to hear the gate bell over the noise of the film.

Across the brick walk from the Andersons, Miss Emily Caine sniffed.

She tightened her lips as Hattie Griffin, who had been in her employ for nearly fifty years, looked out the front door at short intervals with what her employer considered shameless inquisitiveness.

"We will see the woman soon enough, Hattie," Miss Caine observed in her favorite icy tone. "Quite soon enough."

Emily Caine was not pleased with George Tate's decision to lease the manor house at Tapestry Court. She should have been consulted. After all, having Number Two, which was closest, the state of affairs would affect her more than the others. At the least, she should have been able to interview the prospective tenant. Who knew what was being thrust upon them? The woman was arriving by bus...surely not a lady. A widow, George had said. And a friend of Galen Delaney's. Miss Emily Caine did not like that. She didn't like it at all.

She picked up her Bible and turned to a much-read passage. *"For yet a little while, and the wicked shall not be: yea thou shalt diligently consider his place, and it shall not be."*

Hattie Griffin looked around just as her employer gave a little nod at the book in her lap. Good. Miss Emily would be engrossed for a while. Hattie would be free to look for the new lady all she wanted without those censorious eyes burning into the back of her neck.

"How deceptive."

Elizabeth Daily stood motionless at the sight before her. Barely seen behind the pink and white dogwoods that lined the walk, each of the six houses facing one another, three to a side, reminded her of English cottages. And she knew from Galen's description that the manor house at the far end, though hidden from her view by the foliage, was architecturally the same style. Colonel Tapestry had attempted to recreate a small English village environment at the edge of the central Kentucky town that housed his company. Elizabeth had seen enough attempts at grandeur that ended in pretentiousness during her forty five years to doubt that it could be done, but now she nodded her head in tribute. He had accomplished his goal. But the murder put a sudden stop to his enjoyment of the creation.

On her three block walk from Simpsonton's business district she had seen only one small store, one tiny house, and acres of empty but well kept lots. Isolated from the rest of civilization, Tapestry Court appeared to be serene and free from the frenzies of the fast paced world outside its boundaries. And that suited her very well. But then she remembered. Deceptive.

The iron fence, she was told, enclosed the entire six residential acres with only two accesses, this gate before her and another leading from the multiple garage facility at the back of the property. She hesitated just as she inserted the key in the slot. Suddenly she felt like an intruder instead of a person coming to her new home.

"Ridiculous!" Nevertheless she rang the bell hanging above the oversized box that announced in old English lettering that it would receive mail for

Tapestry Court Residents.

She told herself that she rang it only to see what would happen but she suspected that she really wanted to be welcomed.

In seconds, a sandy-haired boy bounded out from between the trees fronting the second house on her left. He stopped a few feet inside the gate.

"Hello." His eyes made a quick sweep from the top of her head to her feet.

"Hello. I'm Elizabeth Daily. I've leased Number One."

"Hi." He grinned. Elizabeth thought she must have passed inspection.

"May I come in?" She turned the key as she asked the question.

"Sure." He pulled the gate open to let her pass through. "I thought it was too early for the mailman's ring."

Concluding that meeting the mailman was a regular task for the boy, she asked, "Do you pick up the mail for everyone?" She closed the gate behind her, careful to latch it back.

"Yes ma'am. Great Aun . . .I mean Miss Caine always did it, but she can't walk too good anymore and so now I do it." He looked up at her. "Can I carry your suitcase?"

"Why, thank you." She smiled at him, resisting the urge to correct his grammar. "Have the rest of my things arrived, do you know?"

"They got here last night. Dad let the men in the house." He paused. "Ms. Daily, is there just you? I mean, do you have any kids?"

Elizabeth laughed. "Sorry, there's just me. I would have liked children but they never came. What is your name?"

The blush made his freckles stand out. Chuck set the case down and stuck out his hand. "I'm Chuck Tate," he said proudly and then his face fell, "Maybe you'd rather call me Charles. Everybody around here does." He made it sound like a sentence of doom.

"Chuck it is." And she grinned at the relief in his eyes.

They continued down the brick path. At one point she saw a movement in a window to her right and wondered how many of the residents of Tapestry Court were watching their progress.

"I'll try to make it up to you . . .about the children, I mean. I bake great homemade bread. And you can come have some whenever you like." She hadn't meant to say that. She'd arrived with great vistas of uninterrupted privacy in mind.

"Really?" Excitement lit his features, but faded in the next moment. He heaved a sigh. "I didn't mean to be rude. It's just that . . ."

"Everybody around here is old?"

He nodded. "My sister's the only other kid and she's boring."

He opened the second gate, and they entered the lawn surrounding the manor house.

A grove of lilac bushes in full bloom grew up to the walk from their right and the fragrance drew her back to a memory of little girls playing dolls on a blanket beneath heavenly smelling blooms in a springtime four decades past.

To the left of the walk, the branches of dogwood trees intertwined to form a pink and white lace screen between them and the house.

A brick walk wound around and through the trees, and then they were there. The house was all she had imagined. A small porch was created by the front door being inset a few feet behind the archway, and another archway to the left made way for the walk to wander between the main house and the guest cottage. The weathered brick and multipaned windows were exactly what she hoped for. It was the kind of house she had seen in pictures and dreamed of living in. Galen was right. She loved it.

"Ma'am," Chuck tugged on her sleeve, dragging her attention from the quaint surroundings. "The key is under the mat. Dad left it for you when he went to work this morning."

As she retrieved the key and unlocked the door, Elizabeth hesitated. She could tell that the boy wanted to come in with her; but she really wanted to have her first moments in this magic place alone. She took the suitcase and said gently, "Thank you,Chuck. Come back and see me soon."

His face fell.

"Let's see," she added hastily, "today is Tuesday. I should have that bread ready by Friday afternoon. Would you like to come to tea around four?"

Interest leaped into his brown eyes. "Tea? Like in the movies?"

Elizabeth Daily winked at him. "In a place like this, one should certainly have tea, don't you think?"

He grinned and nodded. "See you Friday." And he whirled around to leap down the walk. But before she could enter, he yelled back, "Dad said if you need anything, just come to Number Four." She nodded and watched him disappear behind the lacy curtain of dogwood blossoms before she turned and walked inside.

The interior was not a disappointment. Polished wood gleaming in the entrance hall did not look like the house had been shut up for nearly ten years, and she was sure she smelled the fragrance of fresh furniture polish. A beautifully carved newel post and shining banister seemed to warn you to wear gloves when touching their shining surfaces. She set her bag at the foot of the steps and opened the door on her right.

The library was everything Galen promised. It ran the length of the house and smelled of leather and adventures bound with paper chains just waiting to be set free to live again in her mind. A gigantic fieldstone fireplace covered most of the back wall.

Crossing the hallway she peered into the parlor. One wouldn't dare call it a living room; it was most definitely an old fashioned parlor. She was amazed that a man had created this room for himself. A white, delicately carved mantle surrounded the fireplace, and on either side stood a small Victorian rocking chair with a rose velvet seat and back. A Steinway spinet sat against one wall on the deep rose carpet; the couch and draperies were of matching fabric in shades of delicate pinks and blues. Period oval tables held beautifully shaped china pieces, and a freshly cut bunch of lilacs in a Waterford vase rested on the white wicker sewing table which served only as a decoration.

The next room was a formal dining area complete with sideboard and crystal chandelier. From there the hallway led her to the kitchen which she judged to be directly behind the parlor. Peering in an opening to the left of the kitchen she saw a utility room boasting a washer and dryer, ironing board, and folding table.

From the kitchen, the hallway led to the downstairs bath and back to the entrance hall. Elizabeth picked up her suitcase and ascended the stairs.

Immediately at the top of the steps was another bathroom. Two left turns led her down the hallway to what she knew would be her master bedroom as soon as she saw it. Again she found herself intrigued by the man who had lived here. Moss green velvet with gold and white accents gave her the impression of stepping inside the boudoir of a woodland elf queen.

She left the case beside her bed and followed the hallway back until she found another room beyond the bath. Obviously a guestroom, and again exquisitely decorated, this room had a cheerful cherry blossom motif. She could picture her treasured antique yard sale pitcher and bowl sitting at the right of the dresser.

The house was surprisingly perfect. She didn't see one thing she wished to change.

Elizabeth walked back down the stairs. She paused only to purposely leave a fingerprint on the gleaming wood.

"There." She nodded with satisfaction. "I've made my mark on you. You are going to be my home."

Two hours later she had her own teakettle whistling away on the stove and her dishes stacked neatly in the spacious cabinets.

Galen had made sure there were supplies waiting for her, and she laughed when she unwrapped the white butcher paper, discovering fresh steamed crabmeat. He often teased her that one day she would start walking sideways because of all the crabmeat she consumed. She finished putting the salad together just as the water was ready for tea.

Elizabeth looked around at the English country kitchen. Why hadn't she taken the time to find out more about the private life of the man who had designed this house in which she immediately felt at home?

She knew a lot about his public personality. Colonel Guy Raymond Tapestry profited toward the end of the depression as a very young man. He bought a small bankrupt casket factory on the outskirts of Simpsonton and proceeded to build it into the leading casket manufacturing concern in the country. Though he later acquired other manufacturing companies, that first acquisition of Tapestry Industries remained his great love. Eventually an office building was erected near the factory and from there he managed his vast empire. At the same time, on the other side of town, he bought the ten acres bounded by the mountain and turned six of them into the picturesque Tapestry Court.

According to Galen, Colonel Tapestry never married but surrounded himself with a family atmosphere by populating his mini-village with employees whom he trusted. But that didn't explain the romantic personality that permeated this house.

A strange man, a man of paradoxes. Ruthless in business but generous to those close to him. Obviously a man of excellent taste, and a romantic according to the testimony of the house. A man who, despite all his business acumen, left a will which had been impossible to settle during the ten years since his death. A man whom someone had hated enough to kill. A man whose murderer had walked free and undetected for over a decade. A mystery man.

Elizabeth Daily had come to Tapestry Court to unravel the mysteries in her own life.

But while she was here . . .

Chapter Two

Elizabeth dried the cup and returned it to the shelf. She looked around the kitchen, a feeling of deep satisfaction settling over her at the neatness and the atmosphere. She would have a long bath and reread *Murder at the Vicarage*, her favorite Miss Marple adventure.

Mysteries were exciting. Even tame ones like the discoveries she made during her years of researching, both for college work and to make extra money to pay for her education. Her researching skills were what led her here.

Galen wants me to find an heir. Who knows, maybe my lifelong fascination with fictional mysteries will pay off and I'll discover a murderer as well.

It had been six weeks since Galen told her about this place as well as the big question that needed to be untangled regarding the life of Guy Tapestry.

Seated at Mike's, a pile of empty crab leg shells between them, the thought had crossed her mind that other empty shells separated them more surely than those on the table. Her past was confusing but the success of her first and only book had catapulted her into an emotional dilemma that could no longer be ignored.

A lump sprang to her throat at the memory of sadness in Galen's eyes when he recognized that she was now farther away from accepting his proposal of marriage than before. She reached across the table and slipped her hand into his, "I need to know who I am and what my life is all about before I can decide what to do with the rest of it. Please understand."

A chime startled her, bringing her back to the present; her watch showed twenty past seven. Surely the clock wouldn't...

Not the clock. The door bell.

An elderly woman stood on the porch, squarely in front of the door, grey hair knotted tightly, hands fixed on a handbag. An African American woman watched from the walk behind her.

"I am Emily Caine." After making this terse announcement, the elderly woman turned to her companion, "You may return for me in twenty minutes, Hattie."

With a slight nod, Hattie walked off in the opposite direction. Miss Caine gave her no further notice but fixed a stern and slightly disapproving stare on Elizabeth.

Since she obviously was to be given no choice in the matter, Elizabeth opened the door wider and smiled a welcome. "Won't you come in, Miss Cain?"

Miss Caine made her way to the parlor where she chose a spot on the sofa.

"Sit down, my dear." A slender hand patted the cushion beside her.

Elizabeth sat, feeling as she had felt at the gate to Tapestry Court - an intruder.

"I am your closest neighbor, at Number Two." Emily Caine's eyes scanned the room and she gave a barely perceptible nod as she spotted the vase of lilacs.

"I hope everything is to your liking?" But it wasn't really a question. It was obvious to Elizabeth that Miss Caine had no doubt anyone would be pleased with the manor house.

Elizabeth smiled. "Thank you for the flowers. They made me feel very welcome. And yes, everything is lovely."

Again Miss Caine gave her little nod. "I had Hattie cut them. I expect you will want the key." Her thin lips tightened as she opened the clasp on her handbag, and then hesitated as if waiting for a protest.

"Yes, thank you." Elizabeth held out her hand. "Are there others, do you know?"

Miss Emily sniffed as she handed over the key. "I believe George Tate has one. Hattie and I have seen to the house, naturally. But as president of the Company, it is his right to possess one."

"Were you Colonel Tapestry's housekeeper?" As soon as the words were out of her mouth, Elizabeth regretted them. Miss Caine's backbone became even more rigid and the lips became a thin line.

"I was secretary and assistant to the President of Tapestry Industries from its inception until my retirement."

"I'm sorry," Elizabeth said softly. "I thought since you had a key..."

Miss Caine snapped her handbag shut. "Hattie supervises the girls who come in from town to clean. But I have always had a key. The Colonel wanted it that way."

"Of course," Elizabeth murmured. *And woe unto the "girl" whose efforts do not pass the white glove test.* Aloud she said, "May I offer you some tea? It's herb tea, no caffeine."

"No thank you, my dear." Miss Caine's chilling tone belied the endearment. "I came to deliver the key and to invite you to Sunday services. I don't know your religious preferences but I assure you that Simpsonton's

Presbyterian Church is quite correct doctrinally. All the best people attend."

Elizabeth stifled a smile. "I appreciate the invitation, Miss Caine." The expectancy on the woman's face showed that she waited for a promise of attendance, but Elizabeth made no further response.

Both women stared at the flowers during an uncomfortable moment of silence.

Miss Caine spoke first. "As I am president of the Helping Hands Circle, it is my duty to welcome newcomers and also to find facilities for visiting clergy. It has been our custom to house them in the cottage adjoining this house. Will it be acceptable to you that we continue that practice?"

Again Elizabeth received the impression that an affirmative answer was not only expected but demanded of her.

She carefully worded her reply, "I will need to discuss it with my advisor naturally, concerning insurance and liability. I'm sure you understand."

Another sniff, this one expressing a level of high disapproval. Elizabeth glanced out of the corner of her eye at the china clock.

"Hattie will be here shortly," Miss Caine stated dryly.

Evidently Elizabeth's glance had not been sufficiently surreptitious.

"Is there a path between your house and mine?" Elizabeth cast desperately about for a topic of conversation.

Miss Caine looked at her haughtily. "There is an opening in the fence. And the lawn is easier for me to traverse than the brick walk, which has become increasingly uneven."

"Of course," said Elizabeth, silenced again.

At the sound of the door chime, Elizabeth leaped to her feet, fighting the urge to heave a relieved sigh. *Saved by the bell.*

After goodbyes were said, she watched the two women disappear through the trees, Miss Caine leaning heavily on her companion as they went.

"Not a good beginning." Elizabeth sighed as she headed up the steps to her bath.

Her thoughts returned to the night at Mike's when she first heard about Tapestry Court.

Galen had finally given up protesting her need to get away, to take a sabbatical, and made a different kind of proposal.

"I think I've found your answer," he'd announced. "At least a place for you to go and figure out the answer for yourself."

When she showed interest he went on and described the little town of Simpsonton about an hour's drive from Lexington, and the small, gated community of Tapestry Court.

She had known that Galen, as one of the Vice Presidents of a large Lexington bank, was working on a case that involved a missing heir but had no idea until that night the extent of the mystery surrounding that case.

Colonel Guy Tapestry had been found murdered in the small park at Tapestry Court and the local law enforcement officers were convinced that his death was a result of discontent over wages at the factory he had founded. It was never discovered how the shooter gained access to the Court and the perpetrator was never discovered. But the mystery that concerned Galen was not the death but the will of Guy Tapestry.

It provided for his known family and clearly stated they were to receive nothing more from his estate. It made provision for the staff that were with him from the beginning and a few who had given him their loyalty in later years. And it designated the bulk of his estate to go to his son.

The problem was that, as far as anyone knew, there was no son. Colonel Tapestry had never married and indeed had never been known to have any female companion. He had given all appearance of a man consumed with a lust for power and money, with no interest in the passions of less driven men.

No executor was named in the will and the court appointed the Colonel's bank as administrator. After ten years, the bank had exhausted all avenues of investigation. Neither had they been successful in attempting to have the will set aside and assign the properties and stocks to the family or the business. The wording was very cleverly executed and the will stood as written. Recently Galan was asked to take over the case when Bill Stevens, who had been unsuccessfully working on it for a decade, died.

After a relaxing bath in the delightful Victorian clawfoot tub, Elizabeth snuggled into her comfortable new bed, glad that she would not need to replace the mattress as she had anticipated. Mattresses were such individual things and had to be just right or you couldn't relax. Surprisingly, everything about her new home away from home seemed perfect.

A smile curved her lips at the memory of Galen's excitement when he offered her the perfect place for her sabbatical and at the same time enlisted her help in searching for clues to the unknown heir. She knew the fact that Tapestry Court was within easy driving distance for visits and that he had an "in" already with the community aided in his acceptance of her decision. That comforting thought was in her mind as she drifted off to sleep. Galen. What woman could ask for anybody more perfect? If only... She snuggled up to the pillow and pretended her head was on Galen's shoulder.

The next morning gave promise of a beautiful spring day and Elizabeth hurried outside to explore.

The outer premises proved to be as charming as the house. A brick patio, edged with flower beds and surrounded by a hedge, ran the length of the back of the house; and the path which had disappeared so enticingly under the archway led to an enclosed garden complete with gazebo and a now empty goldfish pond.

Though the lawn was mowed, the flowers were shamefully neglected. Perennials were swamped with overgrowth while the plots left for annuals had become a haven for weeds. Elizabeth was unashamedly glad. The house itself left nothing for her domestic instincts to act upon. Now she visualized merry pansy faces here, graceful impatiens there, petunias in that spot. Dreamily she placed a pear tree at the far side of the garden wall and perhaps a wisteria vine...

"What am I doing?" Elizabeth came to with a start. Pear trees and wisteria vines were for permanent homes. Not for temporary residents, perhaps not even here for the full year of the lease. Well, she'd pick up those annuals this weekend and in the meantime she would weed and prepare the earth.

She strolled across the lawn past the lilacs and to the gate that entered on to the Tapestry Court Park. The park was actually another garden, with neatly laid out beds planted in bulbs. The tulips were in bloom now, the park ablaze with red and gold.

In the center of the paths which separated the flower beds stood a fountain with a gigantic bronze T in its center. The Colonel had certainly intended to leave no doubt as to the ruler of this empire. She'd noticed that all the towels and sheets in the linen closet were embossed with an ornate T and it seemed that everything surrounding the Colonel had been marked with the name Tapestry or his initial. Were it not for the sensitivity apparent in his decorating and landscaping, Elizabeth would be tempted to picture the man as a comic megalomaniac.

Here at the foot of the giant T was where Colonel Tapestry had been found with a bullet in his heart. Murder by person or persons unknown.

Elizabeth followed the path through some tall shrubs to another gate which opened into a yard, probably Number Three.

Just then the back door to the cottage opened and a pretty dark haired woman descended the steps, holding a tray of marigolds. She looked startled as she spotted the newcomer.

"I'm sorry," Elizabeth said quickly from her place on the park side of the gate. "I didn't mean to spy. I was just looking over the park and the path led me here."

The young woman set the tray of flowers on the steps and came toward the gate wiping her hands on her gardening apron. Then with a shy laugh, she hid her hands behind her back. "I won't shake hands. I'm all over dirt. Welcome to the Court. You must be Ms. Daily."

"Yes. And please call me Elizabeth."

"My name is Jenny Anderson. I'm glad you're here." The welcome sounded sincere, even heartfelt.

Warming to the young woman, Elizabeth deepened her smile. "Yes, it must have seemed a shame, watching that beautiful house sit empty all these years."

Jenny responded with a comment about the flowers she was planting and the two women discussed gardening for the next few minutes.

Finally Elizabeth announced that it was time for her to leave. "Please come and visit me. Young Chuck Tate is coming to tea on Friday. I've promised him homemade bread. Perhaps you could come too."

Jenny's eyes clouded.

"I...uh..I think I'll be busy Friday. But do come and visit me. I'm always here. I mean, except when I'm away." Then her eyes cleared and Jenny laughed. "That made a lot of sense, didn't it? Oh, Ms. Daily -- Elizabeth -- it's lonely here. I do hope we'll be friends. Please come, maybe Monday morning, for coffee and cake?"

The earnest plea in Jenny's face plucked at a sympathetic chord deep inside Elizabeth. Here was a young woman who needed a friend.

"I'd love it." Elizabeth waved goodbye and walked slowly back to her house, enjoying the scent of lilacs. And wondering.

After a lunch of salad -- oh so healthy -- and preparing a tuna casserole to heat for supper, Elizabeth unpacked books and added them to the well-stocked shelves in the library. Her own favorites looked shabby next to the beautiful leather bound and hand tooled matching set of masterpieces there. But after she had pulled out a few of the exquisite tomes, she realized they had never been read. The pages still cracked and the spines bore no evidence of creases. Her impression of Colonel Tapestry received its first real blemish.

Among the books she found an old leather bound Bible with pages to record Births and Marriages in the front. It didn't look much more used than the matched set, but the blank lines had been filled in. Elizabeth scanned the entries with interest.

Shortly after two, the men from the telephone company arrived to install the land line and internet connection. When they left, Elizabeth placed a call to Galen at his office from her cell phone.

"Settling in?" he asked, after she had given him the house number.

"Yes. You were right. I love it."

"Have you met your neighbors yet?"

"A few. And like a ninny I've already made two social engagements." She laughed. "Miss Caine is not pleased that I am here but she loves the house. Jenny Anderson, on the other hand, does not appear to be interested in the house but is glad I've moved in. And young Charles Tate - Chuck to all who value his friendship - is curious about both the house and yours truly."

"What's the problem with the Caine woman?" Galen's voice snapped with irritation.

"I'm not sure, Galen. She's one of those unbending types whose life seems to be consumed by the past and her church activities. And, I didn't beg to join her church circle. By the way, she's been using the guest house as a missionary haven and wants to continue. I told her I'd discuss it with you."

"So I'm to be the heavy?"

"Please?"

"You've got it. Is that the only problem?"

"Well, I made a giant faux pas. I asked if she had been the Colonel's housekeeper."

Galen groaned. "I should have briefed you more thoroughly."

"Is it important that she like me?

"Oh, nothing like that. I just don't want your time of reflection spoiled by petty worries."

"It won't be. It's all under the bridge now. Jenny Anderson seemed nice but I got the impression she wants me to visit her instead of vice versa."

"I don't know much about her. Her parents were part of the Tapestry ménage. She inherited the house when they were killed in an automobile accident." He added as an afterthought, "Shortly before the Colonel's death, I believe."

"I haven't met the Colonel's sister yet. She would be the most likely to know about his personal life, don't you think?"

"I doubt it," answered Galen frankly. "She married and lived away until her husband retired. I think they'd only been there a few years before Tapestry died."

"When are you coming down?"

"You mean male visitors are allowed in the cloister?" He sounded amused.

"Don't be cute. I don't want total isolation. Will there be talk if you stay in the guest house?"

His low chuckle tickled her ear. "Do you care?"

"Not really."

"I'll be there Friday."

"Not until after six, I hope?" She purposely added a teasing tone to her voice.

"Do you have another date?"

"Yes, sir. I have invited young Mr. Tate for tea, complete with homemade bread."

"Sour dough?"

"Of course."

"Save some for me. I'll bring steaks."

"See you then. And, Galen," She paused. "Thank you. I really love it here."

"And I love you. Kiss your nose for me. See you Friday around seven."

After hanging up the phone, Elizabeth stood still a moment basking in the warmth of being loved. When she returned to the library only half of her mind concentrated on the books she unpacked.

Cloister was an interesting word; Galen was perceptive as usual. She was here to get away from the world and re-evaluate her life. She once ran away from being cloistered, but here she was seeking just that atmosphere.

An unintended sigh escaped. How young and naive she'd been when she made her first big decision about life and God. She believed then that anyone in full time ministry must burn with holy love and single-hearted devotion to service; she was determined to live that way as soon as she became legally of age. When that time came and she discovered within herself another love, another desire, she thought her calling had not been real, that it stemmed from the daydreams of a lonely young girl who had been taught by nuns and had immersed herself in stories of saints and miracles.

Her years of dedication ended when she fell in love with Robert. The subsequent marriage ended two years later when she admitted to herself that Robert was in love only with a bottle. At age twenty, she entered college to become a social worker and then went on to get her Ph.D in psychology. She began writing then, articles and short stories that promptly found markets and resulted in enough financial remuneration to add to the grants, scholarships, and student loans, ensuring that she could devote full time to her studies. It was years later that she realized how unusual her success had been, that most writers collect hundreds of rejection slips to one check. But at the time she wasn't really a writer. It was only a hobby that she could use to make extra money.

She unpacked most of the book boxes and then looked down at the volume in her hand. Only one copy of *the book* made it to Tapestry Court, and she shook her head in renewed awe as she added it to the others on the shelf. *The Fall and Redemption of God* began as an exercise in sorting out her own beliefs after years of study and professional interaction with people. That she was now wealthy, famous- and infamous - as a result of that exercise still astonished her. Of course, Elizabeth Daily wasn't famous. Her pseudonym, Amanda Brady, caught all the public attention. The thousands of letters written in passionate response to her published thoughts were divided into two equal categories and lay in boxes in her

Lexington apartment, all unanswered. Those letters, forwarded to her from the publisher, were the reason she was here seeking haven in Tapestry Court.

It wasn't that the letters upset her. The opinions of others had long ago lost the power to either dismay or delight her. She was her own most demanding critic and her own most loyal fan. The two roles kept her ego in healthy balance.

Her dilemma was a moral one. The letters denouncing her as a heretic would be easily dealt with...read them, extract any real content from the objections, determine if there was any validity in the accusations of blasphemy and respond appropriately ... eventually. She just hadn't been able to make herself tackle the task yet.

It was the other letters that had sent her fleeing from her practice and well ordered life. They had touched a long buried part of her heart and demanded a decision. They were letters from sheep begging for a shepherd.

Chapter Three

The door chime sounded as Elizabeth removed her casserole from the oven. With a glance of regret she set it on a trivet and left the kitchen. "Seven twenty," she observed as she glanced at her watch. "This must be the appointed hour for making calls at Tapestry Court."

This time the open door revealed a man, a gentleman, she decided at once. He had kind brown eyes and that graying at the temples which always made men look distinguished. He was neatly dressed in a suit and tie.

"Ms. Daily? George Tate. I hope I haven't come at an inconvenient time."

She opened the screen. "Come in Mr. Tate. My casserole needs to cool down before I can eat it anyway." She held out her hand. I'm glad to finally meet you. Galen speaks so highly of you."

"And of you." When George Tate grinned, Elizabeth saw where Chuck had gotten his charm.

"Shall we talk in the library?" Elizabeth opened the door to that room and they settled themselves in the two brown leather chairs. "Would you like some coffee?"

"No, thank you, Ms. Daily. I just finished dinner. Is everything all right? Anything you need?"

"Everything is perfect. I couldn't be more pleased. I met your son. He is such a nice young man."

George Tate's eyes glowed with pride. "A good boy, Charles. A very good boy. He said he met you at the gate when you arrived. And that you had invited him...er...for tea?"

Elizabeth gave a soft laugh. "Yes. It seems appropriate here." Her gaze swept their surroundings.

"Don't let him become a pest, Ms. Daily."

"I won't. I enjoy children, really. Especially well mannered ones like Ch..Charles."

George Tate threw his head back against the soft brown leather with a hearty laugh. "Got you calling him Chuck, does he?"

"I hope you don't mind?"

"Not at all. The boy needs a friend who will let him be himself. This is a dull neighborhood for a child. Grew up here myself."

"Oh, that's right. You're Miss Caine's nephew, aren't you?"

"Yes." A grimace twisted his lips. "But don't judge me by that." Then he added quickly, "I mean no disrespect to my aunt but she's a little hard on young people. I never actually lived with her - grew up in Number Four where I am now. Hattie raised us, Charles Simmons and me. But Aunt Emily was always there to make sure we behaved properly. She didn't get religious on us 'til our teen years, thank God."

The phrase piqued her interest and she studied his face. "You're not a church man yourself, Mr. Tate?"

"Please call me George. Oh, we attend church, my family and I. My wife's more involved than I am. But we are pretty much live and let live people. Unlike Aunt Emily." He laughed again. "She wouldn't approve of anybody being here in this house. She's responsible for it all you know. Chose the furnishings, oversaw the landscaping. And she's kept it like a shrine since the old man died."

Elizabeth was speechless. *That little old nasty woman the designer of all this beauty?*

"Ms. Daily." George Tate shifted in his chair and failed to meet her eyes. "I did come to welcome you but I have another reason for being here too."

"Oh?" Elizabeth lifted her eyebrows slightly.

A flush colored Tate's face. "I admit that I, well, I looked into your background before agreeing to lease the place."

"Quite understandable." Elizabeth nodded. "Tapestry Court is so ... enclosed. You would want to be sure of the type of neighbor you were getting."

He relaxed. "Good. You understand. Well, in the course of my - uh - investigations, I found that you have quite a background in research and have written some very scholarly articles on human behavior."

Elizabeth inclined her head modestly.

"I'll come straight to the point. I know Galen Delaney has told you about this will mess. And I want to officially ask if you would look into the matter. It's awkward for the Company to have the majority of voting stock tied up in limbo. The bank has graciously allowed me, as President, to vote the majority shares, but frankly it's uncomfortable for me. I want the thing settled."

A smile played about Elizabeth's lips. "Are you engaging me as a private detective?

"A private researcher, shall we say? A researcher into the human mind. Will you do it?"

She was smiling broadly now. "In your 'investigation' did you also discover my penchant for mystery novels, Mr. Tate?"

"Galen provided that part," he admitted sheepishly.

"And does he know that you were going to offer me this... research assignment officially?"

He nodded. "You're not offended?"

Elizabeth laughed. "No, I'm not offended. I'm flattered, actually. But I'm not sure that I can be of help."

"Galen thinks you can. And I trust his judgment. Old Stevens played with the thing for years and never got anywhere. You will be able to talk to people, listen, find out things. The Board would be horrified if I hired a detective but a researcher, and a lady - that's a different matter. You'll be compensated of course."

"Oh?" Elizabeth smiled. He probably knew nothing about the book and her current financial status.

"The cost of the lease, if that's acceptable. It's not as much as a full time job, of course. But I don't expect you'll work at it full time. And you may solve our mystery in a month and live here peacefully the rest of the year. I'm sure the heir, whoever he is, will be willing to honor that contract. He will have reason to be grateful. Several million reasons," he added wryly. "Please say you'll do it."

There wasn't really any decision to make; the proposal gave her permission to do what she wanted to do anyway.

She straightened in the chair. "The terms are acceptable, Mr. Tate. Do you have any suggestions as to where I might start? Any leads, I think is the proper term?"

"Mrs. Fowler, I think. She's only been here since '90 but she may know of friends or relatives from the past. My aunt would probably know more than anyone but she's incensed at the idea of Tapestry having a son and refuses to believe it. You'd think we made it up as scandal instead of the old man writing it in the will himself."

So Miss Caine was not only protective of her employer's house but of his reputation as well. Interesting. "I understand. By the way, whatever became of the other sister, Lydia? I saw her recorded in Colonel Tapestry's Bible." She nodded toward the bookcase.

Tate's eyes rolled up toward the ornate chandelier as he shook his head. "There's no help there. Been in a home for years. Batty as they come. She won't be any help at all."

Elizabeth was silent, but as usual she was determined to form her own opinion.

George Tate left the library by the side door and Elizabeth called after him with one last question.

"Is my official capacity a secret, or is it to be known that I am engaged on this research project?"

He paused, turned, and lifted his shoulders with a shrug. "That's entirely up to you, Ms. Daily. Whatever you think best."

"No, you know the residents of the Court and I don't. Do what you think best."

She watched thoughtfully as he disappeared down the path. And then she returned to the kitchen to reheat her dinner.

So George Tate and Charles Simmons had grown up together under the auspices of the multi-talented Hattie. She supposed that Simmons must be who George had named his son after. The boys would have been like brothers even though they were not related. But who was Charles Simmons, and where had he come from? She must remember to ask George Tate when she saw him again. All Elizabeth knew about the man was that he was the attorney for Tapestry Industries and lived with his young wife at Number Five.

She was tempted to call Galen again,but decided the question could wait until Friday.

Thursday morning was spent weeding and by 10:30 the perennials stood free from their captors. After a light lunch she settled herself at the large roll top desk in the library and began to make notes. This had always been one of her favorite parts of any research project - deciding upon the questions that needed answering.

1. Who is Charles Simmons - his parentage? How did he come to live at Tapestry Court?

2. Why is Lydia Tapestry institutionalized? Is she able to answer questions?

3. Was the Colonel ever involved with any women?

4. Was there any location the Colonel visited frequently?

5. Who are the stockholders in Tapestry Industries?

6. What were the exact terms of the will?

7. Who chose George Tate to follow Tapestry as President?

8. Does Jenny Anderson have an aversion to the manor house? If so, why?

9. Did something turn Emily Caine from a romantic who created the atmosphere of this house into the bitter legalist that she is now? Or was she just a natural decorator?

10. Does Lucille Fowler know anything about her brother's private life?

As Elizabeth recorded the tenth item on her list, a timid knock sounded at the outside door of the library. She hastily slid the paper in a drawer and went to investigate.

A tiny white haired lady with lively brown eyes stood at the threshold.

"I hope I'm not disturbing you," the woman fluttered. "I probably should have gone to the front, but Guy was always in here and when I did find it necessary to disturb him, he was less irritated if I came directly to this door."

She took a deep breath and added humbly, "I'm Lucy Fowler."

Elizabeth smiled warmly. "Do come in, Mrs. Fowler. I'm Elizabeth Daily and I've been looking forward to meeting you. Let's sit in the parlor, shall we?"

Lucy Fowler crossed the hallway and went straight to one of the rockers. She sat down with a satisfied sigh.

"I always loved this room." Her head moved as her gaze rested on each item of furnishing. "So comfortable."

"It's lovely," Elizabeth agreed. "I thought I would want to make changes but the whole place is perfect just as it is."

"Emily did it, you know." Lucy nodded. "She had quite a flair in her younger days. I was just a girl when Guy built this house. And my, was it a treat to come and visit my rich brother. We were very poor, you see, before Guy's success. After that, things were easier. He saw to my education and moved our parents to a pleasant neighborhood in our old home town. He would have brought them here but they didn't want to leave."

"Miss Caine must have been almost a girl herself when she began working for your brother." Elizabeth was surprised to see a blush spread over her visitor's cheeks.

"Yes. Guy always liked...young people about him." She plucked at an invisible piece of lint on her neat skirt and went on hurriedly. "He was young too, you know, only twenty when he made his fortune. But Guy was so clever."

"I believe you have a sister too?" At her startled glance, Elizabeth quickly explained. "I saw your brother's Bible when I was putting my own books away. All your births were recorded there."

"Lydia, poor woman. Yes, she was the youngest. She came here very briefly when our parents died. She didn't want to but there was no help for it. Harold and I were off in China being missionaries and couldn't take her."

"Your sister never worked?"

"Oh, no. Lydia was always...." Lucy stopped speaking as if she was groping for the right words.

"I'm sorry. I didn't mean to pry. Your sister wasn't well?" Elizabeth went right on prying and hoped it wouldn't be noticed.

Lucy Fowler drew a handkerchief from her pocket and began folding and unfolding it as she spoke. "Lydia was always fragile, not physically you understand. They called it mental back then. But there was nothing wrong with her mind really. Today they would recognize it as emotional instability." She broke off as if she had said too much. "I didn't intend to bore you with our family problems. I came to welcome you to Tapestry Court."

"You are not boring me." Elizabeth assured her. "I find the Court and the family fascinating."

"We're really very ordinary...except Guy of course. He was, well, different. So dynamic. He made things happen."

"Ms. Fowler, I'm going to be honest with you. George Tate has asked me to undertake a research project to attempt to settle your brother's will."

Lucy began fanning herself with the handkerchief. "Oh dear."

"Do you object to that?"

"You seem very capable. I'm sure you could succeed at anything you put your hand to."

"But you're reluctant? Don't you want to find your nephew?"

The fanning stopped and Lucy Fowler leaned forward in her chair.

"My brother was not a nice man, Ms. Daily. He was very generous but there are things...I mean, I would naturally welcome any blood relation. It's just that in pursuing...I mean...oh, dear." The fanning began again.

"There are scandals which might not have anything to do with the will which you would rather not have brought out in the open?" Elizabeth asked gently.

Lucy nodded.

"That's why Mr. Tate asked me instead of a professional investigator. He knew he could trust me not to report anything which did not have a direct bearing on settling the will."

"Yes." The folding and unfolding resumed. "I'm sure you're very discreet, my dear."

"There must be something you could tell me, a place to start," Elizabeth said encouragingly.

Lucy rose from her chair. "I have to think about it. It's all so...so distasteful."

Elizabeth crossed to the older woman and laid a hand gently on her arm. "I'm sorry our first meeting has been unpleasant for you. Perhaps I should have waited to mention the subject."

"No," Lucy protested. "I appreciate you being straightforward."

"And you'll think about...telling me?"

A shadow crossed the elderly woman's features. "Yes, I must...oh...yes, I, I'll think about it."

When she had gone, Elizabeth revised her last notation to read, 'Find out what Lucy Fowler is ashamed of concerning her brother.'

Within the hour Elizabeth stood inside the little store she had passed on her first day. At first she thought the shop was deserted, but then a familiar impish face popped up from behind the counter.

"Chuck!" she exclaimed. "Do you work here?"

He nodded with an air of importance. "Thursdays after school and Saturday mornings. Mr. and Mrs. Archer pay me a whole seven dollars and twenty-five cents an hour."

"Where are they now?"

"They went to pick up some supplies in town. I'm not really supposed to be here by myself, but they trust me and it's not for long. And Mrs. Archers' Dad - he's really old - lives with 'em back there." He pointed to the back of the store. "So if I need something, I'm supposed to go get him."

Elizabeth surmised that the door in the back wall led to an apartment where the owners lived.

"Well then, you can help me. I need some blackberry jam. I'm getting ready for our tea tomorrow."

"Are we going to eat it on those trumpets they always have in the movies?"

Elizabeth suppressed the smile before it reached her lips. "Crumpets? No. I was thinking more of jam cake."

Delight lit the boy's face. "Oh, boy! You want store or homemade?"

"Homemade?"

"Yeah, uh, yes ma'am. We have it here." He ducked into a doorway behind the counter and emerged with a glass jar through which she spied paraffin under the golden screw top.

"Is it...I mean I thought it was against the law to sell home canned goods."

"Oh, it is," answered Chuck cheerfully. "But folks around here would get upset if they couldn't buy Miz Selby's homemade jams. Wait 'til you taste the strawberry on biscuits. Mmmm."

Elizabeth took the jar of blackberry jam and eyed it with suspicion. "You're sure it's safe?"

Chuck laughed. "Our best customer is Deputy Collins. You won't end up in jail. He'd have to arrest himself too."

"But I meant..." Elizabeth changed her mind. "Oh well, when in Rome. How much?"

"Three dollars."

She paid for the jam and they reminded each other again of their four o'clock engagement the following day.

On the way home Elizabeth considered the community in which she found herself.

"Bootleg jam." She shook her head. "I'd like to believe that's the most sinister thing I'll come across."

But after her talk with Lucy Fowler, she knew there were far more ominous things lurking in Tapestry Court.

Chapter Four

On Thursday evening Elizabeth prepared the blackberry jam cake for her tea with Chuck, and a chocolate angel pie for dinner with Galen. All the ingredients for Galen's favorite dessert had been conveniently included in her supply of grocery items. She also added flour, sugar, and oil to the sourdough starter that she fed that morning.

Elizabeth loved the feel of dough beneath her fingers. The house would begin filling with the scent of bread during the night while it rose in the bowl and the aroma would intensify during the day tomorrow as it grew in the bread pans. It should be ready to put in the oven at 3:30 and be fresh and hot when Chuck arrived.

Elizabeth took a relaxing bath before retiring and fell into bed and an exhausted sleep. Friday morning confirmed that the bath had done its job and she felt little effect from the previous day's physical exertion in the garden.

After kneading the dough and setting it in pans on the stove, she spent the morning tackling the weeds and decided to intersperse pink azaleas with white impatiens in the flower beds. Both would grow well in the shade provided by the surrounding shrubs. So what if azaleas were a permanent plant? They would be her contribution to the house when she left.

At 3:30 the bread went into the oven. She placed butter, apple butter, and strawberry preserves on the large silver tray, and orange spice tea bags nestled in the matching silver teapot. Blue and white Haviland cups, saucers, and dessert plates gleamed in the light reflected from the silver, and tiny precooked smoked sausages lay in a casserole dish waiting to go into the oven for warming when the bread was ready.

Elizabeth went upstairs to give a final brush to her hair and touch up her make-up.

"You'll never grow up, Elizabeth Daily," she said to her reflection. Preparing the tea was her way of playing house, pretending that she was part of a world that had never existed for her. But at least she was aware of the pretense. Surely that counted for something.

It had taken Elizabeth years to allow herself to play, to enjoy life instead of feeling that every moment must be filled with accomplishment of some kind. Galen helped a lot. He'd taught her that everything did not have to be meaningful; some things could just be fun. Without realizing what he was doing, the handsome banker had changed her picture of God and what He might want for Elizabeth Daily. Galen continually showed her how to find joy in the midst of everyday life.

The door chime interrupted her reflections and she chuckled as she checked her watch. Chuck was almost ten minutes early.

She let him explore the house alone, excusing herself to make last minute preparations. Everything was laid out on the coffee table in the parlor when he joined her, eyes aglow.

"This is a neat house." he said excitedly. "Those ships are awesome." Chuck shook his head in the wonder of admiration.

Elizabeth had seen the model ship collection which sailed across the mantel in the library. She'd admired the delicate sails and tiny rigging on the clipper but made a mental note to store them in the empty cabinets and replace them with some of her own treasures.

It was on the tip of her tongue to tell Chuck he could have the collection when she realized they did not belong to her. They were the property of Colonel Tapestry's mysterious heir.

"Yes, they are really works of art," she replied. "Now come fill your plate before it all gets cold."

Elizabeth didn't eat much since she would have a heavy meal in less than five hours but her visitor made up for any lack on her part. Her concern that a boy would not enjoy the tea ritual disappeared along with the food, and soon the tray was empty except for a few crumbs. Chuck seemed to have no preference of sweets or savories.

He went out to explore the 'secret garden' while she washed the dishes. When she joined him, he was sitting on the edge of the goldfish pond. Elizabeth knelt beside him.

"Are you going to put fish in it?" he asked.

"Yes. Is there a place here where I can buy them?"

Chuck frowned. "Only little ones. I think you need big ones for outside."

She nodded. "I'm sure I can find them in Lexington next time I go."

"Are you going on the bus?" His voice took on a wistful tone. "I've never ridden a bus."

She laughed. "No I'm going to bring my car here."

"If you have a car, how come you rode the bus when you came?"

"Oh, just for the adventure." The boy nodded. Children understood things like that. She had tried to explain to Galen but he could not identify with journeys into the past. Galen always lived in the present, though she suspected her tendency toward anachronism was one of the things about her that attracted him.

"Mr. Sinclair has a neat car, it's a Porshe."

"Mr. Sinclair?" The name sounded familiar.

"In Number Six." Chuck looked away quickly, his expression vaguely troubled.

"Don't you like Mr. Sinclair, Chuck?"

"Yeah. I mean, yes ma'am. But..."

She waited as the boy made marks on the concrete with a nickel he pulled from his pocket, restraining herself from stopping the graffiti in progress.

"I heard...well, he goes over to see Mindy a lot and Mom said it doesn't look good. I heard her and Dad talking and they were afraid he was going to hurt Uncle Charles or something." The boy looked at her with puzzled eyes. "I don't think he's mean though." His eyes cleared and began shining again. "He took me for a ride once - with the top down!"

"I wouldn't worry about it if I were you. Maybe you misunderstood." Elizabeth ruffled his hair and tapped his nose with her forefinger in imitation of Galen's gestures toward her when she got too serious.

She remembered now that Galen had mentioned that William Sinclair was the top salesman for Tapestry Industries, a young man in his thirties. And she felt distaste. She didn't like to think of a modern affair going on in her beautiful old-world haven. An inner voice mocked her. *But murder is all right? And secret illegitimate sons?*

She stood up, suddenly too restless to remain seated.

"I hope whoever comes to live here when I leave will keep the fish pond full and plant pear trees and keep the garden nice."

"I hope you stay forever and ever," Chuck said seriously.

Something almost like pain shot through her middle and tears sprang to her eyes. "Thank you, Chuck." She smiled at him. "But eventually the person it all belongs to will be found."

"Oh, yeah. I know about that." He kicked a dry branch that had been overlooked by whoever kept the lawn mowed and cleaned.

It occurred to Elizabeth that the boy might have overheard things that could help her.

"Does anybody have an idea who it might be?"

"Mom thinks it might be Uncle Charles but Dad thinks it could be Mr. Sinclair. Dad says if it was Uncle Charles then the Colonel would have made him president instead of Dad. And he said maybe that's why Mr. Sinclair was brought here. Maybe he was training him to take over."

Elizabeth saw the reasoning behind that. Had the Colonel been killed so that he could not reveal the relationship? And wouldn't George Tate have the best motive if that were the case?

She realized with a shock that she had never believed that the Colonel's death was caused by an outsider. Every person she met had been subconsciously scrutinized as a murder suspect.

"What time is it, Miss Daily?" Chuck tugged at her sleeve bringing her out of her daze.

She glanced at her watch. "Why, it's nearly 5:30."

"I've got to go," he announced glumly. "Mom said not to be a pest."

"Never, young Chuck." Elizabeth laughed and rumpled his hair again. "Tell your mother I thank her for letting you come. And tell her I'm looking forward to meeting her."

After he left, Elizabeth retrieved her list of questions from the desk drawer and added number eleven.

> 11. What is William Sinclair's background? Why did Col. T. install him in the Court?

And then she lay down on the couch and closed her eyes, letting imaginary scenarios play across the screen of her mind. Perhaps one of them would be productive.

It didn't make sense that George Tate would kill the Colonel to keep his heir from being revealed and then go to all this trouble to find him. Or had ten years as head of the company installed him so firmly that there would be no threat to his position? No, he himself had said that the majority of the stock belonged to the missing heir. The majority stockholder could vote himself president and no one could do anything about it. She settled herself more deeply into the cushions satisfied that George Tate's actions did not appear to be anything but sincere. Elizabeth liked George Tate. And she liked his son.

Jenny Anderson. There was something there. A deep traumatic fear of some kind, or Elizabeth had learned nothing from the experiences of a fifteen-year practice in psychology. Could the Colonel have been responsible for her parents' death? Could Jenny have killed him as an act of revenge? Her eagerness to reject that thought caused Elizabeth to realize that on some level, she believed the death was related to the mystery of the heir.

Lydia? In an unbalanced state of mind? Again, unrelated to the matter which she was investigating. Or was it? And was Lydia Tapestry even here in the Court at the time?

Emily Caine. Elizabeth was ashamed at the surge of emotion that went through her at the thought of the prim

Miss Caine as an avenging fury, seeing herself as a messenger of a vengeful god, the hand of judgment on fornicators and adulterers. Yes, of all the people she had met so far, Elizabeth would rather Emily Caine be the killer. But Miss Caine refused to believe that the Colonel had ever done anything that would result in a son. Since that fact had not even surfaced until after his death, she wouldn't have had a motive - at least not concerning the missing heir. Maybe there was something else.

Lucy Fowler? She couldn't imagine Lucy Fowler ever doing anything more illegal than...than buying bootleg jam! Elizabeth adjusted the cushion behind her head and let her thoughts move on.

And then there was Hattie. She must make a point of meeting Hattie. Could the Colonel have...? No. Well. She really must meet Hattie.

She mentally went down the list of others she had not met who had been among those Galen listed as living in the Court.

Joel Anderson. But he had not come to Tapestry Court until years after the Colonel's death. And it would be quite a coincidence for him to be the missing son and, without knowing it, marry into the court family. If he were the heir and knew it, he would have declared himself at once.

Linda Tate. George's wife. Could she, believing Charles Simmons to be the heir, have killed the Colonel before he revealed it, in order to protect her husband's position?

Mindy Simmons. Elizabeth was prepared to dislike the young Ms. Simmons; she had formed a picture of a flirt at best, an unfaithful wife at worst. But she could as yet see no motive for murder, and besides the girl would have only been a child at the time.

That left...

William Sinclair, who could be the son. But if he had killed to inherit, surely he would not have let ten years pass before declaring himself. Not a man who liked expensive sport cars.

And Harold Fowler, the retired minister. Surely nothing there. He was not of an age to be the missing son. And a clergyman.... Elizabeth stopped herself. The last decades of the 20th century had proven very publicly by way of the news media that clergymen were most surely subject to 'like passions as other men', as the Apostle Paul put it. But what could be his motive?

Eyes closed, she reviewed her scenarios once again.

After a few moments she got up and added question number twelve to her list.

Chapter Five

"Absolutely not, Elizabeth." Galen was uncharacteristically upset. "We want you to find an heir, not track down a murderer."

"But I really believe the two are linked," Elizabeth protested.

"Then the deal's off. You can go back to Lexington with me right now." He slapped his hand on the table.

"I will not." She glared defiance at him. "I like it here."

"Then marry me and I'll move here with you."

"Galen," she said with forced calmness. "Have you forgotten my main reason for coming here?"

"No. But evidently you have." It was his turn to glare.

Elizabeth smiled sweetly. "I'm staying. And if the deal is off, that is fine. I have a lease and I was prepared to pay rent anyway. I can afford it."

"Then you will give up playing detective?"

"No." She began stacking dishes on the patio table where they had been relaxing over coffee. "No, I won't give it up. I just won't receive any compensation for it, that's all."

He was silent and she knew she had won. Finally he said, in a gruff voice, "I don't like it."

She crossed behind him and put her arms around his shoulders, resting her chin on the top of his head. "I know you don't, but I do. I like it a lot." She straightened and stood looking around her. "I like this place. And I like the challenge. I feel free and energized. And just think, Galen," she teased, "It will be a feather in your cap if we clear this thing up."

He pulled her down to his lap. "I just want you safe."

"Don't be a worrywart. I am safe."

"But a murderer." He shook his head. "Of course, I'm not at all convinced that you're right. The police were positive that none of these people were involved. But if they are wrong, then you could be in danger."

She laid her head on his shoulder. "Nobody but you knows I'm looking for a murderer."

"If your suspicions are correct and the two are linked, you put yourself in jeopardy."

She moved so she could look him in the eyes. "I'll be careful, I promise."

He held her tightly before releasing her. "Well stubborn woman, let's get these dishes inside."

When the plates were neatly stacked in the drainer, they went to examine the guest house. Unexpected. The decor was oriental, the furnishings wicker and brass. Elizabeth recalled that the Fowlers had been in the Orient during one part of their life of ministry. Had they been the source of the Colonel's interest in Eastern art objects? Had he visited there himself? She was quite sure this was not the handiwork of Miss Emily Caine. And yet...Miss Caine housed her missionaries here. Elizabeth decided to make no further assumptions regarding the inner workings of the spinster's mind.

After making sure that Galen had everything he would need, the two walked back to the main house.

"The guest house has a television," she commented. "I wonder why the Colonel didn't have one in his home."

"Maybe he did," said Galen. "Someone could have taken it to use after his death."

She shook her head. "I doubt that. I don't think so much as a book has been moved, except to be dusted."

"Do you miss having one? We can run up and get yours."

"Miss it? I never even noticed there was no TV until I saw the one in the guest house. But I would like a ride back with you Sunday to get my car."

He nodded. "Good. I feel better with you having it here. Want to check out garage space?" They had paused at the hedge surrounding the patio.

"Yes. It's such a pretty night. I hate the thought of going inside."

"I left my car in the parking space by the store next to the Court. The Archers said it was all right with them."

"I haven't met them yet. The one time I went there Chuck Tate was minding the shop for them." She shook her head. "Things certainly are different away from the city." She explained about Chuck being left alone in the store and about the jam. "Would the Archers know anything helpful, do you think?"

They passed through the gate to the park and went through the second gate that led to the parking garage. Security lights insured total visibility throughout the area.

"I don't see how they could. They've only been here a couple of years."

Upon entering the garage, they saw that an empty space ran its length, giving access to any of the six partitions constructed for the vehicles.

"But there are seven houses!" Elizabeth exclaimed.

Galen examined the plaques on each divider. "The stalls are numbered. One, and then three through seven.

Let's see ...Miss Caine has Number Two. I guess she never drove."

"One's empty. Must be mine."

Just then they heard the sound of a key turning in the old-fashioned garage door that opened to the Number One slot. When the barrier was swung upward and rolled overhead, they saw a man standing in the glow from the headlights of a still running automobile. Galen and the other man recognized one another and shook hands. Elizabeth was introduced to Charles Simmons.

She was surprised that he did not resemble George Tate and then realized that although the two men had grown up as brothers, they were unrelated. Where Tate was tall and of a stocky build, with dark hair and dark merry eyes, Simmons was a slightly built man with light brown hair and serious blue eyes. Elizabeth couldn't imagine him grinning or cutting up the way his foster brother had done.

Simmons pulled the car in and relocked the garage door from the inside. He then invited them to his home to meet Mrs. Simmons and join him in a nightcap.

As they accompanied him through the park and down the brick walk to Number Five, they explained what they had been doing in the garage.

"I'm actually using your space, Miss Daily. My wife keeps hers in our slot. The Fowlers and Aunt Emily don't keep a car, but George's family has two. Joel Anderson's and Bill Sinclair's fill it up. We'll work out something. When are you bringing yours?"

"Sunday evening." Elizabeth knew her reply sounded abrupt but she was trying to stop the inner bristling in reaction to his statement 'We'll work something out.' After all, it was *her* parking place.

Simmons nodded. "I'm going to be out of town for a couple of weeks starting Sunday, so there won't be any problem for a while. And I'll leave the key with my wife if you've left for Lexington when I take off."

They followed him through the door to his home, and waited while he went upstairs to announce their presence.

It was a few minutes before Mindy Simmons came down the steps to join them, and only a few seconds after that until Elizabeth had revised all preconceptions about her new neighbor. The obviously sincere warmth in the enormous blue eyes, the long sweeping lashes and hair cropped in golden curls, the petite little body that couldn't have weighed over 100 pounds all belonged more to a child than a *femme fatale.*

Mindy apologized for not joining them immediately. "I was already in bed reading," she confessed.

Elizabeth and Galen hastened to apologize for disturbing her.

"Please don't!" She laid a hand on Elizabeth's arm. "I'm just never sure when Charles is coming home. I'm really glad you're here. I love having company." She looked toward the kitchen where her husband was brewing coffee. "Charles is a workaholic. And I get so lonesome."

"Do you read a lot?" Elizabeth asked.

"Oh, yes!" Mindy's eyes widened and Elizabeth recognized a love of books which rivaled her own. "I wanted to go to college and major in literature. That would be heaven. But I had to get a job and earn a living instead." She shrugged. "But that's where I met Charles so it all came out right."

"Do you still work for the company?" Elizabeth asked.

"No, there's a rule. No more than one member in a family can work there. And Charles doesn't want his wife to work anyway."

Elizabeth noticed that Mindy seemed sad when she said it, but immediately the childlike face lit up again. "So I read." Something in her tone made the statement sound courageous.

Elizabeth instinctively liked the girl and hoped she was not getting herself involved in something unsavory with William Sinclair, as Chuck's report of his parent's discussion had implied.

Galen accepted a cup of coffee and Elizabeth a soft drink, and they all seated themselves in the conversation area. Elizabeth said, "Mrs. Simmons, have you thought about going to college now, since you're not working?"

"Yes!" The eyes glowed again for an instant before Mindy cast a quick glance at her husband. "But it hasn't worked out. And please call me Mindy."

Elizabeth saw Galen's slight move out of the corner of her eye and knew he was sending her a subtle signal to keep out of something that was none of her business.

She ignored him.

"Since your husband is going to be out of town next week, perhaps we could get together. I'm familiar with many of the small colleges within driving distance from here. Why don't you come for supper, say Monday? I baked a jam cake last night so the dessert is already prepared."

She saw the blue eyes dart toward Charles Simmons at her first words and realized that this was the first his wife had heard of the business trip.

"Why thank you, Ms. Daily..."

"Elizabeth," she interrupted.

"Elizabeth. I'd like that very much." She added with a laugh, "But forget dessert on my account. I never eat sweets." Then she looked again at her husband as if hoping he would say something to her. But he remained silent, staring at the ice in his glass.

Elizabeth decided that she had said enough uncomfortable things for one evening and sat silently for the remainder of the visit.

The two women smiled at each other periodically while the men discussed Wall Street, corporate law, and similar matters to which neither Elizabeth nor Mindy Simmons had anything to contribute.

It was almost painful to watch the girl's adoring eyes follow her husband's every word and gesture. He never even acknowledged her presence.

Finally Galen and Elizabeth excused themselves after Galen declined an invitation to dinner the following evening.

As they walked back toward Number One, Elizabeth asked, "Why didn't you want to see them tomorrow? You two seemed to have a lot in common."

He put his arm around her and drew her close. And said, in a Transylvanian accent, "Because I vant to get you all alone, my dear."

"Galen!" She pulled away. "Someone may be watching."

He laughed. "I thought you didn't care what anyone thought."

"You staying in rooms next door and us clutching one another in public are two different things entirely," she jerked her chin primly.

"Clutching in private works for me," he said with a mock leer.

She ignored him with all the dignity she could muster. Elizabeth had dated other men, a few, during the years since the divorce, but she had felt no romantic sparks until two years ago when Galen Delaney came into her life. Because she had imposed celibacy on herself outside of marriage and that decision affected him, Galen became the first person in thirty years to whom she had confided the details of her past. He didn't understand; but he accepted. And he loved her just as she was. But she always suspected that if he knew the depths of her reaction when he took her in his arms, he might try harder to wear down her convictions.

"I was certainly wrong about Mindy Simmons." Her voice cut into the silence as they sat on the patio bench, still reluctant to end the evening.

"What do you mean?"

Elizabeth explained Chuck's recital of his parent's conversation. "I had my sympathies all reversed."

"You don't like Simmons?"

Elizabeth considered a moment. "I don't know. I couldn't see a person behind the businessman. But there must be something or a neat person like his wife wouldn't be so crazy about him."

"He doesn't appear to notice, does he? And such a pretty little thing too."

"Oh?" Elizabeth teased. "Unlike her husband you did notice?"

Galen's comic rendition of "I Only Have Eyes For You" ended in a kiss which made Elizabeth decide that she had better end the night.

When she was safely in her own bed she thought over their visit with the Simmons.

Had the rule about only one family member working for Tapestry Industries been in effect when the Colonel was alive? Was that why the Colonel had not named his son? Because to have him there would be breaking his own rule?

Was the rule the reason for Emily Caine's retirement ...she left when her nephew became old enough to join the firm?

Elizabeth thought about Charles Simmons...so unemotional and business minded. She could see him calmly planning and carrying out a murder to further his career. And then waiting one year or twenty for someone else to declare him the heir so that no suspicions could be attached to him. A part of her mind realized that her assessment was unfair. His lack of warmth toward his wife had prejudiced her. She wondered why Charles Simmons had married Mindy in the first place. He must have remained a bachelor until he was in his forties.

People are strange, she thought for approximately the millionth time in her life.

She was now prepared to look with more favor on William Sinclair. She dreamily envisioned a future where Charles Simmons proved to be the missing heir and the murderer. Mindy and William Sinclair would ride happily off into the sunset to some literary college town.

Were people, meaning Charles Simmons, allowed to inherit the fruit of their own crime? She thought she had heard somewhere that they could not. From Galen's point of view that would be a major consideration. What would become of the Tapestry fortune if the unknown son turned out to be the murderer as well?

And if William Sinclair proved to be the missing heir? In that case, Charles Simmons would have no motive.

But George Tate would.

It was all a muddle and Elizabeth was too tired to think about it anymore. She had learned a lot about the residents of Tapestry Court in the three days since her arrival.

But had she learned anything about herself? Too tired to think about that either, she curled into her sleeping position and let unconsciousness creep over her mind.

Strange dreams disturbed her sleep, brief scenes that bore no relationship to one another or made any sense in themselves.

Mindy Simmons was explaining to Chuck that her child would have blue eyes because both she and her husband did. It was all a question of genetics.

And Emily Caine stood in the parlour over the body of George Tate, with a gun in her hand. She matter-of-factly told Galen, "You see, I am not ready to retire." Jenny Anderson stood watching. And screaming.

Then Lucy Fowler pushed a wheelbarrow down the brick walk away from the manor house. The wheelbarrow was full of jars of strawberry preserves. Galen took one of the jars and handed it to Elizabeth and said, "There. Now will you marry me?"

And Elizabeth said, "Yes" because everything was settled.

Chapter Six

"Fine looking woman." Reverend Harold Fowler fixed his glasses more firmly on his nose as he peered out the window.

"She's only a girl, Harold." His wife frowned as she joined him. Then she stopped short. Harold waited for her to realize that he was not speaking of Reggie Tate who had been sunbathing in the grass between Number Four and Number Six earlier. Elizabeth Daily and a distinguished looking silver-haired gentleman were standing on the sidewalk chatting with Linda Tate and Charles.

Lucy Fowler's hand slipped as she leaned on the table, and the jade figurine fell to the carpeted area below.

"Oh, dear." Harold knew the figurine was not the reason for her exclamation of dismay.

"She looks very nice," he said encouragingly.

"Of course she's nice, Harold. It's just that . . . after all these . . . all that old business . . . I just can't . . . Oh, dear." After replacing the jade, Lucy plopped down in the maple rocker and began fanning herself with the faithful handkerchief from her pocket. Her husband of over four decades understood that there were things she hated to discuss, even with him.

"It can't have anything to do with . . . and yet if there were a . . . I don't see how . . . Oh, dear."

Reverend Fowler let his wife ramble on in her own unique habitual fashion. He learned early in their marriage that rambling aloud was her way of thinking things through and it was useless of him to attempt to persuade her of anything until she had made up her mind as to what she thought herself. After that point had been reached, she was open to consider opposing views.

Her next remarks seemed to be directed at him.

"It has been so nice. I felt quite safe . . . no fear of something nasty happening to embarrass us." Sensing that he was about to comment, she quickly added, "I know that some people think it's embarrassing to have a sister like Lydia but she truly seems content." Lucy often spoke of her sister's contentment. Harold knew it was an attempt to placate her own fears as to Lydia's emotional state.

At least they had gotten her out of the nursing home. Ugly things, nursing homes. The Chinese were much more humane, in his opinion. They kept the elderly and infirm with them. And he read once that some primitive tribes efficiently sent those who were unable to care for themselves off to die alone in the jungle or the desert. While not condoning the unchristian practice, Harold secretly admitted to himself that it certainly saved everyone a lot of misery and bother.

Once a month he and Lucy went to visit Lydia at Moreston Manor, an assisted living center in Lexington. George or Linda Tate always drove them. Lydia certainly seemed glad to see them and he could tell she was much happier there. She had been in the nursing home for years but finally some doctor recognized that she didn't need to be there. Guy had readily agreed to pay for the assisted living center as well as the live-in sitter who was there for when Lydia had her spells.

The little group on the walk dispersed now. Linda and Chuck went into the house and Ms. Daily and the silver-haired man went out the gate.

Harold Fowler turned back to his wife. He hoped that she would make the right decision.

He had absolutely no opinion of his own on the matter.

"I see why you like Ms. Daily so much," Linda Tate said to her son as he replaced the milk carton in the refrigerator. Chuck gulped down a twelve ounce glass full to the brim.

He pointed to the wall clock and grinned at his mother. "Five seconds. That's a second off my record. Uh oh, almost ten. Gotta run or I'll be late for work." And like a whirlwind he was gone.

As she washed the breakfast dishes, Linda Tate recalled the image of Tapestry Court's new resident. Exquisitely slender, beautifully made up in a way which looked like she had on no makeup at all, elegantly dressed with lovely salt and pepper hair which could not be duplicated at the most expensive salon. Elizabeth Daily represented what Linda Tate had always intended to make of herself . . . if only she hadn't been so busy raising children and keeping house. Not that she would trade her life with anyone's.

But lately George had seemed so quiet and withdrawn, so unlike his usual talkative and jovial manner. And when he told her that he had leased the manor house to a woman! Well, Linda had wondered if maybe she should pay a bit more attention to her hair and nails, and perhaps lose that ten pounds.

But it was obvious now that Ms. Daily and Galen Delaney were an item. Linda Tate burst into a chorus of

"Zippedy Do Da" as she scrubbed the plates so hard that her family would be able to see their reflections in them. She refused to care that her pride in that accomplishment would seem demeaning to some of her own gender.

Hattie finished sweeping the walk to Number Two and returned to the house where her employer was waiting for her.

"Were you talking to that woman?" Emily Caine demanded.

"Yes, Ma'am." Hattie walked into the kitchen where she replaced the broom in the closet. In a few minutes Emily Caine joined her, leaning heavily on the cane she refused to use outside her home.

"Who was that man with her?" She seated herself at the kitchen table and tapped her cup against the saucer, a signal to Hattie to refill it with coffee.

"That Mr. Delaney that George been talkin' bout. He's stayin' in the little house. Vistin' Miz Daily this weekend."

"Hmph," Miss Caine said before she sniffed.

Hattie looked at her narrowly. It was a bad sign when her mistress added the "Hmph" to the sniff. It designated not only disapproval but a determination to Do Something About the Situation.

"Now, Miz Emily, they are nice people."

"Hattie," Emily Caine drew her shoulders up haughtily, "I think I have sufficient experience to be a good judge of character. And I tell you there is wickedness in Tapestry Court. First that disgraceful secretary who deceived young Charles into marrying her and flaunts herself half-naked with the Sinclair creature. And now this woman brings her lover right here in plain view of everybody. Wickedness, I tell you."

Hattie liked Mindy Simmons and enjoyed watching the two young adults play badminton in the area between the Simmons and Anderson homes. They were often joined by the Tate children, and Hattie approved of the wholesome fun and laughter. She wished 'her boys' had done more of that kind of thing when they were young.

The Colonel and Ms. Emily had insisted the boys be raised very strictly. Everything was homework and learning the business. Sometimes Hattie played games with them when no one was around—Hide n' Seek or Catch, but there wasn't a whole lot one woman could do alone to help two little boys have fun. Not when she was the only one who thought they should be having fun at all.

When they were twelve they were sent off to boarding school and Hattie hoped they would get to play like normal boys there. But the Colonel had chosen one of those militaristic places and Charles Simmons became even more serious and seemed to forget how to play at all. George, though, and Hattie smiled at the thought of George, he always found a little fun for himself wherever he went. Mischievous, George was. He was Hattie's favorite, though she always tried never to show partiality to either of the orphans. She had been all the family they had. Miss Emily might be George's relative but she wasn't family the way Hattie understood the meaning of the word.

And the boys had become family to Hattie. She started ironing and cleaning when she was fourteen years old to help her Mama feed and clothe her nine younger brothers and sisters, and several Tapestry Court homes were among the Simpsonton residences where she worked. One day after she had proven her dependability and competence, the Colonel called her into his library. After he asked a lot of questions, he told her that Miss Emily's sister and brother-in-law had died in an unfortunate accident, leaving a child only a few weeks old. There were no other relatives and Miss Emily's job was too important for her to leave and undertake the raising of the baby.

If Hattie would move into Number Four and take care of the little boy, she would be assured of a home, food, and a weekly salary as long as she wanted them.

It was obviously the miracle Hattie's Mama had been praying for all those years and the largest part of that weekly salary was sent on to that first family.

A year later Charles Simmons had joined them with no explanation from the Colonel other than that he was a companion for George. Hattie picked up a few phrases from conversations between the Colonel and Miss Emily and understood that although the Colonel had not adopted Charles, he had given him a permanent foster home and become his legal guardian.

Hattie and the boys were left alone except for the nightly visits from either the Colonel or Miss Emily to see that they were 'developing as they should and learning their lessons.'

After they went off to school, Hattie stayed on in Number Four to keep a home for her boys for when they came back at vacation time. Somehow the years passed and her life was so completely entrenched in Tapestry Court that she forgot any earlier dreams of her own.

When George brought his bride to live at Number Four, Hattie moved in to do for Miss Emily. She didn't like the change but it never occurred to her leave the Court. And soon there were the Tate children to help with.

Most important, she was still near her boys when they needed her.

Hattie would do anything for her boys.

Joel Anderson leaned on the shovel and looked wistfully at his wife as she bent over the flowerbed. Beautiful, her body so full of promise.

The first time he'd seen her, he had wanted her. Wanted her more than he had ever wanted a woman. Her shyness and modesty only heightened his desire. She made a man want to protect her; have her only honorably, in the marriage bed. And he'd thought she wanted him.

But the promise that had seemed to be on its way to fulfillment had been violently and heartbreakingly shattered on their wedding night. At first she had responded to his lovemaking just as he thought she would and then, when he was positive she was as eager as he, something had happened. She pulled away from him and sobbed until she fell asleep from exhaustion.

They consummated the marriage the next day but it was with sufferance on her part. And every time he touched her, even now, he felt her body stiffen until she willed it to relax.

Joel had tried to talk to her about it but all she ever said was, "Women are different from men." Once he suggested they go for counseling but her reaction duplicated the scene of their wedding night and he never brought it up again.

Joel loved Jenny, and their marriage was all he could wish for except for the unfulfilled promise of her body.

"I like your friend, Sweetheart. It will be good for you to have someone to visit with."

She smiled and nodded shyly. "I hope we'll be friends. That man seemed nice too. Maybe we could have them over to play cards or something."

"Good idea," he said, returning to the task of overturning the earth. "If you see them on their way back, ask if they're busy tonight."

Jenny watched the muscles in her husband's shoulders and arms as he worked. Joel was so masculine. And she loved him very much. She knew she was a disappointment to him. But she just couldn't . . .

And she didn't know why.

It was nearly noon and Chuck carefully counted the money in the cash register.

He would get paid today. Chuck was very proud of earning the minimum wage, "the same as many grownups" his father had assured him. The Archers were nice people . . . they treated a guy fair.

Galen Delaney's silver Lincoln pulled up in the driveway beside the store and Chuck hurried to the doorway so he could speak to the couple when they passed. He need not have bothered; they came into the store looking for him.

"Is there some kind of wagon we could use to take the carload of plants to the house?" Mr. Delaney asked.

"Sure," Chuck said. "I use it to bring the stock in on Thursdays. The Archers won't care."

"Maybe we should ask them first," Ms. Daily said. "When will they be back?"

Chuck grinned and pointed, as the arrival of the green pickup seen through the window answered her question.

Joe Archer was a big man with a dark beard that reached to his collar. He reminded Elizabeth of pictures she had seen of lumberjacks. The top of his wife's head barely cleared his shoulder. Joe got them all a canned drink from the refrigerated unit and refused their offer of payment.

"This one's on me," he said. "A welcome to the neighborhood present." Then he laughed, a booming laugh that matched his appearance. "I'll get it back, believe me."

"I love your store, Mr. Archer. It has character." Elizabeth gestured at the baskets full of fresh produce and the antique scales sitting on the meat counter. Both of the Archers beamed.

"We're looking for an old cracker barrel," Jane confided.

Galen admired the potbellied stove in one corner with two rocking chairs and a checkerboard directly in front of it. "I'll bet it's really got atmosphere in the winter."

"Oh yes," Joe agreed. "Old-timers with lots of tall tales swapping' stories around the fire. Just like it used to be. That's why we try to recreate the old time general store feeling. People like it. And it's good for business."

Chuck got up slowly and tossed his empty can in the trash container. "I gotta go. I promised Mom I'd mow the yard."

Joe went toward the cash register.

"There's $144.10," Chuck reported.

"Good," Joe nodded. "This boy is quite a businessman." He winked at the others.

They filled the wagon with the first load of bedding plants and Chuck insisted on pulling it for them at least as far as his house.

As they walked toward Tapestry Court, Elizabeth thought about the old-timers talking around the potbellied stove. She would have to get into a long conversation with the Archers very soon.

After they unloaded the flowers and Galen started back down the walk for a second load, Elizabeth let herself in the front door.

At her feet lay a sheet of paper that looked as if someone had slid it under the door. Expecting another invitation for the evening, Elizabeth smiled in anticipation of Galen's reaction. But when she read the words, her hand flew to her throat in a protective gesture.

In crudely printed letters she read,

GO AWAY. YOUR NOT WANTED HERE.

Chapter Seven

The open briefcase sitting on the coffee table before them was a present to Galen from Elizabeth the previous Christmas.

Elizabeth decided on the gift early in the fall and by Thanksgiving she found the exact shade of leather she had in mind. It was when she went to have the initials added that the dilemma presented itself. The very distinguished clerk at the exclusive shop lifted a discreetly startled eyebrow when she gave the order G O D, representing Galen Oliver Delaney. At the sight of the eyebrow, Elizabeth realized that this was probably the reason Galen did not already possess an initialed case.

Hurriedly she said, "No, that won't do. We'll leave out the middle initial." As soon as the words were out of her mouth she pictured Galen walking into a tense conference with a blasphemous briefcase. The clerk evidently envisioned something similar, for the other eyebrow lifted a fraction of an inch.

Elizabeth gave up all pretense of sophistication at that point. She sank into a chair and laughed until tears ran down her cheeks. She redeemed herself slightly in the eyes of the clerk by finally settling on the name DELANEY which cost more than most customers paid for personalization.

The memory of the incident still brought a smile whenever she looked at the bag.

The contents of 'God's briefcase' were now the subject of serious discussion. In it was a copy of the Tapestry will and other data concerning the estate, the corporation, and the employees. Galen knew before he came Elizabeth would have questions. She was glad to have the distraction from the note she'd quickly hidden before Galen could see it.

The answers to four of her questions now lay in front of her. The will was clear about everything except the identification of Tapestry's son. It stated that George Tate was to follow Tapestry as President. It listed certain investments that were to be held in trust, the interest to pay for the care of Miss Lydia Tapestry until her death. At that time the holdings would be released outright to the son of Harold and Lucy Fowler or his living heirs, should he predecease his aunt. Other investment properties and Number Seven Tapestry Court were left directly to Lucille Tapestry Fowler. Number Four was left to George Tate or his heirs; Number Five to Charles Simmons or his heirs.

Elizabeth frowned at the document in her hand. "What about the other houses?"

Galen pulled a notebook from the compartment in the case lid and flipped a few pages.

"Here it is. Number Two was deeded over to Miss Emily Caine in 1984 at the time of her retirement from Tapestry Industries. And Number Three was deeded to Jennifer Crossfield at the time of her parents' deaths." He looked up from the page. "Actually that was the last business transaction Tapestry ever made. He was killed that night . . . or early the following morning."

"When did George Tate come to the firm?"

Galen flipped through a few more pages. "Tate entered the company as a junior executive in charge of Advertising." He looked up again. "The casket industry does not advertise to consumers but this department provides photographic layouts of their product as sales tools when agents approach distributors. And now they also design ads for professional magazines."

He explained further. "The manufacturing company does not deal directly with funeral homes either. Caskets are sold in bulk to distribution firms who sell directly to the mortuaries where they are then sold to customers."

"So many middlemen." Elizabeth shook her head in disgust. "No wonder the cost of dying is so high."

Galen looked back at his notes. "Tate got his Masters in Business Administration in 1985 and immediately went to work for Tapestry."

"Oh!" Elizabeth's voice held a note of disappointment.

"What's wrong?"

"Well, it occurred to me that perhaps George Tate wasn't really Miss Caine's nephew at all, that maybe he was the missing son. But it seemed that if the one family member rule was instigated by Tapestry, he would have made her retire when George started working . . . if he was her nephew. And he did. She left in '85 and George started in '85. So it looks like George Tate is exactly who they said he was."

"Yes. I never had any doubt of that," Galen said gently. Then he asked, "I thought you liked Tate. Why are you trying to give him a motive?"

"Oh, it's not that," she explained hurriedly. "It's totally personal. I'd like to see him maintain his position. And Chuck loves this place so . . ." She waved her hand vaguely indicating the house around them. "It occurred to me that if George were the Colonel's son, it could belong to him some day."

Galen laughed. "Shall we go ask Miss Caine if the Colonel had an illicit affair with her married sister nine months before George was born?"

Elizabeth threw up her hands in mock horror. "Heaven forbid! I have a feeling the lady already despises me." She was quite sure that the note had been written by that disapproving spinster, and probably delivered by an unsuspecting Hattie. She didn't want him to know about it, or even suspect that there was more hostility than that of which he was already aware. So she quickly changed the subject.

"What about this house? It is still tied up in the inheritance, isn't it?" She knew very well that it was; that was why it was available for her lease.

"Yes." Galen looked at her curiously. "This and Number Six are part of the estate."

"Hmm," Elizabeth mused. "And Tapestry moved Sinclair into Number Six. It looks like he might be our man."

Galen turned to the next page. "Tapestry hired Sinclair in '90, three months later made him head of the sales department and installed him in Number Six." He removed his glasses and picked up his coffee cup. "It was an unprecedented move. Up to that point, all the residents of the Court had been relatives or staff who had been with the Colonel since the beginning, like Emily Caine and Thomas Crossfield, Jenny Anderson's father."

"Well, it seems pretty obvious, doesn't it? Why hasn't someone obtained proof of Sinclair's parentage?"

Galen grinned. "There's a problem with that. It seems Sinclair was discovered one morning on the steps of a children's home with a one month old baby in his arms. He was around seven at the time. He'd never been to school and all he knew was his name and that his mother and an 'uncle' brought him and his new baby sister to this place where his mother had told him they would be given plenty to eat and toys to play with." He checked his notes again. "The little girl didn't even have a name. The boy told the staff at the home they just called her 'Baby'."

"How sad," Elizabeth sympathized. "And no one ever found out where the children came from?"

"Evidently, from what the boy said, they were some sort of migrant farm workers, never settling in one place for long. He and the woman had lived with a long series of 'uncles' in truck beds and tenant shacks."

"Whatever happened to the baby?" Elizabeth's sympathies had completely turned her mind from the track of her investigations.

"She was adopted while she was still very young, but Sinclair grew up in the home. He was a smart kid and an excellent salesman. He says he met Tapestry when he was pushing a line of business cards." Galen chuckled. "Says he didn't make the sale, but the old man offered him a job before he left the office." He shrugged his shoulders. "Who knows?"

"Mmmm . . . so many orphans . . ." Elizabeth said.

The portfolio revealed that Tapestry Industries was considered a "closely held corporation'; 51% of the stock was retained by the Colonel, 10% was owned from the onset by Emily Caine, and 10% each was given to George Tate and Charles Simmons on the occasions of their 21st birthdays. The other 19% was on the open market with no more than 5% owned by any one shareholder.

Galen snapped the case shut. "And that's all the information we have to date."

"You didn't mention Charles Simmons." She realized her voice sounded accusing. "No one ever talks about his background."

"Is he your favorite prospect for First Murderer?" Galen grinned.

"Yes, he is." Elizabeth thrust out her chin. "It used to be Emily Caine. But she just makes people in general miserable. Simmons is more selective."

"Come on, Bitsy." Galen tugged at her nose playfully as he called her the pet name. "You can't tell from seeing the couple for one hour what goes on in their marriage."

But she wasn't to be distracted. "What is his background? Why hasn't an investigation been done?"

"It has. And it's all very above board. Charles Simmons was illegitimate and given up for adoption by his mother at birth. She told the agency the father's name, a soldier killed in Korea. Satisfied?"

She eyed him suspiciously. "I still think there's something about the man you aren't telling me."

Galen laughed softly and reached for her. "Stop thinking about other men. It's my last night here."

A steady rain on Sunday put an end to their plans for the day and they left mid-morning to drive back to Lexington.

After a seafood buffet luncheon at Mike's, they went to Elizabeth's condo and spent several hours boxing up more of her belongings. She resolutely avoided the boxes of categorized letters and the new crate of unopened mail forwarded by her publisher.

When the trunk and back seat of her car were full, they said goodbye.

"Take care of yourself, Bits." Galen kissed her gently.

"I will." Unexpectedly, her throat tightened as she realized she would be going back to the manor house alone. "I'm going to miss you," she said in a small voice."

Galen laughed. "Good. I'm glad the computer is going with you this time. Send me love notes by e-mail as soon as you get hooked up."

She grinned and nodded, and then remembered, "Oh, would you find out who Lydia Tapestry's doctor is?"

"Will do." Galen kissed her on the nose and she got in the car.

The downpour presented a problem when Elizabeth returned to the Court. The car had to be parked at the front gate while she got the key from Mindy Simmons before she could drive it into the garage. Elizabeth was soaked by the time she walked to Number One and because of the rain she decided to leave her belongings in the car overnight.

What a shame that the flowers had not been planted before the rain started. They were outside, pots in neat rows on top of the soil where Elizabeth and Galen had intended to plant them that morning. It was going to be a messy job planting them in mud.

Elizabeth took a hot bath and finished reading *Murder At the Vicarage*. Just before she slipped between the bed sheets she remembered her appointment with Jenny Anderson the next day. The quiet reflective life she had envisioned had not yet materialized. *Why do I keep filling up my hours?*

The following morning revealed the sun again; all the greenery and blossoms were sparklingly fresh from their Sunday shower and she enjoyed the short walk to Number Three.

Jenny greeted her with enthusiasm and led her on a tour of the house. She explained that all the cottages had the same floor plan. Elizabeth was surprised to see that the smaller homes had more rooms than the manor house. But the rooms at Number One were over twice the size of Jenny's.

After the tour the two women settled in the kitchen where coffee and bagels and cream cheese were laid out on the table.

"Do you visit with the Simmons very much?" asked Elizabeth. She would have thought that the two young wives living next door to one another, and both home all day, would have formed a friendship. And yet they both professed to be lonely.

"No," Jenny walked to the refrigerator and peered inside. "We . . . we don't have a lot in common." After a moment she closed the door and returned to the table, having accomplished nothing that Elizabeth could see.

An uncomfortable silence pervaded the room.

Elizabeth had made note of the VCR/DVD player and shelves of movies in the living room. "Are you and your husband movie buffs?"

The younger woman's face lit up. "Oh yes! Especially me."

Jenny talked animatedly then for some time and the two discussed old favorites they had in common such as "Gone With The Wind," "Friendly Persuasion," and the version of "Little Women" that starred June Allison, Janet Leigh, Elizabeth Taylor, and Margaret O'Brian. Elizabeth was not familiar with some of Jenny's other, more modern, favorites.

"Tell me about your own girlhood. You grew up here?" Elizabeth looked around at the homey kitchen.

The animation went out of Jenny's eyes. "Yes."

"What was Colonel Tapestry like?"

"Hitler." The resentment was not unexpected but the vehemence of its expression startled Elizabeth.

"Oh?" When Jenny did not say more, she added, "George Tate did say this was a dull place for a child to grow up. But then he had no parents to insure that his life was normal."

"It wouldn't have done him any good if he had," young Mrs. Anderson said bitterly.

Elizabeth said nothing and waited for the girl to continue.

Jenny walked to the sink and began re-stacking the dishes from Joel's breakfast that were waiting there to be washed. "You see, anyone who worked for him had to devote their whole life to the company. And so did their families. Father worked constantly except when he was asleep, and Mother . . ." Here she swallowed with some difficulty and abandoned the dishes before she continued. "Mother devoted her life to Father and entertaining for the Company. If ever I was in a play or had a school event . . . they were too busy . . . never once did they . . ." She stopped speaking and got a tissue from the counter to blot the tears threatening to spill down her cheeks. "Hattie came once . . . she'd made a costume for me." Jenny laughed, a funny choking sort of sound. "I was Joy for the church program . . . but they couldn't come. He had them doing something else. And then I was sent to boarding school in ninth grade. That's where I was when . . ." She stood motionless with her back to the sink and her eyes closed.

"When they were killed in the accident?" Elizabeth felt as though she were probing an abscessed tooth.

Jenny nodded.

"It was very fortunate that he deeded this house over when he did, very kind of him."

"No!" Jenny's eyes flew open with a flash of fire. "He wasn't kind. I wish he had never done it. I hate it here."

Elizabeth pushed on ruthlessly. "I suppose that's why you don't like to come to the manor house, even though the Colonel is no longer there?"

"I . . ." Jenny's mouth snapped closed and a slight shudder went through her frame. She shook her head.

Elizabeth could see that whatever was troubling the girl had deep roots. She said gently, "Is there anything you can tell me about Colonel Tapestry? I'm going to be frank with you. I've been asked by George Tate to assist in finding the missing son and heir."

Jenny seemed calmer now and began refilling their coffee cups. "No, I knew nothing about him really. I'm sorry to have gotten all upset." She heaved a sigh. "I'm all right now." She resumed her seat at the table.

"I thought perhaps you had heard your parents discussing him, something perhaps about his romantic habits?" The face froze before her eyes but it was just for a moment. Then Jenny shook her head again.

"No. No, nothing."

"May I ask you something else?" Elizabeth placed her own hand over the girl's.

"I'm sure the entire period was horribly painful for you, but you were here at the time. You see, I've become convinced that the Colonel's death was linked to the mystery of the heir. So I'm looking into the murder too. Did you see or hear anythi--"

Jenny pulled her hand away and stood up. There was no mistaking the terror in her eyes.

"What are you talking about? You are wrong. It was someone from the factory, an outsider. It was! They said so."

Elizabeth feared that she had gone too far. "Yes, you're probably right. I'm just a silly woman who has read too many murder mysteries." She smiled ruefully. "Oh well, if you think of anything that might help us find the person mentioned in the will, please let me know."

The relief on Jenny's face was as obvious as the terror had been.

"I'm sorry," Elizabeth said, as if there had been no uncomfortable moments, "to have discussed business on what I had intended to be a friendly social visit."

"It's all right." Jenny smiled now. "I'm sorry I can't be of any help."

The visit ended in a pleasant vein with Elizabeth promising to come very soon and view some old movies with Jenny.

But Elizabeth was concerned about the girl. She thought it quite probable that Jenny Anderson needed professional help.

Chapter Eight

Elizabeth decided to wait for Tuesday and the effects of a few more hours of sunshine to dry out the ground before working in the garden. This would be a good time to tackle the Colonel's books and office paraphernalia that she didn't want to use. She found a large storage space under the stairway in which to keep them until their rightful owner put them back out or disposed of them.

She set out toward the Archers to borrow the wagon again so she could bring in her computer, a few more boxes of her own books, and some other knickknacks. On her way she stopped at Number Five to set a time for her supper date with Mindy Simmons.

Just as she was about to knock on the door, the inside door swung open and a young man with his back to her was saying, "And don't worry. It'll all work out."

The face that turned toward her as he started to leave was classically handsome. Elizabeth had heard of men described as resembling a Greek god, and now she knew what was meant by the phrase. It was the combination of good looks and radiant vitality that gave one an impression of a creature surpassing mere mortals.

She suspected that she was about to meet William Sinclair.

He was tall and blonde with a bronze tan and Elizabeth thought that any woman who met him would immediately feel more feminine. The man looked startled briefly when he saw her and then broke into a smile and made a slight bow. "Hello." He called over his shoulder, "Mindy, you have company." And opened the storm door so Elizabeth could enter. "Let me guess. You must be the marvelous Ms. Daily."

Elizabeth replied in the same tone, "And you must be the wonderful William Sinclair."

His laughter was free and hearty. "Come in, Ms. Daily. I'm very glad to meet you."

Mindy smiled at both of them. "No need to introduce you two, I see. Please don't go yet, Bill. Sit down and really meet Elizabeth."

"I can't stay," Elizabeth protested. "I have a lot I need to get done this afternoon. I was just going to borrow the Archers' wagon to haul stuff from my car. I stopped to see if 7 is okay for dinner."

"We've got a wheelbarrow," Mindy offered, after confirming the time.

"And I've got muscles." Bill flexed an arm. "Point me to the boxes."

"Oh, no. I couldn't ask you to--"

Bill interrupted. "You didn't. I offered."

Mindy's eyes twinkled with laughter. "The truth is, Elizabeth, that he wants an excuse to see your house. He was just bemoaning my dinner invitation. Said he'd lived here much longer than I, and it wasn't fair that I should see it first."

Elizabeth was surprised. "You mean you never visited when the Colonel was alive?"

Bill shook his head and grinned. "Tapestry didn't do much personal entertaining. And our relationship was strictly business—all carried out at the office."

With the help of Bill Sinclair and the wheelbarrow, all of Elizabeth's boxes were scattered around the library in a short time and the computer was placed on the desk that was built into the wall. After Sinclair got the computer hooked up and running, the two young people explored the house. They made complimentary remarks but Elizabeth could tell that much of its charm was lost on them. When that generation chose a house for themselves it was usually all glass and sharp angles and wasted space. They were a very lively pair and Elizabeth felt invigorated by their company. But they made her realize the age difference between them and herself.

She watched them push the wheelbarrow out of sight as they walked back toward their own homes. She understood why the Tates might be concerned about the relationship. They did seem very fond of each other. But it was an easy and comfortable kind of fondness; surely the suspicions were unfounded. However, she had to admit it was a dangerous situation for two compatible young people to be so close when one of them was neglected by her husband and the other was single. Innocent friendship could turn into something else when people were lonely.

Elizabeth sighed and turned to the task at hand. She hadn't intended to bring in all the boxes at once but since she had help, it seemed a waste not to use it. She felt a twinge of dismay as she surveyed the library. This was a real move, no longer was everything neat and tidy. She had work to do.

It seemed that the best course of action would be to stack the things from the shelves that were to be packed away on the couch, empty her boxes, and then prepare the others for storage. It would have been a neater task to do it one box at a time but . . .

The American history collections and outdated encyclopedias immediately went to the couch to be replaced by Jane Austin, Dickens, and the Brontes. Most of the leather bound classics she left on the shelves. When all the books had been sorted through, Elizabeth began to open the cabinet doors that ran the length of the inner wall under the bookcases. There were a variety of items stored there; books of coins—both foreign and domestic, yellow edged brochures describing the excellence of Tapestry caskets, old copies of the Wall Street Journal, several display cases full of pipes of varying shapes and sizes, and a scrapbook. The scrapbook was the kind that Elizabeth knew from her childhood. She remembered buying little black corners that had to be moistened and stuck to the pages so that snapshots could be displayed. Besides using the book as a photograph album, she had also taped clippings or cards or flower petals in hers. She hadn't seen one in years.

Positioning herself on the floor Indian style, she opened the scrapbook. It contained several programs listing Colonel Guy R. Tapestry as the main speaker. She glanced through newspaper articles depicting the opening of the new factory under Tapestry's management and later expansions, articles involving Tapestry employees who had gained recognition, certificates honoring Colonel Tapestry himself, clippings of Lucy and Harold Fowler's marriage and the birth of their son, an article about Venezuelan oil wells, and one clipping about a young female evangelist.

This last clipping Elizabeth picked up with trembling fingers. It was not at all what she'd expected to find as the first indication of Guy Tapestry's interest in a female. The column was dated July 27, 1977 and reported that a young girl in her teens had broken into the circle of tent evangelism and was drawing large crowds wherever she opened her meetings. Grace Love, as she called herself, would not give any details of her life before her appearance on the evangelistic circuit except to say that she had "visited an evangelistic meeting with some of my friends with the purpose of making fun of 'the fakes' and found my purpose in life."

A smile lifted the corners of Elizabeth's lips as she read the fervor of youthful dedication depicted in the article and recalled her own teenage passions. The teen years were such an intense period for a young girl, all hormones and glands and looking for ways of self expression.

The article went on to say that Miss Love's meetings were very dramatic and emotional. They always ended with the crowd in tears making vows of renewed spiritual devotion.

The photograph that had once headed the column had been removed.

Elizabeth replaced the clipping on the opened page of the scrapbook and sat back on her heels, a frown wrinkling her brow. *Why would Colonel Tapestry have such a clipping in with his other, very personal, souvenirs? And what happened to the picture?*

Just then the door chime sounded. It was only 4:30, too early for Mindy.

Emily Caine entered the front door as soon as it was opened. Elizabeth wished she had closed off the library because the mess could be seen clearly from the entrance hall, for Miss Caine began making her way painfully to that room. She stopped in the doorway and surveyed the library in silence. Then she turned to Elizabeth.

"I have come to discuss this . . . commission you have been given by George." And she made her way toward the brown leather chairs, which provided the only cleared space on which to sit.

"Wouldn't you like to sit in the parlor?"

"This is not a social call," Miss Caine said stiffly.

Elizabeth glanced at the scrapbook., *I wish I had put that away before I answered the door..* When she looked back at Miss Caine, she saw that the spinster's sharp eyes had followed her own. Emily Caine gave a slightly perceptible but decisive nod.

"George informed me of this ridiculous venture. He asked me to assist you in any way I can." Cold blue eyes stabbed at hers. "He said he advised you of my stand on the matter. Guy must have been insane to put such a thing in his will; there was never a hint of any involvement of that kind."

Then, looking back at the scrapbook, she added with venom, "But if you must persist in this folly, you might find that disgraceful young hussy."

Elizabeth was surprised. "The girl preacher?"

Miss Caine nodded. "It's the only possible avenue of investigation. Guy became interested in the antics of the creature. And even had me write for a schedule of her performances."

Elizabeth bit her lip to hide her amusement at the woman's description of the evangelistic meetings. Emily Caine continued.

"So foolish of him. But he was nearing sixty years of age. Men do get silly at that time of life, I understand. They call it midlife crisis now, I believe." She sniffed. "He even attended one of the things . . . in Kansas City I think. It could be that the girl seduced him and bore a child as the result. I would expect such behavior from a person of that sort. Guy was normally above reproach but it was evidently a vulnerable period for him. I suggest that you find that person."

Elizabeth wasn't sure what to say. Finally she asked, "Kansas City, you say? Do you know where Grace Love might be now?"

Emily Caine shook her head and began her struggle to rise from the chair. "I wouldn't know. All that sort of thing—so distasteful. Beyond the pale of acceptable religious practice. I would never have occasion to hear of her carryings on." She made her way to the front door. "Please inform George that I have done my duty."

Hattie stood waiting on the walk, and Elizabeth apologized. "I'm sorry. I didn't see you standing there earlier. You should have come inside."

Hattie smiled and shook her head. "Miz Emily wanted me to wait."

At that her employer sniffed loudly.

When the women had gone, Elizabeth returned to the library and replaced the scrapbook in the cabinet before going to the kitchen to make preparations for her supper with Mindy Simmons.

Mindy arrived on time and over a dinner of broiled scallops, tossed salad with buttermilk dressing, and au gratin potatoes, the two women talked practically non-stop.

Elizabeth outlined her quest for the missing heir and, for the first time, received a reaction of wholehearted enthusiasm.

"What fun!" Mindy's eyes danced with excitement. "Can I help?"

Elizabeth laughed. "If I discover a trail, I'll unleash you to follow the scent." Then she added in a serious tone. "Miss Caine became indignant when she discovered my purpose and Jenny Anderson acted afraid."

Mindy shook her blonde curls. "Poor Jenny. She's afraid of everything."

"Let's go out on the patio for coffee. Is that okay?

"Sure."

When they were settled Elizabeth directed the conversation back to where they left off.

"Tell me about Jenny Anderson." She leaned back in her chair, relaxed in the stillness of the spring evening and comfortable in the presence of her guest.

"I don't know much. I tried to be friends. We are close to the same age and I thought it would be fun having a real neighbor to borrow sugar from and stuff. And at first it seemed like it was going to work. And then I blew it." Mindy gave a rueful laugh.

"What did you do?"

"Tried to exchange girlish confidences. Not very mature of me, I know. But I was, well, I was confused about some things in my marriage and needed someone to talk to."

When Elizabeth didn't reply, she continued. "Charles is . . . I mean . . . well, it's about our intimate life and all that."

Elizabeth interjected. "It's quite all right. I was married once. I have no virgin ears to shock."

"Good! That makes it easier and maybe you can help me. You see, I love Charles very much. I wish I didn't. It hurts."

Elizabeth waited while Mindy swallowed a few times before resuming her story. "He has always been so formal with me. There was nothing like a courtship. I was his secretary and from the first I adored him. He was the perfect strong, silent man, so secure. But he never seemed to notice or treat me any differently from anyone else. Then one day he asked me, in a very casual way, if I was busy after work. I wasn't and he invited me to drive to Lexington for dinner. I honestly thought he must be meeting someone on business and needed notes taken. We went to the Campbell House and I was really surprised when he told the waiter we were ready to order, since no one else had joined us."

She giggled. "The meal was eaten in total silence and I was in a complete swivet wondering what was going on, although I acted calm on the outside of course. Then, after the table was cleared except for our coffee, Charles—only I called him Mr. Simmons at the time—said, in a very businesslike manner," and here Mindy's face took on a stern expression in imitation of her husband, "Miss Bailey, I am forty two years old. I have had no experience with women but it has been pressing on my mind lately that if I am ever to marry and have a family, it must not be delayed any longer. You are a very intelligent and attractive young woman and must have a wide choice of gentlemen friends but since I know of no serious attachments, it occurred to me that you might be open to considering a partnership of this nature. My assets are considerable and you would be assured of a secure future."

The stern look dissolved as Mindy and Elizabeth both broke into laughter.

"I swear, that's exactly what he said—like it was a speech he had memorized. I remember every word, even though I went into sort of a state of shock. I finally said, 'Mr. Simmons, are you asking me to marry you?' He said he was and I said, 'Well, okay.' How's that for romance?"

Elizabeth laughed again. "A unique proposal, to say the least."

The girlish face sobered. "But it has not changed and it's not funny anymore. Elizabeth, the only time Charles has kissed me was at our wedding two years ago—and that was a very solemn peck on the lips."

"Do you mean you've never . . .?"

"Oh yes, about once a week. But nothing that isn't absolutely necessary to try to insure a child. No kissing or . . . anything."

"Oh, dear. How frustrating for you." Even Elizabeth's failed marriage had not been that void of affectionate gestures.

"Exactly. It would be bad enough if I didn't love him. I mean, I am human. But sometimes I just want to—oh, I don't know what I want to do. Something to make him need me or want me or anything besides act like I am a business obligation he is transacting. I have to bite my lip to keep from saying how much I love him and begging him to really love me."

"Why don't you?" asked Elizabeth.

"He doesn't . . . I mean you don't know . . ." Mindy sighed. "I wouldn't dare."

Elizabeth could not imagine any man considering Mindy Simmons a duty. She shook her head speechlessly. Not one bit of wisdom or advice came to her mind.

Mindy had obviously forgotten that the discussion began with a question about Jenny Anderson, so Elizabeth gently turned it back toward that topic.

"And this was what you tried to discuss with Jenny?"

Mindy pulled herself out of the deep study into which she had sunk. "Yes, and she got very upset. She said 'I don't know about any of that' and left my house as soon as she could without being obviously rude. She has avoided me ever since." She sighed again. "This has not been a warm place to live. If it hadn't been for Bill I don't think I would have survived."

Since Mindy was first to bring up the subject, Elizabeth took advantage of it. "You two seem like good friends."

"Oh yes! He's been wonderful. He recommended me for the job with Charles in the first place."

"Oh, you knew him before you came to work here?"

Suddenly Mindy began fiddling with her hair. "No . . . I mean . . . I had first been one of the pool secretaries in the sales department. He noticed my work and told Charles about me when his former secretary retired."

"I see." She hoped Mindy would say something further about the relationship but she didn't.

They ended the evening in a lively discussion of P.G. Wodehouse, an author Elizabeth would have thought the younger woman didn't know. They each admitted an infatuation for both Bertie Wooster and the enigmatic and capable Jeeves.

After Mindy left, Elizabeth remembered that they had forgotten all about discussing colleges and Mindy's further education.

Later before falling asleep Elizabeth found herself thinking again about Jenny Anderson. She had the vague impression that there was something there, which if discovered, would shed light on other things.

And Emily Caine's visit had been very interesting. It certainly seemed to point the investigation away from Tapestry Court. The whole thing was curious. Why would Colonel Tapestry have taken such an interest in the activities of Grace Love?

As she drifted off to sleep, Elizabeth realized that Bill Sinclair was the right age to be the son of Grace Love. It was a vaguely disturbing thought.

Chapter Nine

On Tuesday morning Elizabeth planted her flowers and surveyed both of the gardens with satisfaction. She'd accomplished a lot in the one week she had been at Tapestry Court. *What a shame I can't just forget everything else and immerse myself in the serenity of these new surroundings.* But even if she tried, the attempt would be futile; she knew herself well enough to realize that she would not be able to relax and get on with the question of her own future until every avenue to solve the Tapestry puzzle had been explored.

The Tapestry puzzle. The phrase was catchy and she lowered herself onto the bench in the gazebo for a few minutes' reflection. The whole situation was like a tapestry, individual complexities interwoven in a sometimes startling fashion, differing scenes that must somehow fit together and make sense.

Drowsiness descended and Elizabeth caught herself just as she was falling asleep. She came back to full consciousness with a start. She saw something clearly in her mind just before she drifted off . . . something to do with the young evangelist. She tried to recapture the impression but to no avail.

After taking a shower she felt more alert and set out across the Court to visit the Archers.

Hattie sighed as she watched Elizabeth let herself out of the gate from the manor property. Elizabeth Daily seemed like a really nice lady, so normal, a breath of fresh air from the outside, like Mindy Simmons and Bill Sinclair. It was a good thing Miz Emily was resting, or Hattie would have to listen all afternoon about the shocking color of Miz Daily's dress.

Hattie liked it—hot pink—lively. Miz Emily never wore anything but beige and brown and sometimes navy blue. Washed out old biddy!

It would be nice to work for somebody like Miz Daily. It would be nice not to have to work at all, have her own home, fix eggs and bacon like she liked 'em herself. Here, if she cooked her own food separately, she'd have to hear a sermon about wasting electricity. It would be wonderful to not have to put up with lectures on the 'proper way to prepare' everything on God's green earth.

Well, this morning she'd shut her up. Finally said "That Bible you're always readin' says not to eat pig anyhow. So don't reckon there be any rules in there how to cook it if you do." And Miz Emily had withdrawn to her room to rest. *Miz Emily in a foul mood today but at least now I got me some breathin' space.*

Harold Fowler was puttering in his garden. And he felt an immense satisfaction in doing so. After they left the missionary field, during his years as a very busy pastor of unruly flocks, he had read of retired men who puttered in their gardens and it seemed to him to be a description of the ultimate in earthly peace and relaxation. He wasn't exactly sure what the word putter meant, and steadfastly refused to look it up in the dictionary and risk the definition damaging his original vision. Instead he acted out the vision implanted in his mind when he first read the words.

His idea of puttering was to walk between neat rows planted by his wife and contemplate the miracle of dry seeds becoming green leaves and eventually moist vegetables, and pick up a vagrant stone or twig if he was in the mood to stoop down.

Stoop, not bend. He discovered a few years ago that bending could be disastrous. One day in a fit of husbandly exuberance, after receiving the revelation that though he had retired from his labors, his wife who was the same age must continue the duties she had been performing for over forty years, he bent over the dishwasher. And then not only did Lucy have to empty the dishwasher herself but she had been forced to carry his meals to him on a tray for a week while he lay on a heating pad.

A flash of pink which was brighter than the dogwood blossoms caught his attention and he looked toward the front yard in time to see Tapestry Court's newest resident pass by on her way to the front gate.

Fine looking woman, he thought again. *Kept her figure. Wonder why she doesn't color her hair? She'd look thirty-five if she did. Most women would have dyed it. I like that! Do the best with yourself but leave everything as the Lord made it. Wonder if she has pierced ears?* Harold Fowler did not approve of pierced ears.

Lucy tentatively mentioned piercing her own ears once and he had informed her with great dignity that it was her body and she could do with it as she pleased. "But don't look over at me for support when you are standing before your Creator and He says 'Lucille Fowler, where is the rest of the body I gave you?' You'll just have to confess, 'Sir, I poked out a few holes so I could hang jewelry on it." Lucy had laughed and called him an idiot. But she hadn't gotten her ears pierced.

The Daily woman probably has more sense too. Harold had not yet presented himself at Number One. *Plenty of time. Only been here a week. Let the others satisfy their curiosity.*

He puttered for a while longer, enjoying the warm sun and slight breeze on his skin, when another figure entered his line of vision on the brick walk. It was Reggie Tate, who surely ought to be in school. She too disappeared from sight toward the gate.

Harold was uncomfortably reminded of something in the way Reggie carried herself, but he couldn't put his finger on the memory. With a shrug, he turned back to his puttering.

Four stoops, one rock, and three twigs later it came to him. Evelyn Howard held her neck and shoulders in just the same manner each time she slipped into the pew to join her parents for Sunday evening service.

They found out later that the girl had been skipping youth group all year to go joy riding with a most undesirable young man.

Jackie Archer was alone in the store and acted glad to see a friendly face when Elizabeth entered. "It's been a slow day. Joe has gone to the Farmer's Market for fresh produce. Mostly peas and onions this time of year but it's fresh. And we like to buy as much as we can from local farmers."

Elizabeth nodded approval at this show of community spirit and then gradually led the conversation around to local gossip.

The Archers never met Colonel Tapestry but they'd heard a lot about him. He'd pretty much held the city government in his pocket, according to the locals.

"There was one bit of scandal," Jackie confided. "But nobody seems to know much about it and nothing ever went to court."

"What's that?"

"It was a long time ago, around forty years, I think. The deed shows that Mr. Bottoms—that's who we bought the place from—he bought the store in 1967. Anyway, the reason she sold it to him, the original owner I mean, was because of something that happened with Colonel Tapestry. Nobody seems to know what it was. The Sheriff's office didn't do anything about it and she sold out, and she and her daughter left town. They say Tapestry could have gotten away with murder in this town."

Elizabeth forbore saying that it was someone else who had gotten away with murder. Instead she asked, "What were their names, the mother and daughter, I mean?"

Jackie wrinkled her brow. "I'm sure I heard it. Let's see Anderson, Andrews, started with an A, I'm sure. Yes, I remember thinking A to B and back to A. You know, the initials of the owners? A something to Bottoms to Archer. Adkins! That was it. Emma Adkins, that was her name, the first owner." She beamed triumphantly.

Before Elizabeth left, she had also extricated the fact that Deputy Collins, now almost ready to retire, had been around at the time the incident happened. She said goodbye to Jackie Archer and promised to return for some little green onions. Then she walked toward town and the Sheriff's office which was only a few blocks away.

Simpsonton was a pretty town. She had noticed some lovely old homes along the tree shaded route she'd traveled when she arrived in the community. Now she wondered who lived in them. In the little corner where she now made her home, one got the impression that without

Tapestry Industries there would be no Simpsonton. That was obviously not true.

The grizzled man who hurriedly removed his feet from the desk at her entrance proved to be Deputy Matt Collins.

When Elizabeth explained her assignment from George Tate he agreed to assist her in any way he could.

He pointed her to a chair but didn't move from his own. "I remember it real well. My first month on the job. And an eye opener. Taught me a lot about the Justice system." He shrugged. "The poor offenders get justice—the rich don't. The rich victims get justice—the poor don't. Shook me up at the time. Gotten used to it now. Don't like it but that's the way the cookie crumbles."

"What was the offense?"

He shrugged again. "Don't know. Nobody knew except Sheriff Ryan. Took the lady in his office and calmed her down. Everything all private like. When she left, he tore up the report, saw him myself. Wouldn't have known who it was about 'cept when she came in she said she wanted to file a complaint against Tapestry."

Elizabeth decided he must be comfortable in her presence now because he put his feet back on the desk.

"Sheriff's wife worked for Tapestry, almost ready to retire. Shook me up at the time. Young, didn't understand how the system worked."

Elizabeth shook her head in commiseration. "Can you tell me about the Colonel's death?"

He removed his feet again and sat up with interest. "Now that was something else. Not a clue. Not one. I know—had a new sheriff at the time, didn't know nothing, elected you know . . . money again. So I did all the work myself. Couldn't find out a thing. Nobody pushed it." He laughed. "Don't think anybody cared. Finally shelved it; didn't really care myself."

He scratched behind his ear. "Would've been nice to catch a killer though. Might have run for sheriff myself, but not a clue. And nobody carin' and all. Dropped it. Figured he got what was comin' to him."

Elizabeth thanked him and walked back to the Archers' store. Joe had returned with fresh produce of the local season - onions, peas, lettuce, collard greens, and asparagus.

And Chuck had stopped in after school.

They had a soft drink, which Elizabeth insisted on paying for this time.

"I haven't met your sister but I saw her the other day, Chuck, and she is very pretty. You must be proud of her."

The boy turned up his nose in disgust. "She's stupid."

Elizabeth supposed all boys of eleven thought all girls were stupid, even – or maybe especially - their sisters.

Jackie Archer came out from behind the counter and joined them.

"I'd have given my eye teeth to look like that in high school. She's gorgeous. I'll bet she has lots of dates."

"Nope. Doesn't date. Just acts silly with her girl friends. They keep me awake giggling when one of them sleeps over. Stupid."

"What does *Reggie* stand for?" Elizabeth asked. She had always associated the name with males.

"Regina." He curled his upper lip. "She says it means a Queen and I should treat her like one. It really just means that she's named after Dad."

Jackie Archer raised her eyebrows. "Your Dad is named Regina?"

Chuck laughed. "No. Reginald. That's his middle name. But Reggie says that was just," and here Chuck lowered his eyelids, stuck his nose in the air, and raised his voice an octave, "the mundane means by which the appropriate nomenclature came to me."

They all laughed.

Elizabeth purchased the onions and some asparagus, and returned to Tapestry Court.

After washing the asparagus and setting it to steam, she went to the library and retrieved her notes from the desk drawer. When she pulled the drawer out, she pulled with too much force and it fell to the floor. And then it would not go back in all the way. She pulled it out again and saw that something was lying flat on the surface of the drawer base and blocking the runner.

It was a small appointment book, one of those kind furnished by insurance agencies and banks. This one was stamped with the name of the Lexington bank with which Galen was associated and the year was 1997, the year the Colonel was killed. There were not many entries.

Presumably Colonel Tapestry had secretaries who kept him informed of most of his appointments. An entry in February of that year revealed that on the 14th there was an 8:30 a.m. appointment with "Riley—teeth" and on April 10th at 4 p.m. a designation for "Walters—back". The last entry was for April 21st and read "CS—will" at 10 a.m.

She caught Galen by phone just as he was about to leave the office.

"God's briefcase with all that information is at home. Since I turned the case over to you, I thought I'd need it more there. Want me to call you later?"

She decided quickly. "No, I want to come and have lunch with you tomorrow anyway. Did you find out about Lydia's doctor?"

"Yes, it's Ed Ramey."

"Great!" She and Ed were friends. They'd kept offices in the same building for years.. "I'll try to make an appointment to talk to him tomorrow. But even if I can't, I want to run up to Lexington for goldfish and some other stuff."

She heard the rustling of papers in the background. "1:30 okay? I've got a luncheon meeting but I'll wait to eat with you."

"Fine. If Ed can only see me at that time, I'll call back in the morning."

"Are you okay, Bits?"

"Everything is fine. I'm finding out lots of facts. Whether they are pertinent or not remains to be seen. See you tomorrow at Mike's."

When they hung up, Elizabeth remembered the asparagus and ran to the kitchen to see if the damage she feared had been done. It had and though over-steamed asparagus was not her favorite, she squeezed lemon on it and spread it with olive oil margarine before she returned to the telephone.

Ed Ramey was out of town until the following Monday but Elizabeth was still looking forward to her outing in Lexington. She would look for some summer clothes suitable for lounging around her new home, meet Galen for lunch, and pick up some goldfish before she headed back to Simpsonton. While she was planning the day in her mind, the telephone rang and Galen, with obvious regret, told her that he had to make an emergency business trip to Boston and wouldn't return until late Saturday.

Elizabeth found herself thinking of other errands with which she could fill her day in the city; and then suddenly stopped herself short in her musing.

"What am I doing?" she asked herself aloud. An uncomfortable realization dawned on her. She had been at Tapestry Court one week and during that week she had entertained, visited, investigated, read, and gardened. But she'd not done what she came here to do.

She had not gotten quiet and searched her own mind and heart to find the answers she needed in order to make decisions about the future.

Avoidance, that's what I am doing. She admonished herself, and determined to begin the sorting process that same evening. With Galen gone and no visible way to continue the Tapestry investigation until next week, she promised herself at least four days of nothing but self discovery.

After a supper of very limp steamed asparagus and broiled chicken breast, Elizabeth washed the dishes and walked out the back door in anticipation of meditative relaxation.

The flowers she planted that morning with such love and care lay among clumps of mud all over the patio. Green leaves and colorful petals were torn from stems and scattered around. Tears sprang to her eyes at the sight of the destruction. It wasn't just the flowers, they could be replaced. It was the malice behind the act and the message that clearly stated "You are not wanted here."

"It will take more than that." She spoke aloud angrily at her unknown enemy as she went to gather up broom and dustpan.

She checked out the garden by the pool and was relieved to find that those flowers had not been disturbed. But her heart was heavy as she realized that the serpent was no longer perched on the garden wall. He had entered her own private Eden.

Chapter Ten

Elizabeth awoke on Wednesday morning with a sense of something wrong. She lay in bed sorting out her thoughts for a few seconds before she remembered the flower disaster from the night before.

She'd cleaned up the mess and replanted the flowers before she allowed herself to go to bed. But there was still something in her heart that was not cleaned up. And she acknowledged again that her busyness of the past week, neglecting the very purpose for which she had come to Tapestry Court, was not just due to circumstances. She was most definitely avoiding thinking through the things she needed to make decisions about, incapable of sorting it all out alone.

Calling a psychologist friend didn't feel like what she needed, but what? As her feet touched the floor she thought of Lucy Fowler's husband. She had not met Harold Fowler but she knew he was a retired minister, first a missionary and then a pastor. Elizabeth needed a pastor.

Maybe he wouldn't be what she needed, and if not, she was under no compulsion to share her heart with him.

She could just ask his advice about what to do concerning the flower incident, whether to pursue it to discover the perpetrator or just ignore it.

As soon as she had her first cup of morning coffee and thought that it was not too early to call, she found the phone book and looked up the Fowler's number. A male voice answered on the first ring.

"Reverend Fowler?" Elizabeth hoped her voice didn't sound as needy as she felt.

"Speaking." Harold Fowler said.

"This is Elizabeth Daily, the new tenant in Number One, Tapestry Court."

"Yes." He sounded pleased. "Forgive me for not having called and introduced myself but I wanted to give you time to get settled in."

"Oh, please don't apologize. That was very thoughtful of you." Then, not wanting to imply criticism of his wife, who had called, she added, "But of course I loved meeting your wife; she is just wonderful."

"Yes, she is. I am a blessed man. What can I do for you, Miss Daily?"

"Oh, please call me Elizabeth."

"Only if you will call me Harold."

"It's a deal. Harold, I need some pastoral advice and I know you are retired but I wondered if maybe . . ."

"Miss Daily, Elizabeth, don't you know that pastors never retire? They are just set out to pasture and graze around hoping the Shepherd will call them from time to time to help tend the other sheep."

Elizabeth laughed. "Well, I think this is one of those times. When would it be convenient for me to come and talk to you?"

"Anytime." He sighed. "I wish I could tell you that I had to check my schedule but unfortunately my schedule is always open these days."

Elizabeth glanced at the wall clock again. "It's 10 after 9 now. Would 10 o'clock this morning be okay?"

"I'll be looking forward to it."

When they hung up, Elizabeth checked her e-mail, answered an inquiry from her agent putting off a decision about scheduling speaking engagements, sent a note to Galen that would make him laugh when he checked his laptop from the hotel in Boston, and went to dress for the day. She shook her head at the thought of speaking engagements. If she did that she couldn't retain the anonymity she so desired.

As she put on her makeup she thought how she hated not sharing everything with Galen. But she didn't want him to worry about her, and the act of violence in her garden would probably cause him to try to persuade her again to leave Tapestry Court. And that was just what she was determined not to do, not this soon anyway.

The floor plan of Number Seven where the Fowlers lived appeared to be exactly the same as Number Three, just as Jenny Anderson had told her, but the ambiance was completely different. While Jenny's family had decorated in Early American reproductions and she had kept things as they were, the Fowlers had many antiques, much of it Edwardian and some Victorian.

After greeting Lucy, being shown around the main floor, and declining coffee or tea, Elizabeth was led by Harold Fowler into his office, obviously meant originally as a bedroom but made over into his own very masculine study.

"This is nice," Elizabeth spoke with admiration as she sank into a red leather chair. Harold went around the desk and seated himself in the matching swivel office chair. Elizabeth tore her eyes away from the books that lined every wall but made a mental note to ask permission to come back some time just to browse.

"Thank you so much for taking time to meet with me," she said with a smile.

Harold Fowler was a pleasant, comfortable looking man. Gray hair and just enough wrinkles to look wise.

"As I said on the phone, the pleasure is all mine. I looked forward to retirement with longing but now I find myself looking backward with the same emotion. In other words, I am bored!"

She laughed. "Well, I don't know that my problems will be very interesting to you but . . ."

He smiled but said very seriously and sincerely, "Every part of every human life is interesting to me."

Elizabeth unexpectedly felt tears prick her eyes. It had been a long time since she had gone to someone that she was looking to as older and wiser than she. And this man obviously cared. "Thank you," she said. And it came out in a whisper.

"Shall we begin with prayer?" he asked.

"Please." With unaccustomed relief that someone else was in charge of a counseling session, Elizabeth bowed her head as Harold Fowler's voice invited the presence of God into their midst.

"Father, I thank you for Elizabeth Daily and for bringing her into our lives here at Tapestry Court. I know you sent her here for your purposes. You know those purposes and you know what you want to accomplish during our time together today. We trust you to guide our conversation and give us your wisdom and guidance. In Jesus Name, Amen."

When he finished praying, he looked up at her and smiled, obviously waiting for her to open the conversation.

She cleared her throat. "Well, first, I am amazed that you prayed the way you did. I wasn't sure that I would discuss this with you but . . ." She paused. "You mentioned in your prayer the Lord having called me for his purposes. That's the main reason I came to Tapestry

Court. I needed to get away from my practice—I'm a psychologist, I don't know if you knew that — and, well, from the busy life I have been immersed in lately. Just get away and have time to hear him, hear what he wants of me . . . what his purposes are for my future. There are things, a calling I believed I had when I was young, but then I didn't seem to fit that calling, or it didn't fit me. I don't know . . ." She paused. "I really truly don't know. I have been a psychologist for a lot of years and I know I have helped people. I always told them up front that I was a Christian and if they didn't object, I prayed with them that the Lord would give us insight. I was much more successful with Christian clients. I just don't believe that there are any real answers outside of Jesus. Aids to coping, yes, but real healing, no."

Harold nodded. "You are a wise woman. It sounds to me like you have been fulfilling your calling . . . or one of them."

She nodded. "Yes. But . . . like I said, I came here to try to sort things out, find out what God wants for my future but I don't seem to be getting anywhere with that. I realized this morning that I'm avoiding being alone and thinking things through. Maybe I don't really want to know what God wants. And yet . . ." She really didn't want to expose her identity as the writer of *The Fall and Redemption of God* but how could she sort it all out and expect him to help her without exposing that key piece of the puzzle that was her life?

Before she could say anything, Harold Fowler said. "I read a book recently. Enjoyed it a lot. It seems like it might be just right for you. It had a lot of psychological insight and would appeal to a psychologist, I would think. I'm not sure what it has to do with your situation but it came to my mind as I was praying before you arrived. It is called *The Fall and Redemption of God*.

He looked startled when Elizabeth laughed out loud.

She quickly apologized and explained, "I wrote that book. That was what I was trying to decide whether to tell you about or not. It is under my pseudonym so you would have had no way of knowing."

It was Harold's turn to laugh.

"Well, it seems the Lord took the decision right out of your hands. Tell me."

So Elizabeth told him, the whole story.

It was a few minutes after noon when she looked up at the clock and began to apologize profusely at taking so much of his time.

Harold Fowler was quick to assure her that two hours was not unusual for pastoral counseling sessions.

"We usually only do one hour for individual counseling in my profession, more sometimes for group counseling," Elizabeth said.

Harold grinned. "We have no time rules in mine. Time doesn't mean anything to the Boss!"

They agreed to meet the next Wednesday at the same time and after saying goodbye and thanking Lucy for the use of her home and her husband's time, Elizabeth left, feeling much more hopeful than she ever had about the possibility of past, present, and future blending together in a pattern that made sense.

Lucy knew better than to ask her husband any questions but Harold knew that his wife was brimming over with curiosity. He allowed himself one comment.

"There is a woman who is as attractive on the inside as on the outside."

His wife nodded, "That helps." And after a moment, as she filled his lunch plate, "I'm going to tell her."

And since her decision agreed with his own newly formulated opinion, there was no need for further discussion of the matter.

After making, and eating, some tomato basil soup for lunch, Elizabeth made a decision.

When she knocked on the front door of Number Two, Hattie answered.

Elizabeth greeted her with warmth and asked if Miss Caine was in.

"Yes'm but she's takin' a nap right now. Is there anything I can help you with?"

Elizabeth rapidly revised her plan. "Yes, I think I'd like to talk to you. Are you busy?"

Hattie answered by moving out of the doorway and gesturing for Elizabeth to enter.

When they were in the kitchen, seated at the table with a glass of iced tea, Elizabeth related her discovery of the evening before.

"I just wondered if perhaps you or Miss Caine might have seen anyone suspicious. Or if you had any idea who might want to do such a thing . . . and why?"

Hattie shook her head in disbelief. "That's bad stuff."

Elizabeth could tell that the woman was shocked. She had believed that even if Emily Caine had wanted her to do it, Hattie was not the type for wanton destruction and Hattie's obvious shock was confirmation of her lack of awareness of the incident.

"Can't think of anybody don't want you here cept' . . ." she stopped, realizing she had said too much.

Elizabeth smiled. "Except Miss Caine? I know, but I don't take it personally. She doesn't want anyone in the Manor House."

Hattie looked relieved. "Yes'm. That's right. She thinks a' that house like her own baby."

"Why didn't she get permission to move in it herself?" Elizabeth asked.

"Don't know. Well, I think she believes nobody 'sposed to live there 'cept the Colonel."

Elizabeth nodded her understanding. "She was very dedicated to him, wasn't she?"

Hattie's eyes looked penetratingly into her own. "Yes'm. Very." The look was filled with meaning but no more words were forthcoming on that subject. They discussed the gardens for a few minutes and discovered a mutual love of gladiolus.

When Elizabeth took the last sip of her tea, she stood up. "Thank you Hattie, for the tea—and the sympathy."

"You want I should tell Miz Emily 'bout those flowers?"

"I don't know. What do you think? I wouldn't want her to worry or be afraid that a vandal might do more damage."

Hattie looked skeptical about Emily Caine's worry and or fear, but said. "Yes'm, I think it best to don't tell her."

That made Elizabeth wonder.

When Elizabeth had gone, Hattie shook her head.

Miz' Emily wasn't in no shape to go cause havoc in the neighboring garden or Hattie would have thought it was her, first thing. How that woman hated Elizabeth Daily. And her such a nice lady.

But suddenly Hattie remembered something else about the previous afternoon. *Surely it couldn't be . . .what would be the purpose?*

Elizabeth left Number Two and returned to the Manor House to get her purse. Suddenly she wanted to leave Tapestry Court. She wanted to go into Simpsonton and see what the town had to offer. As she backed out of her parking slot, she wondered what Charles Simmons was going to do about a parking place for their second vehicle.

Well, Charles was one person that could not be blamed for trashing her garden—he had been out of town.

And she refused to believe that Mindy would have done such a thing, or Bill Sinclair. She couldn't believe it of Jenny Anderson either. She knew for sure George Tate was not the guilty party but what about his wife or children? *Not Chuck; he loved the garden. Reggie?* No teenage girl would be interested enough in the life of an older woman to care whether she was entrenched in the court or not. What about Linda, George Tate's wife? Could she not want her there for some reason?

Elizabeth realized that she was assuming that the note and the flower damage were the work of the same person. And whoever the person was, they were not very mature. It had to be someone who lived in the Court; it was a locked and gated community. It was merely a fact that no one else had access.

Reluctantly she thought back over all the inhabitants. In Number Two, Emily Caine would have the motive to scare her away but not the physical means and Hattie would have the physical ability but would not do it, Elizabeth was convinced of that.

In Number Five, Charles Simmons was eliminated because of absence. Mindy wouldn't do it. In Number Six, Bill wouldn't do it. In Number Four, George Tate wouldn't do it and Chuck wouldn't do it. In Number Seven, Harold and Lucy Fowler wouldn't do it. That left four people . . . Joel and Jenny Anderson in Number Three, and Linda and Reggie Tate in Number Four.

Elizabeth thought with a start that, though she had been going to consult Harold Fowler about the flower incident alone if he appeared not to be the person she needed for pastoral counseling. He had been so exactly what she needed that she had not even mentioned that incident or the note at all.

She glanced at her watch. It was 2:30; maybe she could stop by their home again when she got back to the Court.

Brightly colored impatiens and pansies were planted in the window boxes and displayed on all the storefronts on Main Street of the town. *It must have been a Town Council or Chamber of Commerce decision that all the businesses conform to present a harmonious exterior.* She liked it.

Elizabeth drove by the library and on an impulse pulled around the corner and back into the parking lot. The library was obviously an old church building renovated for that purpose. The bell tower and stained glass windows gave it away and when she went inside, that assessment was confirmed. The original sanctuary had not been subdivided and the spaciousness and stained glass windows created a very pleasant, if unusual, atmosphere for a library. A plaque just inside the door informed the reader that it was originally built in 1875 as the Methodist Episcopal Church of Simpsonton, became the United Methodist Church in 1968, and was sold to the town in 1980 when the congregation bought land and relocated.

Elizabeth went straight to the desk, which was manned by a very pleasant looking woman who looked like she was in her thirties. "Hello, I am new to Simpsonton and would like to get a card. What do I need to do?"

The woman smiled. "Welcome. We are always glad to have newcomers. Have you been here long?"

"Just over a week."

"My name is Glenda Taylor . . . just call me Glenda. I'm glad to meet you." She reached across the desk and stuck out her hand.

Suppressing a smile of amusement at the very masculine greeting, Elizabeth shook hands with Glenda Taylor. "And I am Elizabeth."

Glenda handed her a card to fill out which she did. When she handed it back, the woman said, "Oh! Miss Daily. Of Tapestry Court, right?"

"Yes." Elizabeth was surprised. Tapestry Court seemed so far removed from the rest of the town that she hadn't expected to be discussed outside its fences.

"Mindy Simmons has talked and talked about you. She thinks you are wonderful!"

Elizabeth smiled. "The feeling is mutual. She is a lovely young woman."

She was given a card and a map of the library that made it easy to browse around and acquaint herself with the layout. But she left without borrowing any books. As she explained to Glenda, "I am going to make myself get unpacked and settled in before I allow myself to get immersed in reading for fun."

By the time she got back to her car it was nearly four o'clock and she was beginning to feel hungry. She realized that all she had consumed for the day was coffee and tomato soup. She pulled into the drive-through of the Wendy's and ordered before it hit her that she was doing it again—throwing her healthy diet to the wind.

Give yourself a break, Elizabeth. You brought up a lot of painful memories today. It is not going to hurt you to indulge yourself with comfort food this once.

Chapter Eleven

The rest of her second week at Tapestry Court passed uneventfully and Elizabeth felt that she was finally getting somewhere toward her personal goals by relaxing and allowing herself to "just be" as she put it, gardening, reading, and most importantly doing Bible Study just for personal edification and not with any ministry in mind— either counseling or writing. Harold Fowler advised her to allow no 'oughts' in her thinking or actions and she felt good about obeying that rule during the four days since her time with him. The slow pace was its own therapy and it was almost with regret that she picked up the phone first thing Monday morning to call Ed Ramey.

Since he had been on vacation the previous week, she was surprised that he had an available time to see her on Tuesday.

"I thought you would be tightly scheduled for weeks," she admitted. She didn't know whether to be glad or sad that her phone call had positive results.

"I made them schedule lightly the first few days back . . . it's always such a shock." Ed laughed.

"I know what you mean," said Elizabeth. "Just as you get used to the luxury of vacation time, it's over and the rat race starts again." She couldn't exactly think of her own return to the Tapestry puzzle as a rat race but there was a certain amount of identifying with her friend in the very act of making the phone call.

She smiled as she replaced the receiver, thinking of all the times she had given clients the same advice that Harold Fowler had given her. *I knew what to do; why didn't I just do it?* Then she laughed softly as she mentally answered her own question. *Permission . . . we're all such children. We need permission to relax.*

The day stretched out before her as one filled with the luxury of no demands, now that the phone call had been made. Her eyes fell on the copy of *The Fall and Redemption of God* and she took it from its place on the shelf. It had been months since she opened it but she knew it was time.

After filling her coffee cup, she settled in the leather chair, drew up an ottoman and opened the book. This time, she promised herself, she would read it with fresh eyes, ready and open to see what the critics termed the inherent heresy—new age humanism couched in biblical terms. "And Lord, " she prayed. "Please show me if there is any part of this that is not truth. If You show me heresy, I'll burn every copy I can find. And I'll publicly renounce it." With a sigh of relief, knowing that she had truly relinquished the matter, she turned the page.

Fall and Redemption had begun as her attempt to put into writing, in a way that would firm up her own logical processes of understanding, how the God of the Hebrew Bible, the Christian's Old Testament, could be the same as the Jesus Christ of the New Testament. She had never intended it to become a book and certainly had not seen herself as a theologian. But somehow the book happened and somehow she found herself being hailed as the founder of a new school of theology, unstructured though it was.

She wriggled more comfortably into the chair and became engrossed in her own written words and thoughts. She realized with a start two hours later that the coffee was cold in the cup on the table beside her and it was time to start lunch. She closed the book, half read, and placed it on the table beside the lamp.

Not once had she seen anything that resembled blasphemy, heresy, or new age thinking. Indeed she was more convinced than ever that what she had written was truth. . .and wondered again at the smallness of mind of the detractors of the book. "Father, forgive them," she whispered. "They know not what they do."

Perhaps the perceived heresy was in the second half; she'd find out after lunch. She suspected that it was the title that caused people to become so volatile. She had argued with the publishers over that title. But she had to admit—it had gotten a lot of people's attention who would probably never have picked up the book otherwise. Her working title, *Reconciling The Old and New Testament Images of God*, would not have caused a ripple, much less the tsunami of public opinion caused by the publisher's choice. And, after all, their job was to sell books.

Her own job was to communicate truth. She trusted that God wanted truth told even more than she did. And she believed that He would be faithful to show her His will, even if it differed from her current stand.

She had needed to work through her own pride this past few months, making sure that she would not mind being proven wrong. She really had no problem with that; and in fact would want to be proven wrong if that were the case. Elizabeth Daily had committed her life to further the Kingdom of God, not hinder it with pollutions of any kind.

As she began the process of making Portabella/Roasted Garlic Bisque, she smiled at the Lord's ways. She had admitted her avoidance of the serious subjects that her 'sabbatical' had been formed to address; she'd relaxed and demanded no 'oughts' for the present, including thinking about 'the Book', and here she was, halfway through the evaluation and it wasn't even painful. She breathed a sigh of relief. *God is so good, so merciful, and so patient with me.* The evaluation was the first step in her decision about the future; the second would be more . . . *wait a minute, you don't know if the second step will be one bit harder than the first. Relax . . . remember who is Lord.*

When Miz Emily was down for her afternoon nap and the lunch dishes were washed, dried, and returned to the cabinet shelves, Hattie went to her own room and checked out her image in the mirror. A few strokes with the brush satisfied her and she gave a short nod, squared her shoulders, and marched down the stairs and out the front door, closing it carefully so as to not disturb her employer.

It was a pretty day, in the '70s, not too hot and not too cold. Just right—the kind of day where you didn't notice the weather at all because it just matched your skin.

Hattie turned purposefully into the Fowler's walk and rapped on the door.

Harold opened the door and smiled as he recognized her.

"Come in, Hattie." Then he stopped short as he saw her face. "Is anything wrong? Is Emily . . .?"

"Miz Emily's fine, Revren' Fowler. But I need to talk to you 'bout somethin'. Is that okay?"

"Of course, come on in." He led the way to his study, poking his head in the kitchen and telling his wife that he would be busy for a little while.

When they had seated themselves at his desk, Hattie came right to the point.

"Revren' Fowler, did you know that somebody has been pulling mean tricks on Miz Daily?"

"Why, no. What kind of mean tricks?"

And Hattie told him.

"I don't want to point a finger, like the Bible says, but Revren' Fowler I think I know who's been doin' that."

"Who do you suspect, Hattie?"

" I 'spects Reggie."

"Reggie Tate? But . . ." Harold Fowler stopped short as if he remembered something.

"But why?" he asked. "Why would Reggie want to do that?"

"I don' know, Sir. But I been thinkin' and there just ain't nobody else it could be. An' I thought maybe you could talk to her and find out."

Harold Fowler's eyes narrowed. "That would be butting in for sure. But maybe you're right. If Reggie has been doing those things there must be something bothering her and whatever it is, it would help her to talk about it."

Hattie nodded and stood up. "Thank you, Sir. I prayed and prayed and thought the good Lord tole me 'go see Revren' Fowler'. So I did."

"You did the right thing, Hattie." He patted her shoulder. "Thank you. I'll see to it."

The evaluation was completed. Elizabeth breathed a sigh of relief when she replaced *The Fall and Redemption of God* on the shelf. There was not one unscriptural concept in the entire book. She was now committed to its truth without any shadows of doubt. She was torn between irritation toward herself for letting criticism shake her faith in the revelation she had believed came from God, and a gladness of heart that she had been open to criticism and willing to be proven wrong. But it was over now and settled.

"Thank you, Lord," she whispered. "Now, the next step is up to you . . . what do you want me to do about it? I am not going to try and figure out your will. You'll just have to make it clear to me. I trust you." After supper she decided to go for a walk and berated herself for staying cooped up in the house all day with such perfect weather outside. But then she chuckled, "Forgive me, Lord. Today was Your timing . . . the weather waited for me and I am glad I spent the day as I did."

She wondered who tended to the Tapestry Court Park gardens. They were wonderfully neat and perfectly weeded. Maybe she could get the gardener to do some of the heavy work in her own yard.

Elizabeth sat down on a bench and contemplated the well-ordered scene that was perfectly accompanied by the sound of water from the fountain. She had a flashback of a garden in England, or was it Scotland? Regents Park in London or Culzean Castle, Scotland? Wherever it was, there had been this perfect blend of weather and sound and scenery . . . serenity for the senses. She wondered if she would have been able to recognize and appreciate this moment if it were not for the relief that the day's work had afforded her. Probably not; peace comes from the inside out.

Every now and then Elizabeth had experienced these moments and the only way she could even think to describe them was Edenic, a kind of joy that preceded the fall of mankind. Joy after the fall always included victory over sadness of some kind but there was a pre-fall joy that exulted in Be-ing and was aware that Be-ing meant connectedness with the Creator. She basked in the gift of the moment that was filled with the sound of running water and the sight of merry pansy faces.

The quiet was broken by the voices of Joel and Jenny Anderson coming out to their yard through the kitchen door.

"But I don't want to have jury duty," Jenny was saying.

Joel laughed. "Not many people do, Sweetheart. But that's part of our responsibility that goes along with the privileges of living in this country."

"Oh, I know, but . . . I think it's mean of them not to excuse me."

"I think it will be good for you," Joel said with a more serious tone in his voice. "Get you out of the house, meet new people. You may enjoy it and be sorry when it's over."

"I doubt that." There was a silence for a few seconds. "But maybe you are right. It might be interesting to actually hear evidence and make a decision. It's Circuit Court. What kind of cases do they have?"

"Both Civil and Criminal, I think."

Elizabeth heard some thumps and the sound of the garbage can lid being replaced and realized that the couple had been carrying out their garbage. Since there was no real private conversation going on, she didn't feel a need to make her presence known. The Andersons went back in the house and Elizabeth re-entered the peaceful quiet of the garden.

Chapter Twelve

Elizabeth awakened on Tuesday morning with a sense of expectancy that took a few moments to define. Lexington! Today she was going to Lexington. She loved the charm of Tapestry Court and her condo was very prosaic in comparison . . . but it was home and she missed it.

She would run errands but she'd also go by the condo and visit with Ruth Carrier. The elderly lady who lived right across the hall had been very vocal in her sorrow that Elizabeth was going away, and had extracted a promise of occasional visits.

She realized with relief that it would be at least another ten days before Charles Simmons returned . . . and then she shook her head. Relief! The garage space belonged to Number One and she had no reason to feel guilty for using it. That was an area she still had not worked out in her emotions. Her own needs and rights warred with the Christian principle of giving, and she never had resolved where obedience ended and foolishness began. Maybe that was a topic for discussion during her Wednesday appointment with Harold Fowler.

Elizabeth smiled. Just the thought of Harold Fowler brought peace to her mind and emotions. He was such an instrument of the Lord, a pastor after the Lord's own heart. God really knew what He was doing when He sent her to Tapestry Court. The old fashioned surroundings were peaceful, and then to have someone like Harold Fowler to help her sort out her own heart . . . well, it was just so perfect. She chuckled. Just like God to do things perfectly.

Galen had returned from Boston on Saturday night but had a business luncheon scheduled, as well as appointments all day and a business dinner as well. He would not be able to see her during her trip to Lexington and had groaned loudly about the timing, but eagerly accepted an invitation for the following weekend.

It was a beautiful day, a day that almost made her envy Bill Sinclair his convertible—almost but not quite. She had never gotten used to wind blowing her hair in all directions . . . it made her uncomfortable. *Another phobia?* Elizabeth shook her head impatiently. *There is such a thing as too much introspection.*

She relaxed and enjoyed the colorful scenery on the back roads to Lexington.

She went to her condo first. It was only nine days since she had been there to pick up the last load of things she was taking to Tapestry Court, but it seemed like months. She let herself in with a feeling of homecoming.

Before she could get her own door closed, the door behind her opened and she heard a cheerful voice.

"Elizabeth! I thought I heard you come in. I am so glad to see you. Will you be here long?"

Elizabeth turned and smiled at her neighbor. "I'm glad to see you too, Ruth. I was going to run over for a few minutes before I leave. I have an appointment at 12:30 and then I'm going to run some errands but will be back later this afternoon. Why don't you be making a list of anything I can get for you and I'll stop over and pick it up before I leave."

"Will do. Thank you so much."

When she had closed the door behind her, she smiled at the living/dining room. She'd decorated the condo herself and it bore the stamp of the romantic side of her personality.

Her collection of teapots and teacups filled the shelves of the walnut corner cupboard, and the glass top table by the window was adorned with a graceful arrangement of silk flowers that she had hand chosen and put together. She never got around to having the beige carpet removed and hardwood flooring installed. Now she made a mental note to have that done during her time at Tapestry Court, before her return. As soon as she had that thought, she felt a pang at the idea of leaving the Manor House. *Have I got two homes now?*

She wandered into the bedroom, pulled back the draperies, and for a few minutes let herself enjoy her collection of miniature castles in the glass case that stood there by the French doors opening on to the deck. The light entering through the doors gleamed on the surface of the metallic castles and shined through the crystal ones turning them into prisms through which light rays projected onto the walls of her room. She gave a sigh of pleasure. It was good to be here.

Elizabeth went to the bedroom closet and turned on the light. The rope to the pull down staircase was in easy reach and she lowered the steps to the floor with no problem. Remembering to turn on the attic light before she ascended, Elizabeth cautiously started up the flight of steps.

The trunk had to be pulled out from the wall past the slanting roof before she could open it, but finally she sat on a stool with the album in her hand. There, toward the front, among many other newspaper clippings, was the very article she found among Colonel Tapestry's possessions. Only this time the photograph was still attached.

The image of a very young Elizabeth Miles smiled at her above the heading "Evangelist Grace Love Draws Large Crowds." Elizabeth smiled back at her youthful self and said, "How on earth did you attract the attention of Guy Tapestry?" But of course there was no answer.

Memories flooded Elizabeth's mind as she turned the pages of the photograph album. Her career as Grace Love had only lasted fourteen months before the authorities had found her true identity and returned her to the nuns. It had been exciting for the fifteen year old but she had to admit that, when she was forced to give up that lifestyle, there had been a certain relief.

She remembered her first night back at boarding school and the long talk with Mother Therese. Vocation and call was a serious thing, something that needed to be supervised, not something a young girl could take off and bring about by herself. Elizabeth had sat there glowering, and thought, "But I did. And if you hadn't found me, I'd still be doing it." And yet, she was relieved that the decision had been taken out of her hands. The eternal destiny of the souls of people was a heavy burden for a teenager to carry.

Elizabeth was made a ward of the Church and the Sisters of the Merciful Shepherd when she was eight and her family killed in a fire that swept her maternal grandparents' home during a family summer reunion. She would have been there with them had she not begged to stay with a friend in order to attend a Drama Day Camp that week. In one horrible night, she had been left without parents, brother, grandparents, aunts, uncles, and cousins. That the nuns had gotten custody of the child was due to the fact that one great-great-aunt was a member of the order, albeit by that time a resident of the Infirmary.

Elizabeth was placed in the boarding school and had been a part of the community year round since there was no other family to visit on holidays. There were problems from the beginning. The very pampered child, bereft of everything familiar to her and placed in an alien atmosphere while suffering from shock and grief, did not take kindly to the rules of boarding school, much less the strict life modeled by the nuns. There were doctors and priests called in to help her adjust but she never fit in. It was years before she recognized that part of her inability to adjust to the convent environment was a fierce anger at God and everyone who represented Him. He and The Church combined were responsible for all her losses.

And now in the stuffy attic she smiled. *How foolish we all are, Lord. Thank you for breaking through with your love.*

One day when Elizabeth was a teenager some of the day students had talked about a tent revival coming to the town—in a field right across the road from the convent—and how there were supposed to be 'holy rollers,' people who did strange things and rolled around on the ground and blamed it on God. All the girls were fascinated by the idea of the show and some of them, Elizabeth included, made elaborate plans to escape the watchful eye of their guardians and attend.

Three of them managed to meet at the edge of the campus at dusk and with much giggling made their way across the road to the field where hundreds of residents of the town had come to see the evangelist. Cars and trucks filled most of the mown area and a large tent housed the people who had arrived in them.

When the girls slipped into the back of the tent, a man ushered them to the third row from the front. They looked at each other with horror, for their plan had been to stand at the back for a few minutes and then leave.

The music group left the stage about the time the girls were sitting down and a nice looking young man went to the microphone. He smiled out at those gathered and said, "Let us pray."

Elizabeth was amazed at the way the man prayed. There was nothing written and it didn't sound like he had memorized it either. It sounded like the man was talking to God the way he would talk to another person. He thanked God that every person in that tent had been brought there by Him.

Not me Elizabeth thought. *I came here to make fun of you. God didn't bring me.*

But as she listened to the man's message, Elizabeth began to wonder. It was like the man could see into her heart and read all the questions and all the pain that lived there. And it was like he was talking straight to her. Surely he couldn't do that without God. Maybe God did bring her after all, although she doubted that Mother Therese back at the convent would buy that for a minute. She glanced around at her companions. One was rolling her eyes and an answering shake of the head of the second told her that the other girls were not experiencing the same thing she was. They motioned to her that it was time to leave and pointed toward the end of the row near the side of the tent. She shook her head and motioned for them to go on without her. They looked shocked but eagerly obeyed.

The preacher's talk kept her mesmerized, and when the invitation to come forward and "ask Jesus into your heart" was given, she was the first one up the aisle.

Elizabeth closed the album and shook off the past as she looked at her watch. It was almost time to leave to meet Ed. She replaced the album in the trunk, changed her mind, took it back out, and tucked it under her arm.

After she let herself out of her apartment, Elizabeth picked up Ruth's list of needs, and again promised a healthy visit later in the day.

The weather was perfect for lunch at Garcia's. The little courtyard restaurant in the middle of the city provided a peaceful ambiance for stressed out workers, if the weather was good, and they could manage get away from the office.

Ed was one of the few doctors who actually had an office in the downtown area so that he was handy for the employees of the business world. Elizabeth and Ed's offices were in the same building, when she had an office, and they'd shared lunch at Garcia's on more than one occasion. Elizabeth was not much on Italian food unless it was Northern Italian and Garcia's had some of the best.

She felt comfortable and at home again as she waited for her friend to join her. There was a small indoor dining area but in the winter most of the restaurant's business came from carryout. In the courtyard, the European atmosphere and privacy fence that muffled the noise of the city made it a favorite fair weather spot.

Ed came through the restaurant with a big welcoming smile on his face.

"Hey, Girl! Long time. How are you?" He bent to hug her before seating himself across the table. "Where's Galen?"

"He couldn't come. He just got back from a trip and was scheduled to the hilt today."

Ed grinned. "I bet he wasn't happy about the timing."

Elizabeth laughed. "You got that right."

When they had ordered, Ed asked, "So what is it you want to see me about?"

"I guess I could have asked on the phone, but, well, I thought I'd rather have your undivided attention and some extra time. And I wanted to explain the whole thing to you."

She finished telling him about her "assignment" from Galen to find the missing heir, and her own determination to track down the Tapestry killer, just as the food arrived. After the waiter left, she continued.

"I think that maybe Lydia Tapestry has a clue to the character of her brother that would help. I mean . . ." She blushed. "I guess I've read too many Agatha Christie mysteries but Hercule Poirot believes strongly that the key to a murder lies in the personality of the one who is murdered."

Ed was watching her with a little smirk on his face but said nothing.

"I guess what I want is permission to talk to your patient, if talking about her brother wouldn't bring any harm to her."

Ed nodded. "Yes, I know what you mean. Lydia Tapestry is very fragile. The medication controls a very high level of anxiety. Do you know any of her background?"

"Not really, just that she and her sister and brother were from a poor family and then he made a lot of money, her sister married, and Lydia has never been really normal."

"Actually, Lydia Tapestry could probably benefit from your skills. I think there is some psychological trauma underlying her condition." Ed looked at Elizabeth thoughtfully and nodded. "She didn't become my patient until she was already in the center and there was never a request from the family for anything except maintenance. But if you want, I'll write an order bringing you in on the case."

Elizabeth jerked her head in surprise. "I never meant that. I just wanted to talk to her. I'm retired, remember?"

Ed laughed. "Sure you are. I know you, Elizabeth, you'll never retire from the people helping business."

She relaxed. "You're right. If there is anything I can do to help her, I will of course do it. But I don't want to take her on as a client on a regular basis."

"Fair enough," Ed said. "I'll just alert the facility staff to the fact that you will be coming there to visit, maybe once, maybe periodically, and to cooperate fully with you."

"Thank you."

When they parted, Elizabeth went by the grocery before returning to the condo with supplies for Ruth. After they put the food and paper goods away, they returned to the living room where Ruth began to ask questions about Elizabeth's new venture, or 'the experiment' as she called it.

"So is it helping you sort out things the way you thought it would?" Ruth was a tiny woman with the shade of blue hair that had become a cliché. The two had lived across the hall from each other for over ten years and Ruth was one of the few people who knew about Elizabeth's book and subsequent wealth and career confusion.

Elizabeth told her all about Tapestry Court, her assignment, and Harold Fowler . . . well, not all about Tapestry Court. She didn't want to worry the older woman by relating the unpleasant things that had happened.

"You'll have to go back with me some time and spend a few days." Elizabeth offered.

"I'd like that," said Ruth. "But after you have solved all the mysteries. Otherwise I'd feel like I was taking your time away from important things."

Elizabeth rose from her chair. "You are very important in my life." She hugged her friend and announced. "I really have to go now. I need to stop by a pet store on my way out of town to buy goldfish for the pond in the garden of the Manor House."

Ruth walked her to the door. "You really like it there, don't you?"

Elizabeth hesitated. The question spotlighted her new emotional attachment. "Yes, I do. It felt today like I have two homes—here and there."

Scarlett O'Hara's line came to her mind. *I won't think about that now. I'll think about it tomorrow.*

She'd gone on Sabbatical to bring peace into her life but now there was more chaos than ever. And no foreseeable end in sight.

Chapter Thirteen

On Wednesday morning, Elizabeth woke to the sound of rain. She snuggled more deeply into the pillows. How wonderful not to have to leap out of bed, dress, and hurry to an office on a rainy day. Remembering the goldfish in their new home in the garden pond where she had settled them last night, she wondered if they minded the rain or liked it. It was a gentle rain, no thunder or lightening; she decided they probably liked it.

The clock read 9:03 a.m., over an hour past the time she usually awakened. Giving a luxurious stretch as she sat up, she slid her feet into the slippers there on the floor beside the bed. Then it hit her. Her counseling appointment with Harold Fowler was in less than an hour. She pulled a pair of slacks and a shirt out of the closet and dressed quickly so she would have time for her morning coffee.

By the time Elizabeth left her house and stepped out onto the walk, the rain had ceased, leaving behind only the clean fresh scent that hinted at new beginnings. The lilac blossoms were gone and the dogwood blooms were going but the walk through Tapestry Court was still relaxing. The Tudor style cottages created a cozy atmosphere of village intimacy.

Promptly at 10 a.m. she rang the bell of Number Seven and was warmly greeted by Lucy.

"Come right in. Harold just got a phone call and will be a few minutes. I hope you don't mind."

"Oh, no. That just gives me the pleasure of some unexpected time with you. And that's a treat." She meant it and Lucy's smile showed that the older woman appreciated the compliment. The two women went to the kitchen and Lucy poured out coffee for them both.

When they were seated at the table, Lucy cleared her throat.

"Really this is probably a good thing . . . that Harold got that phone call, I mean. I have been putting off talking to you."

She hesitated. "This is difficult for me, talking about the past, I mean. But I really felt I should tell you." Her eyes stared at her skirt while her hands made a crease in the material.

Elizabeth felt sorry for the woman who was obviously having a difficult time breaking in to the subject.

"Is it something about your brother? About the will?"

Lucy Fowler nodded. "Yes, well, not exactly about the will but, well, you know . . . about the son. I don't know anything, but there is something about Guy . . ."

She gulped before continuing. "It's all very unpleasant. We don't know who could have borne him a son but Guy was, well, he had a problem." Her eyes looked pleadingly at Elizabeth.

"Mrs. Fowler, I don't know if your husband told you . . ."

"Please call me Lucy. And my husband doesn't tell me anything about people who come and talk to him."

"Lucy, I am a psychologist, so there are no problems that are shocking to me. I'd rather no one else knew that right now, about my profession, but I trust you two very much. And also I wanted to tell you that I am a friend of Ed Ramey, though I don't think I mentioned that to your husband. I had lunch with Ed just yesterday and asked him about the advisability of talking to your sister Lydia about your brother. He seemed to think it could be a good thing."

Lucy Fowler was shaking her head violently.

"No! No. Please don't. Poor Lydia has suffered so, and has now found a measure of peace."

Elizabeth waited.

Lucy sighed. "There is a name for the problem that Guy had. A name for people like him, I mean. I can't remember exactly. It starts with a P and it sounds like it has something to do with walking, like a pedestrian or something."

"Pedophilia?" Elizabeth asked the question calmly.

"Yes. That's it. Horrible. But Guy had it. I think some priests have it too— dreadful thing, comes from not being married I suppose."

Elizabeth smiled gently. "There are some married people who have the problem too." *Poor lady, to have that problem in a close relative and not understand it. But that generation was trained to be secretive and not ask questions.*

Lucy nodded. "Well, maybe so. But anyway Guy had it. And poor Lydia, well, she was much younger than he, whereas I was closer to his age. She was, I think his first . . . victim I guess you would call it."

Elizabeth could see tears in the eyes of the older woman and she reached out and took her hand. "I'm so sorry. It must have been awful for her, and for you when you found out."

Lucy withdrew her hand and drew a tissue from the pocket of her housedress and wiped her eyes.

"Yes. It must have been awful. Lydia came here when our parents died. I felt guilty but I couldn't take care of her. I didn't know then about the pedo . . . thing. But I still felt bad about not taking her. She wandered around. And she wasn't in touch with reality they said. And Harold was called to the mission field and we couldn't take her overseas.

"She got worse when she was here, went back to playing dolls, and finally she got so bad that she was put in a nursing home. Guy paid for everything for her, and left money in trust so that she would be taken care of the rest of her life. I know he felt badly about it. But I know there was at least one other incident many years later. I know because that's when he told me about Lydia. And he actually asked me to pray about that new one that happened." She shook her head. "That was unusual, him asking me to pray, I mean."

Elizabeth thought back to her interview with Deputy Matt Collins. She nodded but didn't relate the conversation to Lucy.

Just then the Reverend Harold Fowler appeared in the doorway between kitchen and hall.

"Sorry I'm late." He looked down at his watch just as Elizabeth looked up at the wall clock. It was 10:15.

"That's fine. Your wife and I were talking."

Elizabeth saw the questioning glance from him and the answering nod from her. He knew now that she was aware of the situation about Guy Tapestry's problem. She turned to Lucy.

"Thank you so much for sharing with me. I know it was unpleasant. And I won't question your sister and bring up the past. But do you mind if I visit her? Ed seemed to think it might help her."

Lucy smiled. "I think she would love for you to visit. Anybody would."

When Elizabeth was settled once more in the comfortable chair across from Harold Fowler, and thinking what a lovely couple he and Lucy were, she heaved a contented sigh.

"You have no idea how good this feels to me. Being able to be on this side of the desk."

He smiled. "And you have no idea how good it feels to me to be walking in my calling again, at least partially. And that phone call was about the possibility of filling a pulpit for a month this summer." His face beamed with joy and Elizabeth was glad for him. "So, what is on the menu for today?"

"Well, I think, Galen. He is one of the main reasons I came here—to decide about our future. It's confusing. One of those 'Which came first the chicken or the egg?' things. I hadn't agreed to marry him before the success of the book but now it seems that I am not agreeing because of my reactions to the public concerning the book. I've been thinking about that. The book gave me a good excuse but maybe there is more to my reluctance about marriage than just a career decision."

The Reverend Fowler nodded. "Probably. Shall we pray?"

They both bowed their heads as he led them to the throne of grace.

"Lord, thank you for your mercy and grace to us. Thank you that you have all the answers, even when we aren't sure of all the questions. We ask you to guide our discussion and enlighten our minds about your plan for Elizabeth's future. Guide my thoughts and words. Help me decrease so that you may increase in this time of ministry. Amen."

"Amen," Elizabeth echoed. "Oh, and I thought of something else the other day. I have this thing where I feel guilty. Like worrying about what Charles Simmons will do about a garage when he gets back from his trip. I honestly don't know where Christian unselfishness ends and unhealthy martyrdom begins."

Harold smiled and she got the impression that he had wrestled with that same question.

"Thank God we are called to walk in the Spirit," was his reply.

It was not what she was expecting.

"What do you mean?

"Well, if we just walk in the Spirit, minute by minute, trusting that he will tell us if we are supposed to give up something or take some action, then it will all work out. I find the older I get that I actually trust him to guide me in paths of righteousness."

Elizabeth laughed. "Imagine. And I guess that kind of fits in with the whole Galen thing. I mean, trusting him. I know, at least intellectually, that a call to ministry does not demand giving up a home life and personal happiness. But I think it got so ingrained in me during my Catholic childhood that it seems like an either-or kind of thing."

Harold rearranged some pens on the desk in front of him. "Tell me. What kind of a call do you think is issuing forth because of this book?"

She looked at him thoughtfully and nodded. "Exactly. The problem is that I don't know. I have received a lot of invitations to speak, some from legitimate churches, some from new age groups. I guess I think that if I go to all these speaking engagements, it wouldn't be fair to Galen. And more than one person mentioned that I should start a new denomination and let independent churches join. That idea just about . . . well, it gave me a head rush."

Harold gave a burst of loud laughter. "I can well imagine."

Elizabeth smiled at him and continued. "Seriously, I didn't know whether that was a suggestion from the Lord or a temptation from the devil. Whichever it was, it most definitely produced a strong reaction in me."

"Can I ask you a question?"

"Certainly."

"What was your parents' marriage like?"

The question startled Elizabeth. It seemed so out of context. But she cast about in her memories for an answer.

"Hmmm. I don't know. Mother didn't work. Daddy was a banker. I think . . ." Her eyes narrowed as she looked at Harold. "That's funny. I don't think I ever thought about their relationship with each other. Daddy was into his job and Mother was a typical homemaker. We had supper around the dining room table when Daddy came in from work. I guess our house was like a shadow of Father Knows Best, only . . ."

"Only?" Harold encouraged her to continue.

"Only nobody really seemed as interested in us kids as in the TV show."

Harold laughed. "I think that program may have caused a lot of discontent; nobody's home met up to it."

"You're probably right. But there was something else. Now that I think back, my parents didn't seem to have a relationship beyond running the house and making sure we kids had what we needed. I can't recall them ever going out alone or doing anything just for fun. But I was so young when they died. There could have been things I just don't remember."

"And then your own marriage . . .?" Harold prompted her.

Elizabeth shook her head. "A disaster. He drank every night. Knowing what I know now I can see it had nothing to do with me, but back then I took it personally. Hmm. I think I see what you are getting at. I have never seen a marriage where the woman was really fulfilled. And frankly my clients have not given me any reason to change that opinion." She laughed. "But on the other hand, if they were fulfilled and happy, they wouldn't have been my clients, would they?"

Harold chuckled. "Yes, we who are in the helping professions tend to get a jaded view of life because the happy ones rarely come to us."

"My fears are really not fair to Galen . . . I don't believe he would ever change. He is a gentleman and he loves me." She gave a short laugh. "I know, I know. With my mind I understand that, but it's my heart that is programmed with distrust. You know, this sounds ridiculous since it's so obvious now, but I never realized what my reluctance was before now. In fact, even as we sit here that realization is growing clearer to me every minute. And my fears are looking very weak and unreal."

"No, that's not ridiculous. You and I both know that is what counseling is all about—or supposed to be. In sharing, we bring out and see truths that are there just waiting to surface."

Elizabeth nodded. "Yes, and you know, I have not been to counseling since I finished my doctoral program. And I guess back then it just wasn't part of what I needed to know about myself. Career was my only focus. And the calling thing wasn't something that I even recognized as still valid, so that wasn't addressed either."

Harold smiled at her with understanding, and a twinkle in his eye.

"You really didn't need counseling, now, did you? You just needed to talk out loud."

"No, I needed you to ask the right questions to pull the answers out of me. Thank you so much. You have no idea how much I appreciate your help. Oh, I almost forgot. There was something I wanted to ask you about last week and forgot until I was in town that afternoon." She went on to describe the anonymous note and the damage to her plants.

When she had finished, Harold looked thoughtful for a moment, tapping his fingers together.

"I already knew about that. Hattie came to see me about her suspicions concerning the matter."

Elizabeth was very surprised. "Hattie?"

He nodded. "Yes, and I think she was right. I'd rather not say what those suspicions are right now but if it's okay, I'd like to check into it and I suspect you may have that mystery solved and out of the way very soon."

Elizabeth agreed. She trusted Harold Fowler completely.

When she left, he said in a teasing voice, "And if you decide to start that denomination, let me know."

She rolled her eyes and left chuckling. But she knew they would be discussing the call of God on her life in depth at a later date.

Elizabeth finished washing the supper dishes and was putting some Sleepytime teabags in the pot to steep when she heard the door chimes. Hoping fervently that Miss Emily Caine was not on the other side of the door, she opened it slowly.

It was Reggie Tate, and Elizabeth smiled with relief and delight.

"Reggie! Come in. I am so glad that you've come to visit. I've wanted to meet you. Let's go to the kitchen. I have a pot of herb tea just about ready. Do you drink tea?"

Elizabeth led the way to the kitchen and a very silent Reggie followed her.

"Ms. Daily?"

Elizabeth turned and smiled at her guest and pointed to a chair. But the girl remained standing. Reggie was a very pretty teen, her long brown hair was straight and shiny, her features even, her skin smooth. Elizabeth could see that she was going to become an attractive woman.

"Ms. Daily, you probably won't want to have tea with me after I tell you why I am here."

"Yes, I will. Now come and sit down. Don't worry, I don't bite." And Elizabeth pulled out the chair and got another cup from the cabinet.

With obvious reluctance, Reggie sat down.

"It was me."

Elizabeth paused on her way to the table with the pot of tea.

"The flowers?"

Reggie nodded.

"And the note?"

"Yes. I am sorry, really sorry. Not just because I got found out. Mom was telling me how much she likes you, and Mr. Delaney. And I've really felt stupid. I mean, I wouldn't even meet you one day. I went in the house when I saw you coming."

Elizabeth poured tea into both of their cups and set the pot down on the table.

"Yes, that was the first time I saw you, and was sorry I didn't get to meet you. So, I'm not what you thought I was like?"

Reggie hung her head and then raised it and looked Elizabeth straight in the eyes.

"It wasn't that. I wouldn't ever want my parents to know this . . . not that I did something so wrong and stupid, but the reason I did it." She took a deep breath. "I was afraid that you were Dad's girlfriend."

Elizabeth laughed. "I'm sorry. I don't mean to laugh at your fears, but what a relief. I mean, it was awful thinking either there was someone who hated me personally, or there was some . . ." Here she stopped because she didn't want to let the girl know she had suspected that someone in the court might have a sinister reason for wanting her gone, a reason tied in with murder. She finished her sentence lamely, "somebody that was just, well, kind of nuts."

Reggie laughed then and relaxed against the back in the chair. "Well, I was nuts." She breathed a sigh of relief and then picked up her teacup and tasted before adding two teaspoons of sugar. "Anyway, after Mom told me about you, I knew that I'd been wrong. And I felt really stupid. I wished I could undo it but I couldn't. I didn't know what to do about it. So I just didn't do anything."

"Why are you here now?" Elizabeth's voice was very gentle.

Reggie gave a wry grin. "Reverend Fowler figured it out somehow and talked to me about it this afternoon. He said you would understand and forgive me and that I would feel better. And he said that he didn't think it was necessary for my parents to know, but to ask you."

"I think Reverend Fowler is exactly right. There is no need for your parents to know. In fact it would be embarrassing for all of us if they did. And yes, I forgive you."

"Is there anything I can do? I mean to make it up to you?"

"No, not that I can think of right now. But if I do think of something I need help with, I'll let you know. I understand how you feel—wanting to do something to make up for doing something wrong. It's really not necessary but I understand. Now, tell me about yourself. What year of school are you in?"

Reggie smiled. "I am just finishing my freshman year of high school. Just a few more weeks and I'll be a sophomore, well almost."

"What are your plans for the summer?"

"Lots of swimming and I'm going to church camp this year too."

"That's great. I never went to camp when I was young but always thought it would be fun."

"I've only been for weekend retreats with our youth group at First Methodist but this time I'm going for the week and there will be lots of other kids there. And they have horseback riding too!"

"That does sound like fun."

Reggie spotted the wall clock and drained her teacup. "I better go. I said I was just going to take a walk in the park."

Elizabeth walked her to the door and was surprised when the girl spontaneously hugged her.

"Thank you so much. I feel so much better."

"You are welcome," said Elizabeth. "Come back. Anytime."

She breathed a sigh of relief as she closed the door. One mystery solved. But there were so many more still looming in the shadows.

Chapter Fourteen

Linda Tate was putting on her makeup when George came in to their bedroom.

"You're looking mighty pretty," he said.

His wife beamed. She was happy these days. She still didn't know why George was so withdrawn lately but at least it wasn't because he was in love with another woman.

She turned her face up to him as he leaned down to kiss her.

"I love you." She felt that love with all her heart even after being married for nearly two decades.

"I love you too." He gave her a quick squeeze and turned to the closet. "What should I wear?"

"It doesn't matter . . . something casual." They were invited to have dinner with Elizabeth and Galen at Number One Tapestry Court. Linda had not been in the Manor House in over a decade, not since the Colonel died, and she was eagerly anticipating seeing the changes.

"George?"

"Hmm?" Her husband was looking back and forth between two shirts, obviously trying to make a choice.

"The red one," she suggested. And he immediately put the green back in his drawer. "George, I've been thinking."

"About what?"

"About this whole heir business."

George turned to look at his wife. "You have?" His voice held a definite note of surprise.

"Yes. I guess since Elizabeth Dailey is looking into it, I was thinking about it too, more seriously than I did before. There must be someone who knew about the child that would hear the will. You know, somebody to whom the reference 'my son' would be obvious. It's almost like Mr. Tapestry expected that person to tell who the son is. What do you think?"

He pulled the shirt over his head and nodded slowly. "Well, Honey, I'd never thought about that before. Since everyone was shocked by the reference to a child of his, I just thought that he must have known that everyone was ignorant of the situation. Hmm. Why don't you mention that tonight to Galen and Elizabeth?"

Linda smiled and nodded. "Okay, I will."

"No, I haven't changed a thing." Elizabeth laughed as an afterthought occurred to her. "Well, I added some of my own books and knickknacks to the library. But everything else is so perfect, I couldn't think of anything to do to improve it. I think that's why I got so interested in the garden. I needed to put some personal touches somewhere."

The two men had gone out to the garden while Linda helped Elizabeth clean up the supper dishes. They had both offered to help but Elizabeth shooed them outside and said they could get it done faster without the men.

Linda nodded. "It is a beautiful place. Aunt Emily did an amazing job." She shook her head. "Poor woman."

Elizabeth asked, "Why do you say that?"

Linda tilted her head. "I think she was in love with Mr. Tapestry and decorated the house the way she would want it if he married her. I think she hoped that he would someday."

Elizabeth looked at her new friend with respect. "Interesting. That would explain a lot. About her bitterness and about her attitude of ownership in the house. You know I wouldn't be a bit surprised if you were right. I wonder if we'll ever know."

Linda shook her head. "Where do these bowls go?" As she was stacking them in the cabinet, Elizabeth said, "You called him Mr. Tapestry instead of Colonel. I've never heard anyone refer to him as anything but the Colonel."

Linda let out a short laugh. "He wasn't a real Colonel, just had a Kentucky Colonel certificate, like Colonel Sanders, the Kentucky Fried Chicken guy. I refused to call him Colonel. Oh, I guess I should have, George was afraid at first that it would make him mad, but my family were military people and the title Colonel meant something to us. And you know, I think Mr. Tapestry understood that. He never said a word about me not using the title."

"I understand too," said Elizabeth. "You know, I never thought about where the title came from. For him or for Colonel Sanders."

Linda Tate laughed. "People don't. They just accept a title without really thinking about it. And like Sanders, Mr. Tapestry decided that the title was good for business."

Elizabeth took off her apron and hung it on a hook in the pantry. "Well, that's it for the kitchen. Shall we join the gentlemen?"

Galen and George were seated at the umbrella table on the patio.

"Oh," Elizabeth caught herself as she was about to sit down. "I forgot to make coffee. Does everyone want some?"

Linda said "It would have to be decaf for me."

Elizabeth nodded. "Me too, at this hour."

"That's fine with me," Galen said, and George agreed.

Galen followed her in and left the Tates alone outside. He kissed the back of her neck when she bent over to put the coffee in the filter.

"Galen! Behave yourself." Elizabeth laughed, but the kiss had sent cold chills racing over her body. *Lord, help me.*

"I am behaving myself." His eyes were twinkling.

When the coffee was ready, they joined the Tates back on the patio. Galen set the tray in the middle of the table.

"Linda," George Tate spoke as though he had suddenly remembered something. "Tell Elizabeth and Galen what you said about the will." He turned to Galen. "I think she has a valid point."

"Well, I was thinking that the way the will is written, with no explanation, it seems like Mr. Tapestry expected someone to identify the heir. I mean, it seems to me that he didn't name his son because someone knew who it was and he expected them to say so."

Elizabeth ran the thought around in her head. "Hmm, could very well be. But why didn't they?"

Linda shook her head. "I don't know. And I may be all wrong. But I thought if we figured out who might know, then . . ."

"And since they didn't come forth, the identity of the son could very well be a motivation for the murder."

"Elizabeth." Galen's voice held a warning note. "Tapestry was killed by discontents at the factory."

She sighed. "I know." But she didn't know that at all. She changed the subject.

"Galen, Linda thinks that Miss Caine was probably in love with Colonel Tapestry."

"Linda, you don't know that." Her husband's tone of voice was gentle but reproving.

"I think she is right." Elizabeth tilted her chin up. "Her decorating of this house make sense if she was a romantic back then. And it would explain her attitude of ownership, if she had hoped that one day it would be her home."

After a few seconds pause, she continued. "It would also explain her bitterness."

The two men looked at each other and shrugged.

Elizabeth and Linda both laughed.

"Take our word for it, it's a woman thing." Elizabeth said. "Oh! Galen, I just remembered. When I called you to ask about the date of Tapestry's death, you didn't have your briefcase with you and then we both got so busy I forgot. Do you know the date?"

Galen looked at George. "I've forgotten. George?"

"Can't remember the day, but it was in May of 1997."

Elizabeth nodded. "I was thinking I remembered that he was killed in May. And didn't you tell me, Galen, that he had just deeded over the house to Jenny Anderson the day he was killed?"

"That's right."

"Well, I found an appointment book stuck in the back of a drawer. There was almost nothing in it but the last entry was a date in April that said something about a will."

"Really?" Galen's eyebrows lifted. "Do you have it handy?"

"Yes, I'll get it now." Elizabeth left them and went to the library where she retrieved the book.

She opened it as she joined them. "It was on April 21st, a Monday, that he had the appointment with CS for the will."

George Tate nodded. "Clyde Shrofft. He's the attorney who drew up the will."

Elizabeth asked, "Was he not Tapestry's attorney for other things?"

Galen answered the question. "No. He had several attorneys, but as far as we can ascertain, this one was consulted just for the will."

"Isn't that kind of strange?" Linda sat forward in her chair as she spoke.

George rubbed his earlobe. "Maybe. But maybe he just didn't want any of the business attorneys to know his private business."

"When was the will first made?" Elizabeth asked. "I mean, the first time without codicils and all?"

"I can't remember," Galen admitted. "We need to check that out. And also find out what he changed on that date the month before he was killed."

Elizabeth nodded, and relaxed.

The four of them decided they would like to play a game of cards and Elizabeth remembered seeing several boxes in the library, unopened.

"Good!"

The rest of the evening was spent absorbed in two games of Pinochle, with the women ending up triumphant over the men.

As the Tates were leaving, Galen vowed, "Next time, George."

The other man grinned, nodded, and gave a thumbs up.

Elizabeth felt enveloped in warmth as she stood in the doorway with Galen's arm around her watching the other couple stroll hand in hand down the walkway toward their home.

Galen must have sensed her contentment because he squeezed her arm and said, "It could be this way all the time."

Elizabeth didn't answer but the same thought had occurred to her. She just pressed her head more firmly against his shoulder.

He turned her around to face him.

"I love you, Elizabeth Daily. I love you." His eyes bored into hers as if looking for something.

Then as his mouth touched her own, she let her lips give as much of an answer as she could allow herself at that moment.

"I really insist." Elizabeth and Galen were sitting at the Simmons home on the living room couch. She continued. "I truly almost never use the car and keeping it at the Archers suits me perfectly. I can walk there and get it if I need or want it."

Mindy Simmons said, "I don't mind either, truly. Charles needs ready access to the garage because of work every day but I don't."

They looked at each other with frustration and then burst out laughing. Elizabeth loved the promise of friendship with someone who could appreciate the humor in a fight for garage space martyrdom.

Galen said, "I am going to approach the bank committee about building on to the garage from the estate monies. Most families these days have two cars and I think it is a valid need."

Charles Simmons nodded. "Good idea. That will increase the value of the properties too."

By the time Galen and Elizabeth left, Mindy had won the martyr game and phoned the Archers for permission to park her car in their side lot for the time. The store owners refused an offer to pay for the spot. Charles was going to alert the police to the arrangement so they would know the vehicle was approved to be there, and so they could keep an eye on it as well.

As they walked back to the Manor house, Elizabeth chuckled. "The Archers' gravel parking lot is certainly getting full. Your car and Charles' are both there today. And Mindy's will soon be a full time resident."

"Hopefully not for long," Galen said seriously. "I want to see about getting that garage addition started as soon as possible."

Elizabeth slipped her arm around his and he grinned down at her.

"You are an awesome lady, Bits."

She swallowed a suddenly noticed lump in her throat. "Ditto," she said. Then she laughed. "I mean, you're not a lady, but you are awesome."

Galen then burst into a chorus of "We belong to a mutual admiration society."

And they both laughed as they walked through the front door of Number One, Tapestry Court.

On Sunday morning, Elizabeth and Galen went to church with the Tates. Elizabeth wondered if Emily Caine knew that it was Elizabeth's first church attendance since she moved there. Probably. The spinster knew everything that happened in the court.

The new First Methodist Church of Simpsonton sat on several acres of lush green lawn with a large parking lot close to the church. The sanctuary walls consisted mostly of large windows that looked out on a lawn, fountains and old oak trees, and presented a peaceful natural atmosphere conducive to worship. The pastor was exuberant in proclaiming the Good News of the Grace of the Lord Jesus Christ and Elizabeth thought this would be a good church home. Reggie Tate looked thrilled that Elizabeth had come and insisted on sitting next to her. Chuck glowered at his sister but didn't try to take the other side where Galen sat.

Reggie whispered, during the closing hymn, "Next week the youth choir is singing. Will you come back?"

Elizabeth promised she would. As they were leaving, they saw Joel and Jenny Anderson among the crowd walking down the outer steps to the sidewalk.

Elizabeth smiled. "Jenny! I didn't know you attended this church."

The younger woman smiled shyly. "Yes. I'm so glad you came. I should have invited you myself."

It was hard to say goodbye to Galen that afternoon. The weekend had been filled with warmth and comfort and a sense of belonging that Elizabeth rarely experienced.

Just as Elizabeth started up the steps to draw her bathwater, the telephone rang and she went into the library to answer it.

It was Lucy Fowler. "Elizabeth, would it be possible for you to drive us into town tomorrow if I can get an appointment at the dentist for Harold?"

"I'd be happy to," Elizabeth said. "Is he in pain?"

"Yes, the stubborn mulehead." Lucy's voice held an irritation that Elizabeth never heard from her before. "He refuses to listen to me and go for maintenance. He waits 'til he's in pain—and that could be avoided. I called the Tates but Linda has a meeting and a doctor's appointment herself. I hated to bother you but would really appreciate it."

"No bother." Elizabeth promised sincerely. "Just let me know when you have a time."

As Elizabeth soaked in the hot bath water she thought how glad she was to be able to do a favor for Harold Fowler who refused to let her pay for counseling.

Chapter Fifteen

Harold Fowler sipped his coffee while watching his wife with narrowed eyes.

"I am fine this morning."

Lucy smiled at him. "Yes, dear." But she went right on pushing buttons on the telephone. When she hung up from talking the dentist's office into taking him, she turned around with fire in her eyes.

"They said you have cancelled your last three appointments!" Her tiny body trembled with visible indignation.

Being a wise man, he said nothing.

Lucy then picked up the phone again. "Elizabeth, they agreed to fit him in around 10:30 this morning. Are you sure that is all right with you?"

She nodded pleasantly, said goodbye, hung up the phone and without another word, went upstairs. Harold assumed that she was going to get dressed. He looked at the clock. *8:35. Less than two hours.*

He'd hoped Lucy would never find out about the last series of cancelled appointments. He was very aware of his cowardice concerning the dentist, and his own integrity would allow him to call it by no other name. But he hated when that cowardice was made public knowledge.

He and Lucy had been having this battle for years.

"How many times have I told you that you will have less pain and save a lot of money if you go for your regular checkups?"

He used to argue that people in the dental profession must be sadistic or twisted in some way to choose a career that is all bad breath, decayed food particles, and pain. Of course later he had to repent. God called some people to be dentists to help people, just as surely as He called pastors and missionaries.

Harold sighed. On one occasion his ploy was to inform Lucy that the Almighty was capable of keeping his remaining teeth in working order and that he considered it a lack of faith and an insult to Him to turn to the dentist instead of trusting in Divine Protection.

Lucy did not act at all impressed with his piety and said he'd been watching too much television. With a complete disregard for his convictions, she rescheduled the cancelled appointment.

Harold sometimes thought that Lucy did not respect his convictions as much as she should. And other times he thought that she knew him better than he knew himself. Always he thought that marriage was a very humbling experience for a man. He'd read somewhere that marriage was not about happiness but about holiness. Probably true, though his was happy as well. For the most part. When dentists were not involved.

Elizabeth delivered Harold and Lucy Fowler to the front gate of Tapestry Court around one o'clock. Harold's mouth was full of gauze and minus one tooth. Lucy said she would call later about their planned trip to Lexington the next day to see her sister.

Elizabeth parked the car and walked through the park before going on to Number One. She gazed up at the giant T and thought again about the embroidered towels in the manor house. An idea hit her like a lightning bolt. Surely not.

When Elizabeth got back home, she got out her list of questions again.

> 1. Who is Charles Simmons—his parentage? How did he come to live at Tapestry Court?

According to Galen's information, he had been brought to Tapestry Court from an orphanage, presumably to be a companion for Emily Caine's orphaned nephew, George Tate, and supposedly the son of an unwed mother and a soldier who had died while serving in the military. But Elizabeth wasn't satisfied. What if that had been a trumped up story and Tapestry was really the father? Elizabeth left question 1.

> 2. Why was Lydia Tapestry institutionalized? Is she able to answer questions?

That question had been answered along with question ten, "Does Lucille Fowler know anything about her brother's private life," revised to read "What is Lucille Fowler ashamed of about her brother?" and both had been answered. But Elizabeth had promised not to ask questions during the visit with Lydia tomorrow. She crossed off question 2.

> 3. Was the Colonel ever known to be involved with any women?

It seemed that he had only been involved with forbidden very young women, including his interest in her own younger self. But obviously things were not as they seemed, because he fathered a child. That child could be the offspring of a rape, not a consenting relationship. Question 3 was left on the list.

4. Was there any location that the Colonel visited frequently?

The only people Elizabeth could think of that would know the answer to that would be his employees. She would ask Tate, Simmons, Sinclair, and . . .Emily Caine? She doubted that she would get an answer from that source and decided that the discomfort of confronting the reluctant Miss Caine would not be worth the results. But question four stayed.

5. Who are the stockholders in Tapestry Industries?
That question had been answered satisfactorily and could be crossed off the list.
6. What were the exact terms of the will?
7. Who chose George Tate to follow Tapestry as President?

Questions 6 and 7 were also eliminated.

8. Does Jenny Anderson have an aversion to the manor house? If so, why?

Elizabeth had no doubt that the answer to the first part of that question was yes. Was it the result of the Colonel's perversion? Question 8 remained.

9. Did something cause Emily Caine to turn from a romantic who created the atmosphere of this house into the bitter legalist that she seems to be now?

Elizabeth was almost positive that Linda Tate was right about the spinster being in love with Tapestry and that disappointment in love had resulted in her present state. But there was as yet no proof. Question 9 would stay on the list.

Question 10 had been answered along with question 2 and now Elizabeth looked at the next question.

11.What is William Sinclair's background? Why did Col. T. install him in the Court?

The first part of question 11 was very well documented. But not the second. Why did Tapestry put Sinclair as part of the Court family? Elizabeth left question 11.

12. Did Emily Caine have a reason to hate Col. Tapestry?

What if Linda Tate was also right in her speculation that someone knew about an heir? What if that someone was Emily Caine, but she wanted no rival to her nephew's reign over Tapestry Industries?

With a smile for which Elizabeth knew she would have to ask forgiveness later during her prayer time, She added number 12 to question 9 before renumbering the list to total 6. Then after remembering something, she added a seventh question.

Just as she finished her revisions, the phone rang. Lucy Fowler thanked her again for taking them to the dentist and made final plans about the next morning.

"I am going to insist that Harold stay home tomorrow. He doesn't like to admit that he's older and things like having teeth pulled are harder on him than in former years so I am just going to tell him I'd really like to have an outing with you alone, to talk women talk in the car going up and back." Lucy gave a little giggle.

"That sounds wonderful to me."

They decided to leave at the Fowlers usual time of 9 and plan to spend several hours with Lydia. *I know, I'll take Lucy somewhere special for lunch.* Then she had another idea, went upstairs, got the cell phone from her bedside table and put in a call to Ruth, inviting her to join them for lunch. Her former neighbor accepted with enthusiasm and Elizabeth hung up the phone, pleased that the two older ladies would each have an outing. She hoped they would enjoy each other, and was fairly certain that they would.

The afternoon was spent working in the garden, weeding out the few wild plants that had dared return to their former home and trimming some hedges whose new growth reminded her of a boy in need of a haircut.

When she went into the house she admitted to herself that she was avoiding being alone with her thoughts. For some reason, it seemed like it was time to look at The Letters. She would pick them up from the condo tomorrow while she was in Lexington.

Retrieving her cell phone again, Elizabeth made another call to Lexington, this one to Windsor's Tea Room for reservations at 1:30. That should give them time to spend with Lydia, pick up Ruth, and get to the picturesque restaurant and gift shop. Then she checked the cell for missed calls and discovered that Galen had phoned.

She smiled as his voice came through on the message. "Elizabeth!" She knew that he would be irritated that she forgot to take the phone with her again. She kept it upstairs in her bedroom because there was no extension there and she would have it if she needed to make a call or if Galen called her late at night. But she usually forgot to take it downstairs with her in the mornings. Hence

Elizabeth and not Bits. "Where are you? You don't have your phone with you again. Give me a call when you get this."

She dialed his office number but discovered he was in a meeting and left word for him to call her. She wouldn't call his cell phone and interrupt business except in an emergency, and that had never happened.

It was nearly five o'clock when Galen returned her call.

"I'm sorry. I was in the dentist's office with the Fowlers at the time you called." She was telling the truth, she had been there at that time. She saw no reason to admit that her cell phone was left on her bedside table inadvertently.

"Okay. Sorry I got impatient. I talked to Clyde Shrofft this morning."

"Oh? And what did you find out?"

"The will with Shroff was originally made about five years before Tapestry's death and he made sure that the words 'making all previous wills void' were included. The change in April before he died was to change the disposition of some property, outside the Court, that was originally designated to go to Emily Caine. Instead it was added to the inheritance left to the unnamed son."

"Wow!" Elizabeth felt an excitement rise up within her. "I wonder if she knew that."

She could almost see the grin through Galen's voice as he asked, "Do you want to question her about it?"

"No thank you, Sir. I'll pass on that. Hmmm, do you think this makes any difference in what we already know?"

"None that I can think of," Galen replied.

"Me either," Elizabeth reluctantly admitted.

"And when am I invited back?"

Elizabeth's heart fluttered as she recalled their goodbye kiss. He had looked down at her afterwards and said the same words, "When am I invited back?" She wanted to say, "Just stay." Those kisses could be dangerous.

And yet, it seemed so natural for Galen to be here.

Her answer came out in a whisper. "When can you come back?"

"See you Friday, Bits. I love you."

"I love you too, Galen."

After supper she went into the library to check her e-mail and catch up on some correspondence.

She laughed as she saw one that had arrived at 6:07 that evening.

Somehow Galen had gotten some dancing musical notes to prance around on the e-mail background, and he had written, "I'm in the mood for love, simply because you're near me."

But then she stopped laughing. It was true for her too. She was going to have to make a decision soon. And she suspected that she knew what that decision would be. When she examined her heart, she couldn't find more than one real option. Somehow in her three weeks at Tapestry Court, confusion had almost miraculously dissolved.

And she had Galen to thank for that too.

Before she got in bed that night, she knelt down. "Father thank you for Galen and his love for me, and for all my new friends. Thank you for . . . for loving me and guiding me. I hold up the time with Lydia Tapestry tomorrow and ask You to guide our time together. And help me be a good wife to Galen, if it is your will that we be married. And if it isn't please let me know soon. In Jesus Name, Amen."

It seemed so clear now that Galen was an important part of her life, an essential part. Why hadn't she let herself see that before? The pounding in her chest seemed to be the Lord saying 'Open up.' She laughed out loud. "Thank you."

The sunshine pouring through the window in a golden sheet of warmth woke Elizabeth even before the alarm went off. The birds chirping from a branch that she could see from her pillow added to the feeling that the day was welcoming her and urging her to join nature in celebrating it.

She turned off the alarm clock before the shrill noise could disturb the tranquility of the morning.

After she dressed and made coffee she still had plenty of time before going to pick up Lucy Fowler, so she took her Bible and coffee cup to the patio. Elizabeth smiled because when she was last there Galen had been sitting in the chair she now chose. *I'm so silly. I feel like a teenager.* Her new decision leaped around in her heart like a... A rabbit hopped across the grass in front of the walled garden. *My heart's like a bunny rabbit.*

It was exhilarating to look out on the freshly manicured garden. The dew drops sparkled like diamonds on the grass, reflecting the sunlight for the few minutes before its warmth drew them into itself.

She opened her Bible to Genesis 1 and read "In the beginning God created. . ." When she reached the part in chapter two where God proclaimed that it was not good for man to be alone, she bowed her head. "Lord forgive me for making Galen wait so long. And thank you for setting me free to be your gift to him." Would Galen know without her telling him that she had crossed the bridge? She wasn't sure herself when it had happened. But that it had happened she was very sure.

The light of God's love was the light of Eden and He had shared it with the first man and first woman. And He had shared it with her and Galen.

"Thank you, Lord!"

Chapter Sixteen

Emily Caine sniffed as she watched Elizabeth Daily head down the sidewalk. Since the other woman was wearing another bright outfit, this time a golden yellow, she could just make out through the trees that she turned into Number Seven. The Fowlers had obviously been taken in by her too.

"Hattie!"

"Yes, Ma'am?" The housekeeper appeared at the bottom of the steps.

"I'll have my breakfast in my sitting room up here this morning."

"Yes, Ma'am."

Emily Caine thought Hattie sounded entirely too pleased about that and she was tempted to descend to the first floor simply to impose her presence on the servant who would probably do her duties in a slipshod manner if she wasn't there to oversee.

But there was such a good view of the walkway from here.

After a few minutes Elizabeth Daily came back up the walk but did not return to the Manor House. Instead she entered the Park. Emily assumed she was going out in her automobile. But why would she have gone to the Fowler's first?

She would call Lucy in a few minutes and think of a way to find out where that woman had gone. And if there was time, she'd send Hattie to the library.

Harold walked out with Lucy and waited by the front gate until Elizabeth pulled the car around. He was trying not to be too glad that he didn't have to go to Lexington. His wife's eyes twinkled as she kissed him on the cheek.

"Now try not to miss the trip too much, dear. I'll give Lydia your love."

Drat the woman. She doesn't miss a trick.

He kissed her back and couldn't resist answering the twinkle with a sheepish grin that would let her know she was reading him correctly.

He watched the two ladies drive away and walked back to the house with a youthful jaunt in his steps. A whole day all by himself. It almost made the dentist worth it.

Harold Fowler was immediately ashamed of himself. Lucy was the Lord's gift to him and he wouldn't have had it any other way. If anything ever happened to her, he knew he would be lost. "Lord, protect Lucy, bring her back safely."

But there were times, he admitted, when pure solitude was also a gift from heaven.

As he reached his front door, the phone rang.

The day remained beautiful. Elizabeth made sure the windows were adjusted so that the wind didn't hit Lucy or herself in the face and the two enjoyed the fresh air as they drove the back roads, Elizabeth's favorite route to Lexington. More and more colors sprang forth on the landscape each time she made the trip. Violets peeked out through the new growth of bluegrass on the side of the road, and the trees were glorious in varying shades of yellow and pink and white. Horses grazed in the fields and a few galloped gracefully around the others.

"Oh look." Lucy pointed out the window on her side.

Elizabeth saw a flock of sheep and slowed the car. One ewe had two baby lambs nursing at the same time.

"I love coming this way," Lucy said. "It's wonderful. Linda always takes the expressway." Then she added hastily. "Not that I am complaining. She is wonderful to bring us. It's quicker to go the other way, I suppose."

Elizabeth made a mental note to tell her new friend about the driving preference.

When they entered Moreston Manor, Elizabeth was impressed with the sophisticated atmosphere. Lucy led the way to Lydia's rooms and knocked on the door. A pleasant looking middle aged woman answered.

"Hi, Sandy. How is Lydia today?"

"Fine. She's more than fine. I don't see much of her these days."

"Oh?" Lucy looked surprised. "Oh, I'm sorry. Sandy this is my friend, Elizabeth Daily. Elizabeth, this is Sandy. She stays with Lydia and helps her."

The two women acknowledged the introduction.

"So where is Lydia?"

"Probably in the community room." Sandy smiled and her eyes twinkled. "We have a new resident in the convalescent wing. And your sister seems to be very happy visiting these days."

They found Lydia Fowler sitting in a pretty room decorated in maroon and green. A television was playing but only a few of those gathered appeared to be paying attention. Several women were seated at a table playing cards. Lydia smiled brightly when she saw her sister's face.

"Lucy!" She held out her hand and the two hugged.

"I've brought you a new friend, Lydia. This is Elizabeth Daily. Elizabeth, my sister Lydia."

Lydia nodded but Elizabeth sensed no excitement in her at the idea of a new friend.

Lucy and Elizabeth took a seat at the table where Lydia was settled. There was only one other person seated there. He was in a wheelchair with his leg propped on a pillow-covered chair.

The elderly man was perfectly groomed and dressed, looking like a gentleman ready to go somewhere.

It was Lydia's turn to make introductions. Stephen Richardson was a new resident of the convalescent wing who didn't expect to be there over a few months while he healed from foot surgery. He greeted the ladies with smiles and then offered to leave them alone for their visit.

Elizabeth waited to see how Lucy would react, but before that could happen, Lydia had protested. "No, Stephen, you stay right here. I want you to get to know my sister."

She turned to Lucy. "Stephen is a retired minister. I told him about you and Harold."

Lydia Fowler seemed so normal that Elizabeth was wondering how the term "batty as they come" could have been applied to her by George Tate.

Stephen and Lucy exchanged a few comments about pastoral duties and Stephen asked her about the mission field and how it differed. While they talked, Elizabeth smiled at Lydia and the smile was returned.

"I really like your sister and brother-in-law," Elizabeth volunteered. "And I love the Court."

A shadow fell over Lydia's eyes. "The Court? You live there?"

"Yes, I am leasing Number One, the Manor House. Did I hear them say that you lived there for a while?"

Lydia dropped her gaze to the table and didn't answer.

Lucy stopped mid sentence in her discussion with Stephen Richardson.

"Lydia?"

There was no response.

"Lydia!" Lucy arose from her chair and went to kneel beside her sister. "Lydia, are you okay?"

Lydia Tapestry lifted her head slowly and looked into her sister's eyes. "Where's my baby?"

"In your room, dear. Would you like to go back there?"

Lydia nodded.

Elizabeth swallowed a lump in her throat and blinked back tears. She recognized very clearly that she had caused this change by her prying. She turned to Stephen Richardson who was watching Lucy help her sister walk down the hallway.

"I'm so sorry. I shouldn't have said anything . . ." She stopped, recognizing that to explain would be to betray confidences. So instead she closed her mouth and sat there mute and miserable.

He reached out and patted her hand. "I'm sure you didn't mean to upset her. I wondered why she was here. I hated to ask. She seemed so healthy and able to take care of herself. Of course she's one of the permanent residents, not like me."

Elizabeth nodded. "I was surprised too. She seems perfectly normal."

"But now I know how to pray for her," Stephen Richardson said quietly. "Jesus is the same yesterday, today, and forever. And He is the healer of broken hearts, and the one who sets the captives free."

Elizabeth nodded. And felt guilty. She had been so interested in what light Lydia Tapestry might have to shed on the mystery that she hadn't even thought of the pain thinking of the past might bring. She remembered her joy with the Lord on the patio that morning and was ashamed. *How selfish I am.*

"Don't do it!"

Elizabeth looked up and saw the retired pastor looking at her with flashing eyes.

"Don't let the enemy put a guilt trip on you."

Slowly her hands unclenched. "You are right. That's exactly what I was doing. Thank you."

He nodded and held out his hand. "Shall we pray?"

Elizabeth slipped her hand in to his.

"Father, I thank you for Lydia Tapestry. I know you want to heal her and set her free from the things that torment her. Ms . . ." He paused and Elizabeth looked up to see him looking at her. "I'm sorry, I forgot your name."

"Elizabeth," she whispered.

"Father, Elizabeth and I ask You to heal Lydia Tapestry from the things that broke her heart, and set her free from tormenting spirits. We ask it in Jesus Name. Amen."

Elizabeth smiled as they unclasped hands. "I can tell that you expect that to happen."

"Yes, I do. I believe God sent me here to help her." He chuckled. "Now I don't mean that God caused my foot problems; that's just life in a fallen world. But I do believe that he sent me here, to convalesce in this place, to meet Lydia."

He grinned sheepishly before continuing. "Tell you a little secret. I have thought for the last week or so that maybe she is the answer to my prayer."

Elizabeth was startled and must have shown it because the man continued.

"My wife of 45 years died three years ago and I have been lonely. When I met Lydia a few weeks ago, she seemed so . . . refreshing. And well, I thought perhaps she was the answer to my prayer. And she still may be." His eyes narrowed slightly and his cheekbones tightened. "Just because she has some problems doesn't mean that she's not the one for me. It just means that it may take some work."

Elizabeth thought that if he knew the problems were lifelong, he might think differently. And then she was ashamed of herself. She was limiting God, just as surely as this man was not.

She smiled at him. "I hope you are right."

Within a few minutes, Lucy was back. She sighed as she sat down at the table.

"Poor Lydia."

"I am so sorry." Elizabeth put her hand over the other woman's.

"It's not your fault, dear. But what did you say?"

Elizabeth thought back. "Well, I said I loved Tapestry Court, and you and Harold. Oh, and I said I was leasing the Manor House and asked if I was correct in thinking that she lived there for a while."

Lucy nodded. "That must have been it. Remember I told you that she got worse when she was there. Not that I think anything happened . . ." She stopped and looked over at Stephen Richardson.

Elizabeth squeezed her hand. "I think Reverend Richardson is going to be good for your sister. He and I prayed for her after you left."

Lucy smiled weakly. "Thank you. She's asleep now. Curled up with her doll."

She withdrew her hand from Elizabeth's. "Are you ready to go?"

"Yes." Elizabeth turned toward Stephen Richardson. "I'll be praying that you will know exactly how to help her."

He looked at Lucy. "Is that okay with you? If I try to help her?"

Lucy's eyebrows raised slightly. "Of course."

They said their goodbyes. When Elizabeth looked back just before walking through the door to the hallway, Stephen Richardson smiled and gave a thumbs-up.

Elizabeth was pleased that Lucy Fowler's sunshiny disposition dispersed the cloud that hung over them when they left. She could tell that Ruth never suspected that they had been through a trying time before they picked her up.

Windsor Tea Room was Elizabeth's favorite leisure lunch spot and part of the charm was the gift shop. Lunch was excellent, a light flaky pastry filled with large pieces of chicken and mushrooms in a creamy garlic sauce, accompanied by a crisp romaine salad. After they ate, browsing in the gift shop which specialized in British wares delighted both Ruth and Lucy.

As she hoped, the two older women enjoyed each other too and when they all said goodbye, Ruth extracted promises from them to return soon.

There was not much conversation on the return trip until Elizabeth offered to take Lucy there each month, as long as they both lived at Tapestry Court.

"That is lovely of you, dear. Are you sure?"

"Yes, I'm sure." Lucy and Harold Fowler made her feel like part of a family.

When Elizabeth let herself in the front door of Number 1, she was immediately struck by the position of the oriental throw rug that lay on the entrance hall floor. It was turned at least a 30 degree angle from its normal position. She couldn't remember tripping over it or doing anything that would have knocked it askew.

With slight tingles on the back of her neck, Elizabeth looked through each room of the house to see if anything else was out of place. She found nothing suspicious and decided she must have disturbed the rug herself without realizing it.

"Emily phoned you this morning." Harold folded up the newspaper and glanced at the old fashioned clock. He preferred the big and little hands to those glaring red numbers. "It's after nine, probably too late to call her. Sorry. I forgot earlier."

"What did she want?" His wife was smiling at her souvenir thimbles from the Tea Room, and he was glad she had enjoyed herself on her outing, glad Elizabeth Daily had made the day a real adventure for her.

"I have no idea. She asked what time you would be back and I told her that Elizabeth had taken you to Lexington but I didn't know when you would return."

"I'll call her tomorrow," Lucy Fowler said.

Harold neglected to tell her about the uncomfortable feeling he had when Emily phoned.

Chapter Seventeen

Hattie's eyes narrowed as she watched Miz Emily replace the telephone in the cradle. She didn't like that look on the older woman's face.

Miz Lucy called on the phone and Hattie fetched Miz Emily to talk to her there on the kitchen line. The counters needed wipin' off so she couldn't help but hear what was said on this end, could she?

"I just can't remember." That was what Miz Emily said. "I'm so sorry. Old age is just a trial. One often forgets." Then after a short pause, "Yes, if I remember what it was I'll call you. Thank you dear."

But the sneaky smile on her face when she hung up didn't look like she had forgotten anything or was feelin' no trial. What was the old lady up to now?

Elizabeth sighed as she looked at the library. After bringing order out of chaos the previous week, she had now reinstalled confusion in the room. While Ruth and Lucy visited at Ruth's condo near the end of their day in

Lexington, Elizabeth excused herself to "get a few things to take back". The boxes and cartons of letters were now scattered around the floor waiting to be sorted and added to the piles that already needed answering.

After staring at them for a few minutes, she shook her head and left the room, closing the door behind her. *After all, tomorrow is another day, Scarlett.*

She refused to feel guilty for not leaping into the task. There was time . . . all the time she needed. If she hadn't gotten them sorted by the time Galen came on Friday, maybe he would help her. She had not let him see them before, although she told him they contained both extremes in their opinions. But it was okay now. She had reassured herself that there was nothing in the book that she disagreed with or felt dishonored God in any way. And she was no longer afraid to let Galen see her private communications from the public. If she was going to become his wife, it was only right that she share everything with him.

His wife. She stared dreamily out the kitchen window to the garden and the flowers they had chosen together. *Oh!* A new thought struck her. Where would they live if . . . when . . . they were married? She felt a pang at the thought of leaving Tapestry Court. *Silly. This was never meant to be permanent.*

The phone interrupted her musings and when she answered it was Harold Fowler.

"I just called to see if you're coming this morning."

"I am so sorry. I can't believe I forgot it is Wednesday! What time is it?" She looked over at the wall clock. "Oh, 10:30. I am really sorry to have wasted your time waiting on me."

Harold laughed. "Not another word. I told you I have too much time on my hands, plenty to waste. And to tell the truth I didn't waste it. I began doing a word search in some Hebrew dictionaries and lexicons and didn't realize what time it was myself until ten minutes ago."

"Oh, good, that makes me feel better. Is it too late or can I run down there now?"

"Of course. See you in a few."

When they were again seated in the office that Elizabeth found so comfortable she brought up the previous days visit.

"I guess Lucy told you about our visit to Lydia?"

He nodded. "Yes, and about her new friend, the former pastor. That is interesting."

Elizabeth smiled. "More interesting than you know. I never got a chance to tell Lucy but he is romantically interested in Lydia." She told Harold about her conversation—and prayers—with Stephen Richardson.

"He really seems to believe that she can be normal. Of course he doesn't know that she has not been normal since childhood." She gave a short laugh. "But his faith puts me to shame. He makes you believe that it could happen."

Harold Fowler's eyes twinkled. "I'd like to meet him. It's been a long time since I met someone with that kind of faith. You see it overseas but not here." The twinkle left as he shook his head sadly. "Complacency, that's the trouble with the Church in the United States. Content with the status quo. No passion, no expectation for miracles."

"But you, you expect God to move."

"Not like I should. I've put Him in a very narrow box. I expect him to give wisdom when someone comes to me for pastoral counseling. I expect him to give knowledge when I am teaching. And I expect him to give wisdom and skill to doctors to help people get well. But I expect little else. I often feel very faith-less."

He sat up straighter. "But now, we're not here to examine my conscience. What are we going to talk about today?"

She grinned. "You have worked a miracle in me somehow. I have made my decision about Galen. I can't think now how I could have thought there was any other option. God has obviously prepared us for each other and I feel guilty that I've made him wait so long for me to realize it."

"You are good at that, aren't you? Feeling guilty, I mean."

Elizabeth laughed. "Yes, I am. Forgive me, Father, for I have sinned."

"Our times are in His hands."

"Thank God," she answered. "And there has been another miracle too—or what seems like one to me." She told him about her former concerns about the book and that she had resolved them. "And I think that since I believe now that marriage with Galen is God's plan for me, he and I can decide together what speaking engagements, if any, I will accept."

He nodded.

She added with a mischievous smile, "And then we'll just have to trust the Lord to lead us in the paths of righteousness."

"Imagine." Harold added his laughter to hers.

When Elizabeth returned to the Manor House, it was with a very light heart. She opened the door to the library and looked at the boxes intently. Then she picked up the phone.

Mindy's voice sounded happy when she answered. "Hello, Elizabeth. How nice to see your number pop up on caller id. What's going on?"

"I have something I want to talk to you about. Are you busy?"

"No, have you had lunch? Would you like to come over? I can make grilled cheese sandwiches."

"No, I haven't eaten. But I have some leftovers that need to be gotten rid of – Chinese food if you like it. And I really need to talk to you here if that's okay."

"Great. What time?"

"Any time. I'm getting hungry." The clock showed 12:15.

"I'll be right there."

When Mindy arrived, she was a little out of breath. "I ran all the way. I'm so curious about what you wanted to talk to me for."

Elizabeth laughed. "Actually I want to offer you a job."

"What?"

"I need a secretary. But it wouldn't involve leaving the Court, or even your home. So I thought maybe Charles wouldn't mind and you would like a project."

Mindy's eyes widened and she grinned from ear to ear. "Boy, would I? But a secretary? I thought you weren't working anymore."

Elizabeth smiled. "Well, do I have a story to tell you."

An hour later there were no leftovers and Mindy Simmons knew all about *The Fall And Redemption of God.*

Elizabeth led her into the library and she gasped when she saw the boxes and crates spread on the floor there.

"I guess you do need a secretary."

"I have just put off going through them—except for the ones in the wire baskets. Those are divided into fan mail and hate mail. The rest of the boxes need sorting and they all need answering. If you are really interested . . ."

"Yes!" Mindy interrupted. "I am interested and Charles is just going to have to agree. I won't take 'no' for an answer about this."

Elizabeth laughed. "Okay, wonderful. What I was going to say was that you could either work here or take all this to your house, whichever you'd rather."

"It doesn't matter to you?"

"Not at all."

Mindy smiled. "Then I'd like to take them to my house. It would be awesome to set up an office in one of the spare rooms. They really are useless except for the one I use as a library."

"Wonderful! That will get them out of my sight."

They walked together to the Archers' store and borrowed the wagon because neither woman felt comfortable pushing the wheelbarrow.

Elizabeth thanked Jackie Archer. "You need to have a rental service and hire this thing out."

Jackie smiled. "It's great to have such a good customer; you are a breath of fresh air around here." Then she looked at Mindy with a glance as if apologizing for the implication that Mindy was stale.

Mindy laughed. "I agree."

When they were back in the library of Number 1, they surveyed the boxes and estimated how many trips it would take.

"What's wrong with me?" Mindy moaned. "I better clear out that room before I start carrying boxes in. Let me go do that . . . give me an hour. Is that okay?"

"Can I help?" Elizabeth offered.

"No, it's one of those things that nobody can do for you."

After the younger woman left, Elizabeth breathed a sigh of relief. *Amazing how all the problems are just dissolving. Why didn't I think of a secretary months ago? Oh, yes, Lord. Because you had Mindy in mind for this job all along. If I had thought of a secretary, I would have run ahead of you and hired somebody, and messed up your plan.*

Hired? Oh, no . . . we didn't even discuss salary. I hope she doesn't think I expect her to do it free.

When Elizabeth and Mindy had successfully transferred the boxes, crates, and wire baskets full of letters from the Manor House to Number Five, Elizabeth breathed a sigh of relief and beamed at Mindy.

"I can't tell you how glad I am to turn these over to someone else."

"And I can't tell you how glad I am to have a project. I'll probably be sorry when the job is completed."

"Oh, we didn't discuss salary. We could agree on an amount for the whole job but I have no idea how long it's going to take you . . . and also letters are still coming in. Would it be okay if we just agreed on an hourly amount and you keep track of your time?"

"That would be fine. I'll get everything sorted and then we'll discuss the letters you want sent to the different groups."

"They're already separated," Elizabeth said, eyeing the boxes. "Well, more or less."

Mindy wrinkled her nose. "You will have more than two groups because there will be varying categories of interest and sincerity in each group—pro and con."

Elizabeth looked at her with increased respect. "Hmm. I hadn't thought about that. But from what I've seen you are right. Oh! You were a secretary, weren't you?"

Mindy grinned. "Yep. Years of training—at your service."

When Elizabeth walked back home with a sense of freedom she hadn't felt in nearly a year.

Now, to get on to the task at hand.

She pulled out her list and reviewed the notes, revising according to her latest insights.

> 1. Who is Charles Simmons—his parentage? Why did the Colonel bring him to Tapestry. Question one was supposedly answered and she should

delete it from the list but she just wasn't sure that
the answers were true.
2. Was the Colonel ever known to be involved with
any women?
She really must talk to George Tate some more. He
wouldn't know about the women but he could tell
her who might know—besides his Aunt Emily.
3. Was there any location that the Colonel visited
frequently?

She couldn't ask Emily Caine . . . ah. The attorney.
Galen could ask the attorney who had been with the
company for years.

4. Why does Jenny Anderson have an aversion to
the Manor House?

There was no question about the aversion but nothing
she could do to find the answer unless she became much
closer to Jenny. And she felt guilty doing that just to
collect information.

5. What made Emily Caine so bitter? Did she hate
Colonel Tapestry? Does she know about the
missing heir but doesn't want a rival to her nephew
George?
6. What is William Sinclair's background? Why was
he installed in Tapestry Court with family and long
term associates?
7. Is the overwhelming theme of the Tapestry name
and initial important to the solution of the will - or
the murder?

Elizabeth sighed and put the paper back in the desk
drawer. As she did, she saw that a pen that she kept on
the right side of the drawer had somehow gotten turned

around and rolled toward the back. That had not happened when she opened the drawer to get the paper out, so it must have happened before. Immediately she thought of the throw rug in the entrance hall that was askew the day before when she got back from Lexington.

Someone has been here looking through my things.

"You are wasting so much potato!" Mindy threw a thick peel at Bill Sinclair.

"Hey, I'm cheap labor. You shouldn't complain." He was lifting the peeling from his shoulder and they were laughing when Charles Simmons walked in the kitchen.

"Charles! You're home early. How nice." Mindy started toward him but he walked past her, nodded at Bill, and went to the refrigerator to get a bottle of water.

"Bill was helping me peel potatoes." Charles still didn't look at her. She grimaced and rolled her eyes at Bill. "But he's not very good at it." She chuckled.

Charles looked down at the newspaper that was lying on the kitchen counter.

"Did you have a nice day, Charles?"

He looked up at her finally, with eyes that could have belonged to a stranger. "It was okay."

The chill in his voice slapped at her. Shocked, Mindy stood silently, her heart pounding.

Bill got up from the table. "Well, I think I've done enough damage to your potato budget; I guess I'll get on over to the house."

"Won't you come back and eat with us?" Mindy asked.

Bill looked at Charles but he didn't echo the invitation. "No, I don't think so. Thanks anyway. I'll let myself out. Good night, Charles."

Charles answered with a nod and a grunt, but never took his eyes off the newspaper.

On his way out, Bill shrugged at Mindy.

She knew better than to ask Charles what was wrong. At best he would say 'Nothing.' And at worst he would glare at her and say nothing.

"When you've finished with the paper, I've got some news."

Charles sighed and put the paper aside.

"What?"

Uh oh, I should have waited. This was really bad timing.

"Never mind. I'll wait til after you've read the paper and had supper. It's nothing important. Really. Why don't you go on and have a shower. It will relax you."

He gave her a cold look and left the kitchen, taking the paper with him.

She had just started peeling the last potato when Charles' voice rang out.

"What is this mess?"

Uh oh, I left the door open.

She hurriedly washed her hands and joined him in her new office.

"That's what I was going to tell you about. I have a job!" She beamed and tried to act like her insides were not quivering.

"A job?" He was frowning.

"Yes, a job. Elizabeth needs a secretary to handle all her mail. It turns out she wrote a really famous book and she wants someone who can sort through the letters and answer them for her." She couldn't read his expression so she hurried on. "Isn't that great? I'll have a project and yet I don't have to leave our home." She could tell that the look she gave him was pleading for approval and he had to know that.

Finally he nodded. "Yes, that sounds good. I'm glad you have found something to keep you occupied." He turned and left the room and she heard him mutter.

"Though you seem to find plenty of entertainment without a job.".

He sounded like he might actually be jealous of Bill. *Wow. Is this wishful thinking? Could he really care? No, if that's what it is, it's probably just a pride thing. After all I'm his property . . . bought and paid for.*

But if what she hoped would happen . . . would it make a difference?

Chapter Eighteen

The courtroom was packed, and the combination of outdoor heat coming through the windows along with people inside generating heat already made the atmosphere more than a little uncomfortable.

Jenny Anderson was not happy that her name was drawn for jury duty but she reported that Thursday morning to the Courthouse. She was even less happy when she was one of those selected to be interviewed concerning her fitness to be included in the first jury, those who would be trying a murder case.

That beginning process took hours while names were called and people were excused. The chair she had to sit on was hard and so were the faces of the attorneys, both prosecution and defense. *I wish I could be excused. Joel said serving would be good for me so I need to have a better attitude. That lady in the red shirt and slacks looks nice. Maybe we could be friends if we both get chosen.*

Evidently the case was well known among the population of Simpsonton because the attorneys spent a lot of time talking about the problem with all the publicity.

They called the potential jurors one by one into a conference room for questioning. After a short lunch break, the afternoon dragged on and many potential jurors were excused. It grew hotter in the courtroom. She could see people fanning themselves, those up front with her whose names had been called for further interviews and also among those waiting to see if they would be called when others were excused. Jenny got out the book she had in her purse and began fanning herself. She would like to read but thought that would look too rude.

At last her name was called to enter the little room. The prosecutor, the defense attorney, and the judge were all seated at a small table and she was invited to sit in the empty chair. The first question asked was if she had discussed the case with anyone at lunch or prior to today.

"No, I didn't know anything about it until I got here this morning."

They all looked at each other ..*They don't believe me.*

The defense attorney asked, "You never read accounts of the case in the newspaper?"

"No, Sir. I don't read the newspaper."

"But on TV. You heard about it on the news last summer, surely?"

"No, Sir. I don't watch the news." *They are shocked. Good. Maybe they'll think I'm so stupid that I'm not fit to serve on the jury and they'll let me go home.*

They asked a few more questions concerning her opinions on some subjects that seemed completely unrelated and about her willingness to sentence someone found guilty to prison. When the questions were over she noticed them looking at each other and nodding.

She was dismissed back to a hard chair and sweltering heat. Finally the announcement came and Jennifer Anderson was on the list of jurors chosen.

"You are all admonished again not to discuss the case with anyone, and to report it if anyone tries to discuss it with you."

They were dismissed and told to return at 8:30 a.m. Friday morning. Jenny sighed but determined to voice no discontent to Joel.

It was 4:30 Friday afternoon when Elizabeth's home phone rang. Harold Fowler was on the other end of the line.

"Elizabeth, are you busy?" His voice held a serious tone that kept her from telling him that she was preparing supper for Galen who was expected to arrive around six.

"What's going on? Is something wrong?"

"Jenny Anderson collapsed at the courthouse today— she was on jury duty. They took her to the emergency room and she's there now. Joel called to let me know and ask for prayer. I knew that you had some contact with her and thought you would want to know." He paused. "Either to pray, or maybe go to the hospital."

"Oh!" Elizabeth mentally rearranged her evening. "Yes, of course I'll go. Do you want to ride along?"

"No, if you don't mind. I'll just stay here and pray for her. Let me know when you find out something about her condition."

"I will. And thank you, Harold, for calling me."

Elizabeth looked regretfully at the lamb roast and promised herself they would have it tomorrow as she placed it back in the refrigerator.

On the way to the hospital, she called Galen from her cell phone and told him of the change of plans. He said he would come straight to the hospital instead of the house.

"I'll call and let you know if I leave before then. I'm sorry about supper."

"Don't worry. If you're not needed all evening, I'll take you out to dinner."

"It's a deal," she said. "We'll have the lamb tomorrow."

When Elizabeth arrived at the hospital she went straight to the emergency room and inquired at the desk for Jenny Anderson. A busy nurse pointed to a doorway through which a curtain could be seen protecting whatever was behind it from view. When she pulled the material back, Elizabeth saw a worried eyed Joel Anderson holding his wife's hand in one of his own and stroking it with the other. Jenny was lying on the hospital bed looking very pale and confused. She was hooked up to an IV. Her lips formed a slight smile when she recognized Elizabeth's face.

Joel dropped his wife's hand and stuck out his own. "Ms. Daily, how nice of you to come."

She took his hand and nodded but quickly turned to Jenny. "What happened? Are you all right? Rev. Fowler just said you had collapsed. Do they know what caused it?"

Jenny shook her head but Elizabeth saw the hesitation in her eyes.

Joel said, "They think maybe the courtroom was overheated. The air conditioning was broken and there were so many people crowded in there for the murder trial."

Just then a young doctor pulled the curtain back and joined them, paperwork in hand. "Okay, Mrs. Anderson. It looks like your blood work is fine. Potassium level okay. I've ordered that the IV be discontinued when this bag is through." He turned to squint at the device. "That should be in about 30 more minutes. And then you can go home."

Joel protested. "But what caused her to pass out? I don't want it to happen again."

The doctor shrugged. "We don't know why it happened. But all her vital signs are good and her blood work shows no problem. We have no reason to keep her in the hospital." He turned to Jenny. "You just take it easy for a few days, don't go out in the heat. Get lots of rest."

"Can I get an excuse from jury duty?" Jenny asked in a quivering voice.

"Sure. I'll have the nurse write something out . . . how long for?"

Joel said, "The term was for about six weeks, I think. And yesterday was the first day."

"I can legitimately write an excuse through the end of next week." And he left.

Elizabeth could tell by Jenny's face that she was disappointed.

She grinned sheepishly. "You can't blame a girl for trying."

"You didn't want jury duty?"

She shook her head. "I asked to be excused but they wouldn't let me. Joel thought it would be good for me but . . ." She looked up at her husband.

He smiled tenderly at her. "Guess I was wrong."

Elizabeth asked them. "Is there anything I can do? I don't want to intrude. But if there's anything . . ."

"It would be great if you could stay here with Jenny for a few minutes." He glanced at his watch. "I'll be back in half an hour, in time to pick her up, but I don't want to leave her after we get home and we need some things like 7 Up and . . . what do you want, Jenny?"

"I don't know. Whatever."

When he had gone, Jenny turned to Elizabeth and held out her hand. Elizabeth took it and saw Jenny relax. "You are so kind. Thank you for coming."

Elizabeth smiled. "You're welcome."

"I need to talk to somebody. And I think you're the one."

Elizabeth settled on a stool beside the bed without pulling her hand away from Jenny.

"I remembered something. There in the courtroom, I mean. Someone was testifying. I can't even remember exactly what they were saying, it was a witness I think. To the murder, I mean, not just a plain old witness. It's that murder case that happened at the apartment complex near the High School last summer. Anyway, this woman was talking and suddenly I got dizzy and there was like a brown swirling thing in my mind and I saw something and then I woke up in an ambulance with the siren going."

"What did you see?" Elizabeth asked.

"I don't remember. But I knew it at the time. And I'm sure that's why I fainted."

"Jenny, I have spent most of my life as a psychologist and just recently closed my office. I'd be happy to help you work through this if you want help."

Jenny's grasp on her hand tightened. "Yes, I do want help. I feel like I've been sick for a long time. But I didn't even have a clue why. There are lots of things that I'm not normal about." Elizabeth could see the blush spring to Jenny's face.

"It's okay." She chuckled. "There are no 'normal' people, you know. Normal is a myth."

Just then, Galen's face peered around the curtain.

"Galen!" Elizabeth jumped up and pulled him into the enclosure. "Jenny do you . . .?"

"Yes, hello, Mr. Delaney."

"Please call me Galen. And how are you?"

"She's going to be fine," Elizabeth answered for her. "Joel's gone to pick up some things and I'm staying 'til he gets back to take her home."

"I wish I'd told him to get me Wendy's. I'm a little hungry now." She smiled up at Elizabeth as if to say that getting the memory out in the open had made a difference in her physical well being.

"Tell you what," Galen said. "Why don't we, when Joel comes back, go pick up Wendy's for all of us and meet you at your house." And then he added as an afterthought. "Or would you rather go home and rest? We don't have to come . . ."

"Oh, no!" Jenny protested. "It would be awesome for you two to come. I'd love it."

"Okay then, it's settled. I'll wait out here in the waiting area and Bits, you'll come and get me?"

She agreed and he left.

"He seems like such a nice man," Jenny said.

Elizabeth gave a contented sigh. "He is. We are both blessed with very nice men, aren't we?"

"Yes," said Jenny. "And I want to be the wife that my husband deserves."

Elizabeth didn't say, "Me too." But she thought it. "We'll work through it, Jenny, whatever it is. Maybe Monday morning we could start?"

"Yes." Jenny's voice was filled with gratitude. "At least now I know there is something . . . I mean something real, not just me being . . . being nuts."

Galen and Elizabeth stayed at the Andersons for several hours. The young couple seemed starved for company and they didn't want to disappoint them. They watched a DVD of *My Big Fat Greek Wedding* which Galen and Elizabeth had never seen, and enjoyed thoroughly.

It was nearly ten o'clock before they said goodnight.

"Oh, no!" Elizabeth said. "I forgot to call Harold Fowler."

Since they left by the front door, they could see the lights still on at Number Seven so they walked toward the Fowler's home.

Lucy invited them in enthusiastically even though Elizabeth explained that she just wanted to apologize and tell them that Jenny Anderson was at home and doing well.

Harold's face appeared over his wife's shoulder and joined her in asking the couple to join them. They didn't know Galen, and Elizabeth was happy that these people she loved were finally meeting.

As they headed into the living room, Harold threw a questioning look toward Galen and then at her. She shook her head and gave a little shrug. There just had not been time or the right atmosphere to let Galen know about the decisions she reached.

Harold asked Galen about his job, Lucy asked for more details about Jenny Anderson, and then Elizabeth stood up and said, "We really have to go. It's been a long day and I haven't even gotten the guesthouse ready for Galen." She realized she wanted them to know that he was not staying in the Manor House with her. *So much for not caring what people think.*

As they were leaving, Elizabeth turned to Harold, "I am meeting with Jenny on Monday morning at 10 so you might be praying, if you have time."

Harold laughed, "I told you time is my greatest commodity. Gotcha covered."

Galen took Elizabeth's hand in his as they walked through Tapestry Court to the Manor House. "I love you, Elizabeth Daily."

"And I love you, Galen Delaney." Then she added with a touch of mischief in her voice, "Do you realize that when I marry you, my initials won't change?"

They had taken two more steps before Galen stopped short. He turned her to face him. "When? You said 'when' not if. Bits?"

She laughed softly. "Yes, I have finally come to my senses.

And there on the walk right in the middle of the front doors of the Anderson's and Emily Caine's, they kissed. It was the kind of kiss of which Elizabeth knew Emily Caine would not approve. But she didn't care.

Chapter Nineteen

Elizabeth snuggled luxuriously in the comfort of her bed that Saturday morning, putting off getting out of it as long as she could. She smiled as she remembered the look on Galen's face when he realized she was really going to marry him. *How blessed I am, Lord.*

Galen! He is here! She leaped out of the bed, hurried into her clothes, and gave her teeth a quick brushing.

She could see Galen already seated on the patio when she came into the kitchen. She started the coffee pot before she joined him.

He put his book down when she opened the back door. "Good morning my future wife."

Elizabeth could feel herself blush. *I can't believe me.*

"Good morning my future husband. Sorry I'm just getting coffee started."

"That's okay. I'm still high from last night's adrenalin rush."

She laughed and leaned down for a morning hug. "Me too."

"So, what's on the menu for today?"

"Well, I thought we'd have the lamb roast for supper but . . ."

He chuckled. "No, I meant what are we going to do? Any plans?"

She settled herself in the chair beside him. "Visit the Andersons and see how Jenny is? They seem so grateful for company. I don't think they have many friends."

Galen nodded. "Anything else?"

"I guess we ought to discuss the mystery some more. I had questions I wanted you to find out for me but Jenny's crisis drove all that out of my mind. I've got my list though." She was just about to tell him about the moved pen and rug when he reached for her hand.

"Would it be possible that I have some input into our day?"

"Of course. I'm sorry." *How selfish I am. He really is a saint.*

Galen leaned over and kissed her nose. "Just kidding you. I asked, remember? But your future groom would like to discuss wedding plans. How soon can I talk you into making this final?"

Elizabeth blushed again. She knew that part of his eagerness was their physical relationship. And she understood. Very well. It had been difficult for both of them to separate last night.

"I can't see any reason to put it off long, can you?"

"Absolutely not. So—you want to get married this morning?"

She laughed. "Well, I wouldn't mind but I don't think we can get a license this quickly. And, Galen, I don't want a big wedding but I would like it to be special. Could we plan just a little one?"

"Anything you want, Bits. I've waited this long. I think I can handle a little longer."

She moved over to sit on his lap. "You've been wonderfully patient with me. Thank you." She nuzzled his neck with her nose.

"You'll make it up to me, right?" His voice became husky as he traced her ear with his finger. *Well, maybe not a perfect saint.*

She jumped up. "*After* we're married. I'll get the coffee."

When they finished their coffee, and toast spread with bootleg jam, Elizabeth put together a quick banana pudding and divided it into two plastic containers. One went in the refrigerator and with the other in hand, they left for the Andersons.

"Let's go through the park," Elizabeth suggested.

It was pretty. Someone had planted pansies in the beds in between the perennial hostas that were growing back and filling the place with a lush green forest floor atmosphere.

When they reached the fountain they stopped and looked up at the giant T. The sound of the water was soothing. What a shame the spot had been the scene of violence.

Galen broke the silence. "He sure did like his name, didn't he? I never saw so many monogrammed towels and stationary. Even the note pads at the guesthouse have a T on them."

"Yes, and you know, it made me wonder . . ."

Just then a hearty voice reached them. "Hey neighbors. Why don't you come over?"

Joel Anderson smiled at them across the hedge by the far gate.

Galen yelled back. "We were just on our way."

Joel was back in the house and opening the kitchen door for them when they arrived.

At the table, seated with a cup of tea in her hand, Jenny looked happier than Elizabeth had ever seen her.

What a relief it must be to know there was a real cause behind her anxiety.

She handed Jenny the refrigerator dish. "It's just a mix with fresh bananas but I thought maybe you might be able to use it."

"Thank you. Yes, we'll love it." She got up and put the dish into the refrigerator just as the front doorbell rang.

"I'll get it." Joel left them and soon returned with George and Linda Tate.

"Hi!" Linda Tate smiled at Elizabeth. "Looks like it's block party time, huh?" She handed Jenny a glass casserole dish. "We're having lasagna for supper tonight and I thought I'd just make a little extra. We heard about your accident." She suddenly looked confused. "Or whatever it was."

Jenny took the dish and added it to the shelf that held the banana pudding. "Well, Joel. Tonight's supper is supplied." She turned to her neighbors. "Thank you all so much. You can't imagine how much we appreciate it." She gestured to the table. "Please sit down. I was having some tea and we have coffee too."

When they were seated she said, "This is the first time ever that all six of these chairs were full." Her exuberance made them all laugh.

Elizabeth and Linda joined Jenny in having herb tea and the men all drank coffee.

"I fainted," Jenny said to Linda. "It was at the courthouse during the trial and something was said and I fainted."

"Oh." Linda said the one word but nothing else.

Jenny took a deep breath. "I think that I have buried something in my mind and whatever that woman said, it tried to come out and scared me." She looked at Elizabeth shyly. "But I'm going to find out. Elizabeth is going to help me."

"How wonderful." Linda turned to smile at her. "We were all very blessed when you came to Tapestry Court."

"So was I," Elizabeth said. And she meant it from the very depths of her heart.

Linda turned back to Jenny. "Is there anything I can do for you? I mean, I'm not an expert like Elizabeth but if there's anything at all . . ."

Jenny smiled at her shyly. "There is something. Sometimes I've seen you and your daughter sit on the swing in your side yard and talk. Through the window I mean, and I've thought how nice that would be. To talk with you, I mean. I wouldn't want to butt in on a personal conversation but sometime when you're just hanging out, I'd really like that."

Elizabeth was amazed at Jenny's boldness, even though her blush was obvious. And she could tell by the look on Linda's face that Jenny was going to be included in more than just a few conversations on a swing.

Just as the two couples were leaving, this time both using the front door that opened onto the Court, Bill Sinclair walked past on his way to the parking garage.

"Hey, Sinclair. How's it going?" George Tate greeted his employee.

Bill's nod included all of them. "Fine. And you?"

"Just fine," George said.

The single man walked on without further comment or backward glance.

George watched him and then said, "Don't know what's wrong with him lately. Bill's always been the life of the party type. And lately he's so quiet . . . seems to have something on his mind."

Linda changed the subject. "We were going to call you two later. Would you like to come for supper? As you know, we're having lasagna and I've got lots and lots."

"Oh, I'm sorry," Elizabeth said. "It sounds wonderful but I have a lamb roast that didn't get eaten last night because we went to the hospital for Jenny, and I really have to cook it tonight."

"What about cards later?"

Elizabeth looked at Galen. Would he want to spend part of their time with the other couple?

He answered. "Sounds great to me. What time?"

Linda said "7:30?"

"Perfect. We'll be there."

After the Tates had turned toward their house, Elizabeth slipped her hand into Galen's. "I wasn't sure if you wanted to spend the evening with them or not."

He grinned down at her. "Safer."

When they were settled in the library she told him her latest news.

"I have a secretary."

"What?" Galen looked shocked and she laughed.

"Mindy Simmons now has all the letters. After she gets them sorted, we'll get together and agree on the responses she'll write."

"Impressive. She sounds efficient and I'm proud of you for turning that mess over."

Elizabeth laughed. "I should have done it a long time ago." She caught herself. "No, I'm sure it was God's plan that Mindy be the one to handle it."

"What does Charles think about it?"

"She phoned me Thursday and said he is fine with it. But she didn't sound happy. I feel so bad for her. She's such a sweet girl. But he doesn't seem to care about anything but work."

She pulled the list out of the drawer and found the notation she wanted.

"Here it is. I wondered if there is any location that the Colonel visited frequently. Emily Caine would know but I can't ask her. I thought you might ask the attorney that was with him for years."

"You mean to try to find the location of the mother of the missing son?"

"Yes."

"Phelps is an old man. I'm not sure he'd remember. He joined up with Tapestry in the fifties, I think. And since we have no idea how old this son is, we don't even know what time period we're talking about."

"Let's start with Charles Simmons age and go down to, well I guess a little younger than Bill Sinclair. I just keep thinking it must be one of them. Guy Tapestry would not have left his fortune to somebody he didn't trust. And you have to admit it is strange that he gave a house to Bill Sinclair when the other houses in the Court were filled with long time connections."

"Yes, that was unusual behavior for him." Galen scratched his chin. "It's Saturday but I could call Phelps at home. I don't think he would mind."

Elizabeth beamed. "Great."

She went to prepare the crab salad for lunch while Galen searched 'God's briefcase' for the attorney's home phone number.

She was just pulling the plates out to take to the patio table when Galen joined her in the kitchen.

"Phelps can't remember any particular place the Colonel visited a lot. He said Emily Caine would know. He remembers Tapestry sending her somewhere, Alabama maybe, for an extended time. So maybe he had interests there."

"Emily Caine again." Elizabeth shook her head. "I'm not asking her. That's for sure." She looked at Galen with a question in her eyes.

He quickly dispelled that hope. "Not me either. When the Colonel first died she was questioned extensively about the son and denied knowing anything. I can't see her changing her story now."

Elizabeth sighed. "You're right.

"Did you ask Mrs. Fowler about the DNA testing?"

Elizabeth shook her head. "I couldn't bring myself to do it on our day together and then there didn't seem to be the right time."

Galen laughed. "It's okay. You'll know!"

Chuck answered the door when the guests arrived that night. He wasn't sure if he wanted his parents being friends with Miss Daily or not. He kind of liked it when he was the only one who knew her. And he was sure he didn't like it when his sister hugged their new neighbor as if they were close friends.

But Miss Daily was cool. When she saw him her face lit up and she said, "So, young Mr. Tate, when are you coming for tea again?"

He could feel his own face turning from a frown to a smile. "Anytime you say."

He had not been back in the house since her first week at Tapestry Court and he wanted to get another look at those ships.

Linda Tate set a bowl of peanuts on one corner of the card table and a bowl of grapes on another. She was so happy to have company. It had been a long time since she and George had friends to play with. There was a couple that worked for the company who used to come over and taught them how to play Pinochle. But they moved away over a decade ago. *I sound like a child. 'Friends to play with' indeed. But lately I feel like a child. George is still a little preoccupied but he loves me. And I like Elizabeth Daily and Galen Delaney. I wish they would stay here always.*

Then she thought of Jenny Anderson. *Poor child. What have I been thinking? I've not been a good neighbor to her at all. But that is going to change.*

It was a good night—women against men. And the women won again.

Galen and Elizabeth went to church with the Tates again the following morning and Elizabeth decided that she had found the place for her to worship. At least while she was in Simpsonton.

"I wonder how long I'll be here," she said during the walk from the garage back to the house.

"That's one of the things we're going to discuss this afternoon before I leave, right?" Galen squeezed her hand.

She laughed. "We're going to set a date, huh?"

He dropped to one knee there on the pathway. "Please?"

"Get up, silly." She laughed again and shook her head.

They made sandwiches and took them to the patio table which had become their favorite spot.

"Okay," Galen said between chewing. "How soon?"

She thought a minute. "I always thought I wanted a church wedding. And I thought it would be at my home church in Lexington. But . . ." She looked out at the lawn and garden. "This would be a lovely place to get married."

Galen looked surprised. "You're right. I just thought that you'd move back to the condo now."

"I know. I thought that too, before I came here. But . . ." She looked out at the lawn again. "I feel so comfortable here. And I love the people. I feel like I've come home."

She looked down at her plate, avoiding Galen's eyes. He couldn't possibly understand. He grew up with both parents, two brothers, and a sister. He couldn't know the loneliness of never really feeling like you belonged that started in the convent school and continued throughout her adult years. Ruth had been the first person who felt like family and though she decorated the condo with her special treasures, something was missing. But here at Tapestry Court, nothing was missing. Mindy and Linda were beginning to feel like sisters. Jenny Anderson was a dear, and Joel too. George was great. Bill Sinclair was friendly and helpful. Reggie and Chuck provided a youthful touch that was missing in her life. And Harold and Lucy Fowler . . . she swallowed a lump at the thought of losing the Fowlers. *Parent substitutes.*

Elizabeth laughed out loud. "I'm analyzing myself. Why I love it here so much."

Galen reached for her hand again. "Why is that, Bits?"

Galen was more understanding than she'd assumed. When she hesitated in her response, he continued. "There is no hurry. We can both live here until you are ready to leave."

"What? But the drive . . ."

"Bits, my commute in Lexington is almost the same as it is to get here. Remember my bank is on this side of Lexington."

Elizabeth breathed a sigh of relief and something relaxed in her stomach. Tears sprang to her eyes.

"Oh Galen. To be here in this house with you and surrounded by these people. Why, it would be like heaven on earth."

"That's exactly what I intend to make life for you, O future Mrs. Delaney."

The kiss was prolonged but finally Galen pulled away.

"Date?"

"Let me get a calendar."

"And we need to make a guest list."

Finally it was settled that they would be married three weeks from the previous Saturday. Here in the garden. The guest list would include the residents of Tapestry Court, Ruth Carrier, Ed Ramey and his family, and Galen's family.

"And who is going to perform the ceremony?" Galen asked.

"I'd like to ask Harold Fowler if that's all right with you."

"Perfect." Galen said and kissed her again.

Chapter Twenty

Elizabeth knocked at the door of Number Seven. Her appointment at Jenny's was in 30 minutes but she was eager to share with Harold and Lucy about her wedding plans.

Lucy opened the door and a smile lit her features. "Elizabeth. What a nice surprise. Come in."

Elizabeth followed her into the kitchen where Harold sat with a cup of coffee in front of him. His face also lit up. It occurred to Elizabeth that they might enjoy the friendship with her as much as she did. They never had a daughter, and their son and his family lived in another state.

"I can't stay long," she explained as she took the seat next to him. "I'm due at Jenny's at 10." She laughed. "I guess that's the time for counseling appointments at Tapestry Court, huh?"

The couple nodded and looked at her expectantly, as if they knew she must have some reason for the unannounced call.

"I have something to tell you. And something to ask you." Suddenly Elizabeth felt shy. *I am so silly.* "Galen and I are going to get married. You're the first to know."

Lucy clapped her hands that were as small as a child's. "Oh, I'm so happy for you. Such a nice man and so in love with you."

Elizabeth looked at Harold. "Thank you. Thank you for helping me figure out what my heart wanted to do."

He smiled at her. "To God be the glory."

"We want to get married here, in the garden behind my house." Elizabeth stopped abruptly. "I know it's not my house but you know what I mean."

Lucy said, "It's yours while you live in it, right Harold?"

He nodded.

"Anyway, Galen and I want to know if you will do us the honor of performing the ceremony."

Joy sprang into his eyes. "Of course, when?"

"Two weeks from Saturday if that works for you."

He frowned. "I'll have to check my schedule."

Lucy's mouth dropped open. "Harold!"

He laughed. "Just kidding. Everybody knows I have no schedule anymore."

Elizabeth reached over and hugged him. "Thank you. That will make our wedding perfect."

Harold grabbed both her hand and Lucy's. "Now let's pray for your time with Jenny Anderson." He led them in a short prayer.

As soon as he said the Amen, Lucy spoke, "Poor Jenny. It must be awful to have something that you almost can remember but not quite. Something big I mean. You know, it's so frustrating when you can't remember a little thing, like where you put your coffee cup or what you meant to tell somebody about. But a big thing, something big enough to make you faint and push it back down again. That must be horrible."

"Yes." Elizabeth nodded in agreement. Then she pushed back her chair and stood up. "I better go now so I won't be late. Thank you for praying with me."

Lucy went on talking, almost as if to herself. "I wonder if Lydia remembers. Or if she has horrible scenes in her own mind that she pushes back down."

Elizabeth stopped. Something clicked in her mind. She turned to face Lucy. "What did you say?"

Lucy looked at her, a question in her eyes. "I was wondering if Lydia has that problem, if she has buried the memory of Guy and all that."

Elizabeth stared. "You mean, you don't know?"

Lucy shook her head. "Why no, we've never discussed it. I've never told anyone except Harold. Until you. Should I have asked her about it?" She blushed. "I don't think I could do that."

"And she's never mentioned it to you?"

"No."

"Did anyone ever tell her doctors about it?"

Lucy said, "No, I don't think so. We didn't know it when she was young and first started having the trouble. And then when I found out, it didn't seem important to tell them."

Elizabeth looked at Harold. "Repressed memories?"

Harold nodded. "I hadn't thought of that." He looked at Elizabeth apologetically. "She's been...she's had problems ever since I've known her and we didn't know back then about the abuse." He shook his head. "I should have realized."

Elizabeth went over and hugged him. "We can't always think of everything.

Then she hugged Lucy. "I have to go now. But you know, you may have just hit on the key to Lydia's miracle. The one Stephen Richardson believes that God will do." She looked up at Harold. "I'll call Ed Ramey this afternoon."

Jenny's hands trembled as she ran a wet cloth over the kitchen table.. She was excited to have Elizabeth Daily coming over, but the shadow of the brown swirly thing haunted her and spoiled the pleasurable expectancy.

Finally the door bell rang and Elizabeth was there on the threshold, looking fresh and competent as usual. Jenny hugged her new friend and felt some of the shakiness go away.

"Where do you want us to be?" Jenny asked.

"Wherever you're comfortable."

"I don't need to lie down on the couch?"

Elizabeth laughed. "No. In my office in Lexington, I didn't even have a couch. Most of my clients preferred sitting at a table in the corner so we could drink tea or coffee while we talked."

Jenny sighed "Oh good."

When they were settled at the kitchen table with cups of Chamomile tea, Elizabeth opened with prayer. Her face looked like an angel's. Some more of the tension left Jenny's muscles. It was comforting to trust someone who was an expert and also relied on God.

"Now, tell me about the murder trial."

Jenny was surprised by the quick transition from God to murder, but she answered. "A man was stabbed in the parking lot of his apartment building. His girlfriend was arrested for the murder and is on trial."

"And what was going on in the trial when you fainted?"

"I don't remember." Jenny got up and filled the teapot and put it back on the stove. She stayed by the stove instead of coming back to the table.

"Jenny." Elizabeth's voice was gentle. "I think you can remember if you try."

Jenny closed her eyes. She could see the courtroom and the witness stand. "It was a woman. On the stand, I mean. An older woman. She was really nervous." She opened her eyes and looked at Elizabeth with triumph.

"And what did she say?"

Jenny took a deep breath. "Okay. Let me think." After a moment, she swallowed hard. The brown swirly thing was back, there at the edges of her mind. It was hard to swallow.

"I can do this."

"Yes, you can."

I am not crazy! With a determined effort, Jenny pushed the swirly thing away and concentrated on the memory of the courtroom.

"She said that she had heard something and got up to look out the window. Her apartment is on the second floor and she could see down into the parking lot. It was night but the security lights were on. She recognized the couple, had seen them before going in and out of the apartment below hers. And she'd heard them arguing."

"And?"

"That is it. That was all." Jenny shook her head. "I wonder why I fainted."

"You said that something came to your own mind, a memory that you blocked."

The tea pot started its shrill whistle. Her hands trembled as she refilled their cups with hot water and more teabags. Embarrassed, she tried to steady them but the tremors seemed to come from somewhere deep inside that she couldn't touch. Didn't want to touch.

"Can we stop now?" Her voice came out as nearly a whisper.

"Yes, of course." Elizabeth added Splenda to her tea and settled back in the chair.

"Are you okay?"

Jenny nodded.

"I have something to tell you." Elizabeth's eyes sparkled. "You are invited to a wedding at the Manor House two weeks from Saturday."

"You and Mr. Delaney?"

"Yes. And Reverend Fowler is going to perform the ceremony."

Jenny clapped her hands. "How wonderful. I'm so glad for you. Mr. Delaney seems like such a nice man."

"He is." Then Elizabeth said gently, "And so is your Joel."

Elizabeth walked back home through the park and again stood at the fountain in the center. It was such a peaceful place. No hint of violence lingered there.

She needed to call Galen and get the addresses of his family and run into town and pick up some invitations. No need or time to have printed ones made, just something a little wedding-y. Oh, and ask Galen about the time; they hadn't settled that yet.

He was in the office and sounded glad to hear her voice. "If we have it at night, we'd have to bring in lighting," he said.

"That's right. I would like to have it in the afternoon, maybe about four? And then we could have everyone stay for a wedding supper?"

"Sounds good to me—an early wedding supper, and then they can all go away. Right?"

She giggled. "You!"

When he had given her the addresses of his parents and brothers and sister, she asked. "Won't they need to stay in the guesthouse?"

"No way." They can go back to my place in Lexington. Well, could some of them stay at your condo? And they could take Ruth back too."

"Yes, that would solve the problem of getting her back. I was thinking she could probably stay with Lucy and Harold but I hated to impose on them."

"That's great. I'll bring her when I come down that afternoon and they can take her back. Actually I'm not sure how many of them will come. I'm sure my parents will. It's just a two hour drive for them. They'll probably come in on Friday and spend the night with me."

"Oh." She hadn't thought about that. She was so used to Friday nights with Galen. But after that, she'd have him all the time. "Okay."

He laughed as if he knew what she was thinking. "My sister and her family may come in from Indiana but I doubt that either of my brothers will make it. I was thinking that my sister could stay at your place."

"Okay. I'll get the invitations done tonight and in the mail tomorrow and that will give them two weeks to decide and plan."

When they hung up, Elizabeth called Ed Ramey's office but he was out to lunch. She called his cell phone and he answered on the second ring.

When she told him the situation with Lydia Tapestry, he responded just the way she thought he would. "You could be right on. That would explain why her mind seems fine most of the time."

"Do you think it would be dangerous to confront her with it?"

He was silent for a minute. "I really don't think so. From what I understand seemingly unrelated things can send her into the regressed state. And the anxiety is handled with medication. Of course we'd want to be prepared for a reaction. But I don't think it would hurt to try."

"Okay then. I'll talk to her sister and brother-in-law and see what they say. I'll get back with you."

"Okay. You all right?"

She couldn't resist. "More than all right. You'll be getting an invitation in a few days."

"You and Galen?"

"Yes."

"Judy will be thrilled. She has wondered why you two didn't tie the knot a long time ago."

"Talk to you later." Elizabeth hung up. *I don't know why I'm bothering with invitations. I'm telling everybody I talk to.* She grinned at her own happiness.

Before she left for town, she called Harold Fowler and told him what Ed had said and what she suggested. He agreed to talk to Lucy about it and call her back later that evening.

When Hattie left the room, Emily Caine turned away from the window. She'd seen Elizabeth Daily go to the Fowler's house earlier. Later on she watched her go into the Crossfield girl's door. *Anderson now. Anderson.*

But she hadn't seen her come out. *Could it be . . .?*

She looked down at the pills in her hand. And nodded.

She had made the right decision.

The invitations lay on the desk in the parlor. It had been fun writing them out here in this old fashioned atmosphere. She hadn't found any do-it-yourself wedding invitations but the bouquet of pink and blue flowers on the ones she chose seemed appropriate. Male and Female joined together. She remembered the scripture from Ecclesiastes. "A three-fold cord is not easily broken." *The ribbon holding the flowers together is the Lord. Perfect.*

She put them into the addressed envelopes and sealed and stamped them.

Tomorrow would be four weeks since her arrival at Tapestry Court. All of her own problems were solved. She had Mindy to deal with the letters. Her thoughts were firm about the rightness of marrying Galen. And she felt complete confidence that together they would know the right thing to do about any calling the Lord might have for her in ministry.

But she had progressed no further in discovering the missing heir to the Tapestry fortune. Or the murderer of Colonel Guy R. Tapestry

The phone ringing disturbed her musings. It was Harold Fowler.

"Lucy is not happy about it but she agrees that you and she can talk to Lydia about the past."

"When?"

"She would just as soon get it over with. How soon can you go?

Elizabeth thought a minute. "The only thing I have to do tomorrow is put these invitations in the mail. How about ten?"

"Sounds good."

When they hung up, she called Ed Ramey to report. He said he would alert the staff at the Moreston Manor.

Chapter Twenty-One

Harold liked Stephen Richardson immediately. The two men went outside to the grassy enclosure in the center of Moreston Manor. What a great architectural design. All the inside rooms looked out on the garden that was filled with brightly colored pansies and impatiens along with azalea bushes.

"Always a relief to get outside." Richardson smiled as he looked at the neatly laid out paths and stone benches.

Harold nodded his head. "Glad it's just temporary for you, being here, I mean."

The other man laughed. "Yes. Thank God I don't have to be here long, just until I'm able to walk enough to get around the house by myself. I have a housekeeper that comes in every week to clean. It's just daily things I need to be able to do for myself." He patted his leg. "But the doctor says I am healing wonderfully for a man my age. So I hope it won't be long now. Of course it could be worse. Much worse. This is a nice place."

He looked back toward the part of the home where Harold knew Lydia's room lay.

"But I'm going to miss Lydia."

Harold was surprised at this man's interest in his sister-in-law. She had always been so quiet around him. Sweet spirit, but he had never seen her display enough personality to think anyone could miss her presence.

"Maybe you could come back and visit her."

Richardson nodded. "Oh yes. I intend to."

When Harold arrived at the center with Lucy and Elizabeth, they'd found Lydia sitting in the public area with Stephen. After greetings and introductions, Lucy asked her sister if she and Elizabeth could steal her away for a little while. She looked surprised but agreed. The three then went into a private lounge that Ed Raines had arranged to make available for them.

But no one told Richardson what it was all about. Harold didn't want to get the man's hopes up. *Listen to me. Not get his hopes up? When faith is the substance of things hoped for? Shame on me.*

"Would you mind if we prayed together?" Harold asked.

Richardson said, "Of course not. Anything in particular?"

Harold didn't want to expose Lydia's private life, even to this man who seemed to care about her. And even though he was a man of the cloth.

"My wife and Elizabeth, who is a psychologist, think they may have some information that will help Lydia, maybe resolve some of her emotional problems. They are talking to her right now about that."

Richardson's face brightened. "Let's get to it."

Harold hesitated a moment and then said, "Why don't you pray first?"

Richardson was quiet for a moment as if listening to an inner voice. Then he nodded and bowed his head. "Father, we are here before your throne of grace seeking mercy and grace to help Lydia in her time of need. Lord you are the God of miracles, the one who shines light into darkness, shatters chaos, and establishes order—in the universe and in our hearts and minds. We ask right now for an anointing for Lucy and Elizabeth to be your voice of light and shine your truth, your love, and your freedom into the dark places in Lydia's mind. You are the one who heals the broken hearted. Please heal her broken heart and set her mind free. Help her to become all you created her to be. We ask this in Jesus' Name. Amen."

And because there was nothing left to add, Harold simply echoed, "Amen."

Her sister was seated beside her on the love seat while Elizabeth was in the armchair facing them. Lydia looked around and nodded. "What a nice place. I've never seen it before." Then she realized this was an unusual visit. "What is going on?" Suddenly her stomach tightened. "Is there bad news?"

"No, no," Lucy said soothingly. Then she looked over at Elizabeth.

Elizabeth smiled. "Lydia, did you know that I am a psychologist?"

"No. I don't think so. So you're *Doctor* Daily?" For some reason that fact made her stomach tighten again.

Elizabeth grinned. "Well, technically, but I never use the title if I can help it."

Lucy said, "You know I never thought of that. Doctor Daily."

Lydia folded her hands and fixed her eyes on Elizabeth. "So, you are here professionally?"

"That's up to you. Lucy has some information that could be a root cause of your disability. And if you want, we can discuss it. If you don't want, we can just have a pleasant visit."

Lydia looked at her sister. "Lucy?"

Lucy gulped and twisted the handkerchief she held in her hands. "I'm sorry I never thought to talk to you about it before. I didn't think . . ."

"Well, now I am very curious."

Elizabeth reached across the coffee table and touched her hand. "But the information could be painful to you. It might even bring on another one of your attacks."

Lydia sighed. "You know, the last spell I had was the day you two were here last week. I don't remember what brought it on. I never do remember." Then she turned to her sister and smiled. "But that was the first one in weeks. Oh, Lucy, I have been so happy. Stephen Richardson is the nicest man. He has made me feel like a whole person for the first time in . . . well I guess for the first time ever." She frowned. "Or at least since I can remember."

"I'm so glad." Lucy leaned over and hugged her.

"So do you think you want to take the chance that you might get upset?" Elizabeth asked.

"Do you think that this information will help me get better?"

"I honestly don't know," Elizabeth answered. "It's possible."

Lydia nodded. "If there is any chance at all, however slight, that I could get better, I will risk anything. I've never had any hope. Ever. But Stephen has given me hope. He treats me—he treats me like there is nothing wrong with me at all. I can't remember anybody ever treating me like that." She paused. "And even after my spell last week, he still treats me that way."

Elizabeth leaned forward in her chair. "Stephen Richardson believes in miracles. He thinks you can be completely well."

Lucy hugged her again. "And maybe telling you what I know is part of God's miracle for you."

Lydia nodded. "Then tell me."

Her sister took a deep breath. "This is hard for me to talk about." She drew out the handkerchief and began to fan herself. "It was a long time ago—fifteen years or so before Guy died . . ."

Lydia felt the dizziness begin. *No, please God, not now. Please help me. Please.*

Lucy was staring at her.

She reached out and took her sister's hand. "Go on. I'm okay."

"Wait a minute," Elizabeth interrupted. "We didn't pray."

The three joined hands and Elizabeth invited the Lord to guide their every word and to join them in His role of healer.

After the prayer, Lydia nodded for Lucy to continue.

"Guy came to me and asked me to pray for him. He was in trouble because he had been caught trying to molest a young girl."

Lydia squeezed her sister's hand more tightly. *I can get through this. Remember Stephen. Remember Stephen.*

"And then he told me that he always had a problem. And that he had molested you when you were a child."

After a few seconds of silence, Lydia looked at her sister and then over at Elizabeth. She could see them watching her intently. "I'm still here!"

It was so unexpected, such a relief from the scene that could have happened, that they all three burst into laughter.

"Did you remember it?" Lucy asked.

Lydia shook her head. "No. I have no memory of that."

"How does it make you feel?" Elizabeth was looking at her with interest.

How does it make me feel? Hmmm. I feel nothing. "I don't know. I don't feel anything at all."

"Does it make you remember anything, bring any scenes to mind?"

She shook her head. "No, nothing. Should I have scenes come to mind? I don't want to remember that if it happened." Then she asked the question most on her mind. "Must I have scenes come to mind? To get well, I mean?"

Elizabeth sighed. "To be very honest with you I don't know. I do know that to accept the fact of trauma is important to healing. Some people say it is essential for the memory to surface. But I don't know."

"I'd just as soon it didn't." Lydia gave a short laugh. "Isn't that what all this sickness has been about all these decades? If we're right about this being the cause, I mean. Haven't I been trying to keep the memory from coming out?"

Elizabeth smiled. "Yes. You're right. And I don't blame you. If I were you, I wouldn't want to remember the details either."

"Perhaps it's enough just to know what the problem was?" Lucy sounded hopeful.

"We'll find out." Elizabeth sounded very professional. "I'm going to leave my cell phone number with you and you can give it to Sandy. Ed Ramey has told the staff about me and that I am a consultant for you. If you need to talk, you have someone call me anytime, day or night. And I am going to tell Sandy to call if you do have another spell. Okay?"

Lydia nodded. "Okay."

"Another thing. Dr. Ramey will probably start slowly reducing some of your medication. And he will carefully monitor that."

Lydia nodded again.

"And we'll be back once a week." Elizabeth stood up.

"And if you want to come and stay with me a while, you know that offer always stands." Lucy got up from the couch.

"I know I'm not ready for that. The very thought of going to the Court makes me shaky." For the first time, that was beginning to make sense.

When they returned to the recreation room they didn't see the men at first. Lydia finally spotted them in the enclosure and led the others through the doorway. "That's Stephen's favorite place."

Harold stood when they joined them and Stephen straightened in his chair, his eyes searching her face. Then the Simpsonton group said their goodbyes.

After the others left, Stephen reached over and grasped Lydia's hand. "Okay?"

She smiled. "I'm going to be." And for the first time, she believed it. At least almost.

That night as the news was going off, Lucy Fowler burst into tears. Harold immediately got up and went over to her chair and pulled her to her feet.

"What is it, Honey?" He put his arms around her.

"It's all my fault." Her voice was muffled against his chest.

"What's all your fault?"

"Twenty five years of Lydia's life wasted because I was embarrassed."

"Don't be silly."

"I'm not being silly. Why didn't I realize that what Guy did was the cause of her problems?"

He pulled back so he could lift her face and look into her eyes. "Because you were so used to Lucy being emotionally ill that you took it for granted. You didn't think of it having a cause back then."

She nodded. "You're right. I didn't. But oh, why didn't God tell me?"

Harold hugged her again. "I think that the redemption of Lydia Tapestry is happening in God's timing."

Lucy stiffened and said angrily, "Why would God make her stay sick all this time?"

"He didn't make her stay sick. I didn't mean it that way. What I meant was that there are always different ways that each of us can be healed and set free. Remember Jesus spit on dirt to heal some and only spoke to others. I suspect that Stephen Richardson and Elizabeth Daily are what God needed to begin the healing for Lydia."

Suddenly Lucy grinned. "I wonder which is the clay and which is the spit?"

Harold laughed. "That sounds more like my Lucy."

Elizabeth called Ed to tell him the results of their visit to Lydia Tapestry. He said he would give her a few days and then begin a slight reduction in the anti-anxiety medication. "And we'll see what happens."

"Wouldn't this be awesome, Ed? If she could get well enough to live a normal life?"

"But remember her age, Elizabeth. She's never lived on her own. She wouldn't know how."

"Well, who knows? Maybe she won't have to," Elizabeth said happily.

Chapter Twenty-Two

It started little by little, a flash of a scene at a time. While she was dusting. The brown swirly thing would make its presence known and then open in the center for a split second and show flashes of things she knew had really happened. Panic seemed to spread from her mind to her whole body and she could barely make her fingers punch the buttons to call Joel's work number.

"Please come home. Please. I'm remembering things. Please."

His voice was strained but calm. "I'll be there as soon as I can. In the meantime I'm going to call Elizabeth and see if she can come and be with you 'til I get there."

"Okay." Jenny gasped more than spoke the word.

It was only a few minutes by the clock but it seemed like an hour before Elizabeth rang the front door bell and opened it without waiting to be let in.

"Jenny?" She smiled and came to the couch and sat beside Jenny and held out her arms. Jenny leaned into them.

"Thank you. Thank you so much for coming. Joel is coming too."

"Yes, he called me."

"Oh, of course. I can't think straight."

"It's okay. That's normal. You're going through some heavy duty emotional . . . well the best word I can think of is 'stuff.' You've got some heavy emotional stuff happening."

Jenny gave a little half laugh. "That's for sure."

"Do you want to wait for Joel before we talk about it?"

Jenny nodded. "Yes, I do."

Elizabeth smiled. "I'm glad."

Joel arrived before much more time elapsed and now he was on one side of Jenny and Elizabeth was on the other, protecting her with their very physical presence from any fear of being alone and vulnerable.

Jenny leaned back against the couch cushion, breathed a sigh, closed her eyes and said. "Okay."

Elizabeth asked gently. "Can you see it? The scene in the brown swirly thing?"

Jenny held tightly to Joel's hand as she nodded. "I remember now. I remember it all. A teacher at school was supposed to come home with me." She looked at Elizabeth. "I was a sophomore at boarding school when my parents died. But at the last minute her child got sick and she couldn't leave. So I was alone. I was at the funeral alone and stayed at the house alone. I really didn't mind. I always spent most of my time alone anyway. I was looking forward to going back to school but I wasn't scheduled to leave for two days.

"That night, not the night of the funeral but the day after, I was watching TV when a knock came on the front door. I couldn't think who would be visiting that late but it was him. Colonel Tapestry. I always resented him for taking up all my parents time and he had never paid any attention to me at all. I can't remember that he ever spoke to me before. But I saw him staring at me during the funeral.

She paused, fighting panic with another deep breath before continuing.

"He apologized for interrupting me so late but said he had seen the lights on and knew I was still awake. He said he had something very important to show me but it was at his house. He wanted me to come with him. He saw me glance toward the television and offered to wait until my show was over. It was almost 11 p.m. But I said that it was a rerun and I knew the ending. I turned the TV off and went with him.

"I didn't like it when he put his arm around me while we walked to his house but I could tell, or thought I could tell, that he felt badly about my parents and was trying to comfort me. I just wished he didn't hug me so close. And then . . ." She swallowed with an effort.

Elizabeth said calmly. "It's okay. We're right here with you. You can talk about it. Nothing can hurt you now."

Jenny nodded again. "He led me into the library . . .."

She could see spit in the corner of his mouth as he put his arm around her shoulder and showed her the deed. Gross.

"Now see, you don't ever have to worry about having a home. You can continue to go to school and live here in the summer and at your holidays. Miss Caine and Hattie will be happy to help you with anything you need from a female."

His eyes searched hers. "And I will always be here for you."

His hand slid down and squeezed her waist and then settled on her right hip.

"Always."

She felt frozen. What does the old coot want from me? He is ancient. Surely not . . .

He led her to the couch and pulled her down on his lap.

"I know you are upset over the loss of your parents and I want you to know that I will always be here for you. I will comfort you always." His hand started caressing . . .

Suddenly chimes sounded. Col. Tapestry grunted. And she took the opportunity to leap up off of his lap.

"You go on home. I'll be over later to check on you." He practically pushed her out of the library door.

With pounding heart she ran home as quickly as she could, out of the yard, into the Park, through the gate to her own yard, and into the house through the kitchen door. She turned the light on. Lock the door. But what if he has a key? Pull the chain lock on. Check the front door—chain lock on it. Safe.

The lights were still on in the living room. No! Turn all the lights off and pretend to be asleep when he comes.

She quickly turned off the living room and kitchen lights and groped her way through to the stairs. No, not upstairs where he can trap me if he gets in. Where to hide? Behind the couch? In the coat closet?

She stepped into the closet and pushed aside the galoshes and other things on the floor so there would be room if she needed to sit down. Ah, an umbrella. There's a weapon if I need one. But surely he is too old and weak to break the chain lock. *Her heart was beating so hard she was sure that if anyone came in they would be able to find her by the noise. But he couldn't get in. She'd just have to wait 'til she heard him knock and then go away.* Oh! The windows. If he's really crazy he might come in a window.

With trembling fingers she took the flashlight from the hook in the closet. Mother had put it there in case of power failures. She went to each window on the first floor and made sure the lock was turned. What if he gets the ladder out of the storage building in the back yard?

She made her way up the stairs and began to check the upstairs windows. Her bedroom, the bathroom, the guest room, and finally her parent's room. She hadn't been in there since their deaths. Oh, Mother, Daddy. Help me please. Don't let him hurt me.

She went to the last window in their room, the one overlooking the park. The moon was so bright that the security lights were almost unnecessary. She saw him coming through the gate from the Manor House property. Her stomach turned over.

Dear God, help me!

And then someone else came through the gate. And followed him. The Colonel had just reached the middle of the park at the giant T in the center of the fountain when he stopped and turned. He saw the person following him and he saw the gun. He held out his right hand as if to stop the action. But a muffled shot sounded into the night and he fell there in front of the fountain. She could see his body jerking as if in protest. After two more shots Colonel Tapestry lay still.

Jennie's hand flew to her mouth as she watched Emily Caine look down at the gun in her hand. The woman nodded her head, and turned away.

"I don't remember leaving the room or going to bed. And I never remembered anything about the evening. Honest. It was Hattie who came the next morning and told me about Col. Tapestry's death. And it was news to me."

She stared down at her hands, which had stopped trembling. "I guess I must have blamed myself for his death and couldn't face it. I had cried out for help, to my parents and to God. So it was my fault. Miss Caine was only the instrument, like the gun."

"Can you see now that it wasn't your fault?" Elizabeth tone was very gentle.

"I'm not sure. But it's good that I remembered, isn't it?" She looked up at Joel.

"Yes, Sweetheart, very good." He squeezed her hand tightly.

"And I think that my fear of the house was because he said that he would be there always. He said that more than once. I guess inside I was afraid that he really would still be there."

"Now you can begin to heal." Elizabeth said matter-of-factly. "And you do know that neither your parents or God had anything to do with the murder, don't you?"

"I th . . . think so. But . . . it was still because of me, wasn't it? Miss Caine was trying to protect me?"

"I'm not sure about that." Elizabeth frowned slightly. "Her motive remains to be seen. But it will all come out. The important thing now is for you to get well."

"And if you want to move away from Tapestry Court, we will do it. I promise." Joel looked at her with so much love in his eyes that tears sprang to her own.

"What will happen to her?" Jenny was surprised to hear the shaking in her voice. "Miss Caine?"

"That will be up to the police."

A thrill of horror shot through Jenny. "I'll have to tell the police about that night?"

"I don't think you will have to tell about the whole night. Just about going to your parents room and looking out the window and seeing the shooting."

Jenny took a deep breath of relief. "I can do that."

What will happen to her? Jenny's question echoed in Elizabeth's mind. What indeed?

Elizabeth called Galen as soon as she got back to the Manor House.

"Whoa!" His voice revealed that he was as shocked as she was. Even though something in her had wanted the villain to be Emily Caine instead of any other resident of

Tapestry Court, she was still stunned. "So what now? Did you call the police?"

"No, not yet. I don't think there's any rush. Jenny doesn't need to have to explain it to a stranger just yet. I'd just as soon give it a day or two. Do you think that's all right?"

"Yes, unless Jenny's in any danger from the Caine woman."

Elizabeth considered it. "I don't see how. If she hasn't suspected that she was seen all these years, why would she suspect now? And Galen, the woman is so arthritic and unwell, I don't see how she could harm anyone. In fact as awful as it is that she murdered somebody, I hate to think of anyone having to go to prison at her age and in her physical condition."

"Yes, I know." Galen paused and then went on. "Tomorrow you can talk to Joel and Jenny about it and see what they think about waiting."

"That sounds good to me." Elizabeth's muscles relaxed.

Emily looked at the green numbers of the digital clock. 3 a.m. The pain shooting down her left arm wakened her from sleep and made it difficult to lie quietly. *Must have slept on it wrong.* She took a deep breath and adjusted the pillow. That was when the pain went up to her neck and jaw. Her chest felt very tight. *Is this it?*

It was important that she know. She reached over with her right arm and opened the drawer to the bedside table. When the envelope was in her hand, she sighed. It was all there, what anyone needed to know of her story. But it must not be delivered until she was gone.

Guy, Guy. Will I see you? I'm afraid not. You didn't repent. And if you were a believer, no one ever knew it.

She dropped the envelope back in the drawer and closed it most of the way. She didn't have the energy for the final push.

As she lay there waiting, she thought back over the years. She met Guy Tapestry when she was only sixteen years old and all alone in the world.

She walked in the little storefront office on a side street right off Main in Simpsonton because a sign in the window announced 'help wanted.' He was sitting at a desk cluttered with papers and his hair stood up in places as if he had been tugging at it. It was love at first sight.

"Excuse me. I saw the sign, that you need some help. I can type and..." She nodded at the desk. "I'm good at organizing."

He looked up at her but didn't say anything. The look in his eyes was admiring but she suspected that the admiration was due to her physical appearance instead of her proclamation of clerical skills.

Guy Tapestry was slightly built and wiry but Emily thought he was the handsomest man she ever saw. She couldn't believe he was looking at her like...well, like he thought she was pretty.

"And I need a job." She smiled and shrugged her shoulders. The way he returned her smile made her stomach do flip flops. He hired her on the spot.

By the end of the week the office was completely organized and they were lovers.

A wave of nausea rippled through her body. *Don't think about the sickness. Think about Guy.*

She and Guy were inseparable for years. They worked together all day and he visited her almost every night. But the older she got, the less frequent the visits grew. She would see him looking at young girls with that same look he gave her at first.

She was jealous but finally came to realize that it was a sickness with him. He was incapable of loving one woman. Incapable of loving mature women at all. Maybe incapable of loving anybody.

Their relationship solidified but not the way Emily wanted. One last hope arose when Guy built Tapestry Court and asked her to decorate the Manor House in which he would live. She believed that he was going to ask her to marry him and wanted her to have her new home just the way she liked.

But it didn't happen.

Guy almost never came to her at night after the first decade of their relationship - but when he did she couldn't turn him away. On one of those occasions the unthinkable happened. Past the age of forty, after twenty five years, she became pregnant. Surely now, he would marry her.

When he laughed at the idea and refused to even consider it, it was as if a knife entered her heart. But she laughed along with him.

For the benefit of neighbors and business associates, Guy announced that she was going on a business trip to establish some new enterprises for him. Soon after she returned, the public was sorry to hear that her sister and brother-in-law were killed in an accident, leaving an orphaned child. She never had a sister but no one questioned their story.

She left town again to bring her one month old nephew back to live at Tapestry Court. And she began going to church. After a while she established herself there and rested in her reputation as a good Christian woman. Since Guy never came to her again in that way, church became the main focus of her life.

Emily adjusted her pillows behind her head again but nothing made her more comfortable.

"Emily Caine Tapestry." She said it out loud again just as she had in moments of longing over the past 70 years. *Maybe this is the last time I'll ever say it.* "Emily Tapestry."

She remembered the last time she saw Guy. She went to the Manor House because she saw him taking the Anderson girl there and knew what would happen. When she knocked on the door, Guy answered but stood in the doorway blocking her from entering.

"What do you want?"

She pushed past him. "I came to talk to you. And to stop you from making a terrible mistake."

"What do you mean?" He narrowed his eyes as he stared at her.

"You know exactly what I mean. Is the Anderson girl still here?"

"No, she left."

"Good." She started to leave too, but his next words made her turn back.

"While you are here I might as well tell you. I changed my will a few weeks ago and left those properties and stocks to George instead of you - well, it said I left it to my son. But I have decided I'm going to change it again. I'm going to name him as my son."

"You wouldn't dare. You promised." Like Job, she felt the thing she

greatly feared had come upon her. Her reputation would be ruined.

"I no longer trust you to let it be known in your own will. And George is doing a wonderful job. His business mind shows he is truly my son."

"Did you ever doubt it?"

He shrugged his shoulders. "Not seriously, but it's good to see and be sure."

He took her arm and guided her back out the door. "You go on now. I have some things I need to do."

She went back home and got the gun. She'd never used it, just kept it for protection. But she got it and put the bullets in it and went toward Number 1. She saw him passing through the gate to the park and knew where he was going. He was going to that child.

The thought that she was not only protecting her reputation but saving Jenny Crossfield gave her additional courage. She was the hand of God to stop evil.

Guy passed the fountain just as the gate closed behind her. He turned and when he saw the gun in her hand, he threw his arm out in protest. But this time he didn't get what he wanted. She shot three times.

The pain in her chest grew stronger. *This must be it.* She resisted the temptation to call out for Hattie. This was what she wanted. The only way. She knew from the notes she found when she went to the Manor House that the Daily woman was very close to guessing the truth.

The numbers on the clock said 3:37.

Lord, forgive me. For loving Guy too much. For not loving George enough. For ... for killing Guy. Thank you that Jesus died for all my sins and I can come and be with you now. Safe. And loved. Amen.

Chapter Twenty-Three

Elizabeth looked at the clock when her cell phone rang and woke her up. It was only 7:15 a.m. *Who on earth?*

The number on caller id was vaguely familiar but there was no name, obviously not programmed in.

"Hello?"

The gentle voice of Harold Fowler apologized for waking her. "I'm really sorry to call so early. But I thought of you first thing. There has been a tragedy. And I'd like you to come. Hattie just called. She found Emily dead in her sleep this morning."

Elizabeth stifled the urge to laugh at the phrase *dead in her sleep* and mentally berated herself for her irreverence. "Oh, I'm so sorry. Of course. I'll get dressed and meet you there right away."

"I'm going on over to be with Hattie."

"Of course."

She threw on her clothes as quickly as possible, gave her teeth a quick brushing and hurried to Number Two Tapestry Court.

Hattie, still in a bathrobe, let her in and pointed to the stairs. "Revern' Fowler up there now."

Elizabeth patted Hattie's shoulder before she began climbing the steps.

Harold Fowler stood near the head of the bed looking down at Miss Emily's body.

He nodded to her and then straightened the blanket and patted one of the folded hands. Elizabeth saw the tears in his pity-filled eyes.

"Poor soul." He said softly. "Poor tormented soul."

For the second time the thought came to Elizabeth *A truly holy man.*

"Let's pray." He bowed his head and Elizabeth did likewise.

"Lord, I believe you have received Emily Caine into Your merciful Presence. She is your child, and she trusted in the blood of Jesus shed for her sins and iniquities. We agree with that, Lord and thank you. We praise you for your mercy that endures forever. Amen."

Just as he said the 'Amen' they heard the footsteps on the stairs and soon the room was filled with EMTs who took over the scene. Elizabeth didn't know what she thought about Harold's assurance of Miss Emily's destination. And she wondered if he would think the same thing if he knew what she now knew about the spinster.

Elizabeth followed him downstairs to join Hattie in the kitchen. A few seconds later one of the emergency personnel came into the room.

"We've called the coroner and as soon as he gets here, we'll remove the body. Where do you want her taken?"

Both Elizabeth and Harold looked at Hattie.

She shook her head. "I don know. Wait! Seems like Miz Emily said something 'bout pre-paying for a funrel. Le me see." She went to a drawer and pulled out a notepad with some phone numbers written on it. "Yes, here it is— Ransdells Funrel Home. I reckon she must've set it up there."

"I'll call." Elizabeth took the pad out of Hattie's hand and picked up the telephone. She verified that Emily Caine pre-paid for her funeral through that mortuary and they had all the details for the service and burial on file.

Hattie made coffee for them all and soon the coroner arrived. Shortly afterwards the EMTs departed with the body. Hattie, Harold, and Elizabeth watched from the front of Number Two as Emily Caine left Tapestry Court for the last time, rolled out on a stretcher, covered with a blanket.

Elizabeth could see that every house had someone stationed in front of it, as if in salute to the departure of the oldest resident of the Court. At Number Three, Jenny and Joel Anderson stood watching from their door. At Number Four, Linda Tate viewed the procession from her walkway. Mindy peered out from Number Five. Bill Sinclair halted on his way to somewhere from Number Six. And Lucy sat at the bench by the flower bed in front of Number Seven.

"Poor tormented soul," Harold Fowler repeated. Then he turned to them. "I better get back to Lucy."

When he left, Elizabeth hugged Hattie. "Are you going to be all right?"

"Yes'm. I be all right. Not sure where I'll go yet but I got me a little piece of change saved up. I be all right."

"Would you like me to stay with you a while?"

"No Ma'am. I wants to clean up Miz Emily's room now."

"Okay. Call me if there is anything I can do. Please?"

"Yes'm I will. And, thank you."

Hattie pulled the sheets off the bed and put them in the washing machine. Then she dusted the dressers and straightened up the clock and Bible, pen and pad that lay on the bedside table.

"Gonna be strange wi Miz Emily gone. Didn't like her, Lord. You know that. No use tryin to fool You. But I'm used to her. Gonna be awful strange."

As she turned away she noticed the white corner of an envelope sticking up out of the drawer to the bedside table. When she slid open the drawer, she saw an envelope, a big one and pretty thick. Scrawled across the front in Miz Emily's spidery script was the name Harold Fowler.

"Sure would like to know what's in here, Lord. But I don't think You'd want me to open it." She stood listening for a moment. *But maybe you do. Do you, Lord?* There was only silence. With a sigh, she took the envelope and went down the stairs.

In the kitchen she picked up the pad of paper that had recorded the name of the funeral home and with both things in hand, she walked out the front door.

"And I ain't lockin' the door either. Silly to lock the doors. Nobody can get in this place from outside and if you can't trust your own neighbors, well then that's just too bad."

She went straight to the Tates and Linda greeted her. "Yes, he just got home. Lucy called us with the news. I think he was about to come to see you."

Hattie sat in the living room while Linda went to get George. He came in and hugged her. "I was just getting ready to come there. Are you okay?"

"Yes sir. I'm fine. You okay?"

"Yes, it's a shock but I'm okay."

Hattie held out the pad with numbers on it. "I thought you'd want this, being her nephew and all. It has a number on there that says lawyer and I figgered that he'd have a will or something."

"Thank you, Hattie. I appreciate that."

She held out the envelope. "And I found this too."

He took the bulky packet in his hands and looked at the name on the front. "It's addressed to Harold Fowler," he said unnecessarily.

"Yes, sir. It was in her bedside drawer."

"Well, I think you should take it to Rev. Fowler. Don't you?"

"Yes, sir. But I didn't want to do nothin without you knowin about it."

"I appreciate that, Hattie. But what's this "sir" all about? I'm still just your George."

She smiled tenderly. "Yes. You still my George."

"And you're still my Hattie. No more sir, okay?"

She nodded. "Okay, George. Okay."

They hugged again.

She made her way out the door and down the walk to Number Seven.

Harold looked around at the group gathered in their living room. Elizabeth and Galen were seated together on the couch, George was in the captain's chair by the desk and Linda sat in the rocker. On the opposite side of the fireplace from his chair, Lucy perched in her customary place.

"As you all know, Hattie brought me this letter the morning Emily died. I have thought long and hard about what to do with it. I knew it had to be shared because of some of the things it reveals. However, it also reveals some things that I don't think need to be public knowledge." He paused to clean his glasses on his shirt sleeve. When he had put them back on, he resumed. "Emily trusted me with this information and I believe that the best thing I can do with it is to give it to you—George, because you are the one most affected by it and Galen, because you are the person in the official capacity looking into the matters concerned here on behalf of the bank as executor. I trust that the two of you will make the wisest decisions about where else any of the information is given."

He straightened his shoulders and took the letter out of the envelope. When it was unfolded he began reading aloud.

Dear Reverend Fowler,

I am writing this letter to you because you are a man of God. And because you are part of the Tapestry family.

I loved Guy Tapestry from the time I was sixteen. I thought he loved me but he was incapable of loving anybody. I believe I am forgiven for all my sins with him, for him, and to him.

I am the one who killed Guy. He was going to announce a secret we agreed on many years ago and I couldn't allow that to happen. I believe that secret is about to be exposed now and I can't kill again to stop it, nor can I face the future if it becomes known. It is better to quit taking my medication and let nature take its course.

I hope you will tell people that George Tate is the missing heir, Guy R. Tapestry's son. And I hope you will not tell the public that I was his mother. You can tell George if it seems best to you. This letter should be proof enough to settle the Tapestry estate.

My own will leaves my house to George, though it does not speak of our relationship. Let him continue the deception that he is my nephew, if he wishes.

Thank you for tying up these loose ends of my life for me.

Sincerely,

Emily Caine Tapestry (I always wanted to write that)

Harold dropped the hand holding the letter into his lap and looked around the circle. The first person to move was

Lucy. He wasn't surprised. She crossed the room and put her arms around George

"My nephew, my own nephew. And Reggie and Chuck, my own flesh and blood. How wonderful."

George's arms moved slowly, as though numb with shock. He hugged her back and when she returned to her chair, he looked at Harold. "The Colonel was my father? And Aunt Emily my mother?" He shook his head. "I can't take it in."

Linda got up and moved to his side. She put her hand on his shoulder but didn't say a word. He reached up and covered her hand with his own.

Galen broke the silence. "Since Emily is dead herself, and we know the missing heir now, I'm not sure we really need to make the circumstances of his death known to the rest of the world. Do we?" He looked at Elizabeth.

She told the others, "We already knew about the murder."

Mouths fell open. Harold could hardly believe his ears.

Elizabeth continued. "The afternoon before Emily died, Jenny Anderson had a flashback. It had been trying to come through for days, ever since the trial when she fainted. She saw Emily kill the Colonel. She witnessed the murder from her parent's bedroom window. We were trying to decide when to go to the police but the very next morning Emily died. And frankly, now that she has admitted it, I'm still not sure. Does it really need to be made known to the public? How would it help anybody?"

George just shook his head. "I still can't believe it." He looked up at Linda, "It seems that I don't have very good blood, do I?"

Linda's eyes widened and she threw her shoulders back. "You have the best blood in the world. Look at you and look at your children. I don't ever want to hear that again."

For the first time George sat back in his chair. And he laughed. "Yes, ma'am. I mean No ma'am. Never again."

"Poor Emily." Lucy shook her head. "What a sad life. And we thought she was a passionless old spinster. Just goes to show, doesn't it?"

"Goes to show what, dear?" Harold was always interested in the way his wife's mind worked.

"Goes to show we know very little about what really goes on in other people's hearts and minds."

He nodded. "Yes, it does."

Elizabeth spoke up. "I would like permission to tell Jenny and Joel Anderson."

Harold, she and Galen exchanged a glance. "Jenny was afraid that he was killed to protect her since he was on his way to her home and she was alone. She felt responsible for his death."

"That is fine with me," George said with a shrug.

Harold was glad that Elizabeth didn't feel it necessary to explain why Jenny believed she needed protection. Poor George had enough shocks for the day and there was no reason for him to know about his father's perversions.

"Then it's settled." Harold leaned back against the chair with a sigh of relief. He handed the letter to Galen.

Galen said, "Congratulations, George."

George, still looking dazed, nodded.

Elizabeth spoke again. "I think we should tell Deputy Collins about the matter. Let him decide what must be done."

George rubbed a hand across his forehead. "You're probably right. Do whatever you think." He shook his head. "I'm really flabbergasted. All this is too much at once. I'm the missing heir, the owner of Tapestry Industries."

"And the Manor House," Elizabeth said.

"And Number Two," Galen added.

"Hattie," said George. "Hattie has to be allowed to live there as long as she lives."

Galen assured him. "That's no problem. An attorney can draw up that agreement."

Elizabeth said, "And I won't hold you to my lease."

Linda looked horrified. "No, we don't want to move there." She backed up and sat down in the rocking chair again.

George looked over at her. "We don't? I would think you might want to."

She shook her head vehemently. "No, I don't. I love our home." She paused for a minute. "Well, it might be nice for the kids to have a bigger place. But definitely not right away." She smiled at Elizabeth. "Please stay for a while."

George looked at Elizabeth and grinned. "Looks like you are stuck with the lease then."

Chapter Twenty-Four

The Tate family, Charles and Mindy Simmons, and Hattie rode in the family limousine from Ransdell's Funeral Home to the cemetery. George insisted on including Hattie with the family.

Elizabeth took Harold and Lucy Fowler in her car. Bill Sinclair attended the funeral but did not go to the graveside service. Joel and Jenny Anderson did not attend either. Elizabeth understood why Jenny's newly uncovered emotions couldn't face the ceremonies.

That Monday morning was warm, with temperatures in the low 80's. The Presbyterian minister was mercifully brief in his remarks at the cemetery but Elizabeth was aware of the discomfort of the Tapestry Court residents when he praised the virtues of Miss Caine. She was glad that she had Harold Fowler's words entrenched in her mind *Poor tormented soul.* And she was glad for his prayer at Miss Emily's death bed reminding her of the mercy of God.

After the short service of committal, the small crowd dispersed. Elizabeth thought of other funerals, every one she had ever attended, where family and friends gathered afterwards to eat and talk about the deceased. No one wanted to celebrate the life of Emily Caine. *How sad.* But somehow the thought of just going back to the Court and going on with the day as if nothing had happened didn't seem right.

When she came to a stop light, she turned to Lucy in the back seat. "Would you like to go to lunch somewhere, my treat?" She glanced at Harold to include him in the question.

A silent communication passed between the couple before Lucy answered. "That would be very nice, Elizabeth. How lovely of you to think of it."

"Is that okay with you?" She asked Harold.

"More than okay."

Elizabeth's cell phone rang. It was Linda Tate asking if they wanted to meet the rest of them for lunch at Loury's On the Lake.

Elizabeth laughed. "Wonderful, we had just decided to go to lunch ourselves but hadn't discussed where."

"We have to be taken back to the funeral home to get our cars, and we're going to drop the kids off at school, but we'll meet you there. Do you want to go ahead and get a table for seven?"

"Okay, see you there."

Loury's was a beautiful place. Floor-to-ceiling windows in the dining room looked out on the lake and across to the other shore which consisted of trees and wildflowers as far as you could see. The other walls held built in aquariums with exotic fish and murals of lush Kentucky forest land.

Everyone except George and Charles, who had been there before, was entranced with the place. Elizabeth pictured herself and Galen there on their honeymoon. They hadn't even discussed that. The wedding itself was such a joy that a honeymoon would seem like more than icing on the cake. *Cake! I need to contact a bakery. My wedding is in 12 days!*

The restaurant offered a small buffet in addition to the menu. Roast beef in gravy, sliced ham with pineapple, and grilled chicken breast were available along with several vegetables, salads, and desserts. The whole party opted for that.

It was a pleasant meal. Emily was not mentioned, but Hattie talked a lot about when George and Charles were young. And they both laughed as they remembered her trying to play softball with them, and failing miserably. Once she hit the ball and it missed the back window of Number Four by an inch.

Over dessert George said, "I guess this is as good a time as any to tell you all something. Harold already knows because Aunt Emily left a letter." He nodded toward Hattie. "Hattie found it addressed to him and she took it to him. It seems that I am the missing heir, Colonel Tapestry's son."

Elizabeth knew that it was news only to Charles, Mindy, and Hattie. But she was glad that George didn't tell them that she, an outsider, already knew.

"Sho nuff?" There was a glow on Hattie's face. "That's good news."

"Also, it said in the letter and was verified by her attorney, that she left Number Two, Tapestry Court to me."

He turned to Charles. "That all seems unfair, the way we grew up and all, sharing everything."

"No." Charles said. "I called her Aunt Emily but she was your real blood aunt."

"Well." George cleared his throat. "Not exactly." He looked first at Charles and then at Hattie. "It's been quite a shock but . . . it seems that not only was the Colonel my father but Aunt Emily was my mother."

Hattie sat back in her chair abruptly. "Well, if that don't beat all."

"And Hattie, I have discussed with an attorney some options for you. If you want to remain at Number Two, it's yours for life, rent and utility free. You will be given an allowance for food and personal items as well as an upfront cash bonus in appreciation for your services."

Hattie's mouth dropped open like something in a movie, but no words came out.

"If you don't want to remain there, we will make other arrangements."

His substitute mother shook her head. "No need for that. I want to stay there. Why, I've lived so long at Tapestry Court—long as you. I wouldn't know how to live anywhere else."

They all laughed.

"Thank you." Hattie added and smiled at George.

Elizabeth was glad that the announcement of Emily as the killer of Colonel Tapestry was not mentioned. Deputy Collins was really glad to see the letter when she took it to the sheriff's office, but didn't think it was necessary to reopen the case. He said in his slow drawl. "Like I said, nobody cared."

Dear Lord, Please, please, please let him be in a good mood. Mindy felt like she was going to crawl out of her skin all day long, ever since Charles left for work and she found out. She wasn't sure how he had taken yesterday's news about George being the missing heir of the Tapestry fortune. *Did it upset him? Make him envious?*

She worked hard all afternoon making his favorite dinner, stuffed pork chops, broccoli casserole, and salad with homemade bleu cheese dressing, just like Hattie taught her. Instead of the regular dishes on the kitchen table, the good china was laid out in the dining area of the front room and the candles stood ready to be lighted.

She looked at the clock for what seemed like the zillionth time that afternoon. 5:40. He should be home any minute. Had she forgotten anything?

Perfume! She ran upstairs to her dresser and sprayed behind each ear and on one wrist. As she rubbed her wrists together, she studied herself in the full length mirror on the back of the closet door. *Can't tell any difference.* She turned sideways. *Nope, no difference at all.*

She heard the front door open as she started down the stairs and her stomach turned over. *Here goes.* Charles looked up the staircase and his glance traveled from her head to her feet. *He can't help but notice that I'm wearing my party sundress.*

He looked away and then noticed the table set with china and candles. "Did you forget I was coming home this evening?" Sarcasm dripped from his voice.

Mindy didn't try to disguise her hurt. "What do you mean? I wanted to have a special dinner for you. I made all your favorites."

He looked at her for a moment and then brushed past her and started up the stairs without answering. "I'm going to take a shower. What time is supper?"

Her voice was shaky when she answered, "It's ready anytime. Whenever you want to eat."

"About twenty minutes." He disappeared into the bedroom.

Her teeth clenched until she forced herself to relax. *Lord, please make this okay. Please make him be happy with me.*

The minutes crawled by but at last they were seated at the table with the candles lit and Charles' favorite foods on their plates. Soft music played in the background.

They ate in silence. Mindy picked at her food, shoving it around on the plate. Her stomach was not in any shape to digest.

Finally Charles lay his fork down and pushed back his chair.

"Okay, what's all this about?"

Mindy swallowed, her mouth suddenly dry. "I—uh-- I have something to tell you."

He waved his hand at the serving dishes and candles. "Obviously. What is it? What do you want?"

Hurt warred with anger and the anger won. She stiffened her spine against the chair back. "I don't want anything except a husband who might be happy that I'm going to have a baby."

An unfamiliar look . . . *joy?* sprang into his face and quickly left to be replaced by a frown.

After several seconds of silence as they stared at each other he spoke. "Who's the father?"

This time the tears could not be held back. They rolled down her cheeks. Panic rose from her stomach and filled her chest until she could barely breathe.

She stood up and stared at him. "Isn't this why you married me? So you could have a child?" Half of the words were full of air and didn't come out quite right.

"Who is the father?" He repeated calmly.

"I c-c-can't b-believe you. You are so hateful to me. I wish I'd never married you!"

His calmness made her even more hysterical. "That's obvious," Charles said.

"Wh-what do you mean?" She was yelling but she couldn't seem to stop herself.

"I mean you and Bill Sinclair."

"What?" Mindy stared at him in disbelief. "No! It's not like that." Then the sobs started. "It's not."

"Then you have fooled me and most everyone else. I hear your *tete-a-tetes* discussed at the office."

Mindy was on her feet, wordless sobs catching in her throat as she shook her head.

"So now I guess you are pregnant with his child and expect me to raise it as my own." His eyes narrowed. "Or do you want a divorce so you can marry him instead?"

Mindy dropped to the floor and sat like a child with her head down and her arms around her knees. She heard the sounds emanating from her and one part of her mind thought of the word 'keen'. *That must be what I'm doing.* But she couldn't make herself stop.

Suddenly Charles was there on the floor beside her. And his voice was gentle now.

"Mindy, Mindy." His arm went around her shoulders. "Whatever it is, I'll help you. No matter what you want. Don't cry like that. It'll be all right."

"I l-l-love you." She gasped between each word. "I love you. I always have." *There, it's out. It doesn't matter anymore if he despises me for it.* "From the time I went to work for you, I loved you. Always, always, nobody ever but you."

She couldn't seem to stop the words flooding out of her mouth between the gulps and sobs. "You don't care . . . so cold to me . . . but I love you anyway. I've wanted you to kiss me, to love me. But . . . all you wanted was a child. And now you have it. And you don't even believe it's yours." The wailing started again, forced from her throat.

At that, both arms went around her and Charles pulled her close to his chest. "Sweetheart, Mindy, don't. Please don't. I'm sorry. So sorry."

He rocked her gently until the wailing became sobs and the sobs became hiccups.

Then he pulled away and looked into her eyes. "I . . ." He stopped. "Do you think we could move to the couch? This is a little uncomfortable."

At that she smiled; this was an unusually undignified position for Charles Sinclair to occupy. She hated to move;

it had been wonderful being so close, him holding her like that.

When she sat down, Charles sat on the cushion next to hers instead of at the other end of the couch. And he turned her to face him by taking both of her hands in his.

"I can tell we've got a lot of catching up to do. Did you mean it? You love me, really love me?" When she nodded, he shook his head for a moment before continuing. "Mindy, I thought someone like you could never be interested in me, not like that. I thought that if I gave you a home you might become fond of me but I never thought you could love me." He cupped her face in his hands and looked deeply into her eyes. Had he ever looked at her like this before? Mindy hoped he would never look away. "I love you. I always have. But I never dreamed . . ."

She pulled her hands away and threw them around his neck. And stopped his words with a kiss.

When their lips parted, she couldn't stop a shy grin. "There, I've wanted to do that for over three years."

"What a lot of time I've wasted." Charles shook his head. "I owe you an apology. Those accusations about Simmons. But you seem to have so much fun with him. I thought, well, I couldn't blame you but . . . well, it just seemed like you love him."

Mindy's eyes dropped. "I have to tell you something but I'm afraid you'll be mad at me."

Charles' mouth tightened but he said, "Mindy, I don't want you to ever be afraid of me. Whatever you've done, it's my fault for being such a . . . well it's my fault. I should have been a real husband to you. Whatever it is, we'll work through it. And I'll understand."

Delighted laughter spilled from the depths of her happy soul. "It's nothing like that." She kissed him again but when he started to respond in kind, she shoved him away.

"Bill's my brother." She said it abruptly.

Shock filled Charles eyes. "Wh—what?"

"Bill's my brother. We were taken to an orphanage when I was a baby. I got adopted and he didn't. Later he got into the records and found out who and where I was. And we've been close ever since he was able to contact me."

Charles was speechless.

"He worked at Tapestry but because of the no relatives rule we couldn't tell or I couldn't get a job. And then he recommended me as your secretary and that would have made it look worse. And then when we got married, I was afraid you would hate me for lying. And it's all been such a big mess."

Charles face became a mask of shock.

"And yes, I do love Bill and we do have fun. But it's not like you think, or anybody else either. He's my brother and we've both wanted to tell people."

Charles surprised her by laughing out loud. "Bill? Bill Sinclair my brother-in-law?"

She smiled hesitantly. "Yes. Is that funny?"

"Not funny . . . wonderful! I never had a family. And then I thought you were just my family for convenience. And now all of a sudden in one hour I have a wife, a baby on the way and a brother-in-law." She heard joy in his laugh, something she had never sensed in him before.

"Oh, Charles!" She fell into his arms again. After another of the kisses she had longed for, he pulled away.

"Is there any dessert?"

Where did that come from?

"Are you hungry?"

"No, I just thought maybe we could invite our brother over for dessert." He grinned at her. "We'll send him away early but I don't want to make him wait another moment to know all is well with our family."

Mindy stared at him. Was this a stranger wearing the face she loved? In all her dreams she never—The thought ended abruptly. Yes, in her dreams she *had* hoped that Charles would one day love her this way. She didn't bother to stop a giggle. "That would make him so happy. But is he home?"

"I'll find out." Charles picked up the phone and from the kitchen she could hear him talking.

"Hey, brother. Would you like to come over and have dessert with Mindy and me?" Even his voice sounded different. Lighter, somehow. When he winked at her, Mindy's heart flipped in her chest. "We've got something to tell you."

She laughed out loud. That would get Bill over here in a hurry.

Chapter Twenty-Five

Linda Tate was all smiles as she packed the box full of homemade pies and cookies. George came into the kitchen and announced that the card tables were all set up on along the walkway between the six houses leading to the Manor House. "Waiting for you ladies to decorate."

He crossed the room to put his arm around her shoulders and squeezed tightly. "This was a great idea you had, Sweetheart. Elizabeth is going to be surprised and very happy."

She kissed her husband on the cheek. "I just hope Galen succeeds in keeping her at home while we're setting up."

"He will," George assured her.

Elizabeth thought they were coming at 6 p.m. that Saturday a week before her wedding to have dinner and play cards with the Tates. Everyone else knew that there was a surprise wedding shower and dinner and all the Court residents would attend. It was a huge potluck and it was all Linda's idea. The morning they ended up at the Andersons the same time as Galen and Elizabeth, she'd made a joke about it being block party time and ever since then she had wondered why they had never done something like that.

But now she realized that there had been too many strained relationships. Emily Caine herself—hard to realize that woman was her mother-in-law—caused a strain on any gathering.

Charles and Mindy had been, *embarrassing* was the word that came to mind, to be around. Mindy always tried too hard to please Charles and never succeeded. But whatever had been the problem with them was completely gone. They seemed like newlyweds, looking at each other with special "we have a secret" looks.

Jenny Anderson was blossoming like spring flowers thrusting out of the snow. Linda had visited with her often and invited her over. She wasn't old enough to be Jenny's mother—well, maybe, if she'd had her very young—but she was filling a motherly role that was pleasant for them both.

Hattie was just plain fun these days, relaxed, always making jokes. Linda could tell that George enjoyed Hattie's company very much. And when she thought about it, Hattie was the closest thing to a real mother, a nurturing mother, that George ever had.

Harold and Lucy Fowler—*Uncle* Harold and *Aunt* Lucy—were always the same but they seemed much happier this past week.

It was time, everything was just right to begin having block parties at Tapestry Court.

George picked up the box of desserts and Linda grabbed the table cloths, Chinet dishes, and plastic ware. They left through the kitchen door.

"George, I have a question."

"Sure, what?"

"I was really getting worried about you the past few months. You seemed so distracted and almost worried. You don't seem that way anymore. What was it?"

He grinned. "To tell you the truth, I was worried about the future. I did my duty—everything I could to find the missing heir, including working with Galen and asking Elizabeth's help. But honestly I was scared. I thought when they found the Colonel's son I would be out of a job. And I didn't know how I would support you and the kids. And with college coming up in a few years . . . well, I was just scared."

Since her hands were full, she couldn't hug him, but she did lean her head over to caress his shoulder with her cheek. *I'll never let him know what I was scared about.* The very idea of George being in love with Elizabeth seemed silly now.

"Can we tell them tonight?" Mindy kissed her husband's neck as he sat at the table with the newspaper. The potato salad and baked beans were in the canvas carriers ready to take outside.

"Tell them what?"

She slapped his head playfully. "You know. About the baby."

Charles put the newspaper down. "I kind of hate to spoil Elizabeth and Galen's time in the spotlight."

"Oh." Mindy's face fell. "I hadn't thought about that."

"And George has already said that tonight would be a good time to tell everyone about your relationship with Bill Sinclair." He turned his chair around and pulled her down on his lap. "That might be enough exciting news for one evening."

Mindy put her arms around his neck, kissed his nose, and then each cheek, and then his forehead, and then his chin. Charles laughed.

"On the other hand, if you just can't hold it in, go for it."

Then Mindy kissed him on the mouth. And he kissed her back.

Hattie took the fruit salad and the 7 layer salad out of the refrigerator and laid them on a tray. She'd get Chuck to carry them out for her.

This was a good thing, this party. As she went to close the refrigerator door, she saw the bacon and a smile of satisfaction came to her face.

Bacon, I can cook you anyway I want now. Nobody's business but mine.

And Hattie burst into the chorus of "Happy Days Are Here Again."

Joel Anderson watched his wife cut sandwiches and put them neatly in little plastic bags. *So lovely. And all mine. I am a lucky man.*

As if she could read his thoughts, Jenny looked up at him and smiled. "I love you."

"I love you too." *Not lucky. Blessed. Thank you, Lord!*

Lucy Fowler was lifting a squash casserole out of the oven when the phone rang. While she answered, Harold took the cooler full of canned drinks to the front door. *Stationed!* He recently read some Vietnam era reminiscences and learned that in the military service things were stationed in readiness for removal elsewhere. So now he found himself stationing things instead of just putting them someplace.

This is a happy day. Good Spirit in the Court today. I guess that's you, huh Lord?

He chuckled at his own wit. He and Deity often shared little jokes.

"That was Lydia," Lucy announced as she came into the living room. "She is feeling wonderful and thinks she'd like to go out to lunch next time we come up. She said Stephen can now maneuver in and out of cars. I told her we'd try to work it out. But I'm sure Elizabeth won't want to go for the next few weeks. She'll be getting ready for her wedding and then on her honeymoon after that."

"I'm sure Linda would take us, but you remember that day at lunch after the funeral Mindy Simmons said she would be happy to take us anywhere we needed to go. I guess she just hadn't ever thought about it until she saw us riding with Elizabeth."

Lucy sighed. "Everything and everybody seems so nice these days. I'm not glad that Emily is dead but I have to admit . . ."

"Lucy!" Harold looked at his wife sternly.

She jerked her little chin up at him. "Okay I won't say it . . . but you know it's true anyway." And she marched off into the kitchen to get the casserole.

The trials of being a husband. But Harold Fowler smiled.

"You want to walk to the Tates a little early?" Elizabeth asked Galen. "I'm ready."

They were seated in their favorite spot at the table on the patio. He looked at his watch.

"We've got another fifteen minutes. Sometimes it's just as rude to be early as to be late."

"Well, I was thinking we might stop and check in on Jenny on our way."

"Oh, let's not. You have everything lined up for next weekend?"

Elizabeth settled back in her chair. She guessed Galen wanted to discuss their wedding instead of doing good deeds. "I think so. I ordered the cake from the bakery and they recommended a caterer who furnishes all the tables and decorations. I'm so glad we decided on a sit down dinner, even if it is going to be early." She winked at him, remembering his desire for everyone to leave them alone for most of the night.

They were going to spend their first night together here in Tapestry Court and then beginning that Sunday they had reservations for a week in a cabin at Loury's on the Lake.

"I've been meaning to ask you something." Galen looked at her with curiosity.

"What's that?"

"The last question on the list you showed me, something about the Tapestry theme having to do with the murder or mystery. What did you mean by that?"

Elizabeth smiled. "Well, I wasn't going to say anything but I had figured out who the son was. I knew it was George."

Galen looked shocked. "You did? How?"

"The Colonel's obsession with his initials. It crossed my mind once when I was looking at the T fountain in the park and it really hit me the time you said something about the notepads and towels all having a T on them."

"I don't see how that pointed to George."

"Chuck said something one day about Reggie being named after George—that his middle name is Reginald. Don't you see? GRT . . . George Reginald Tate. Guy Raymond Tapestry. The egomania of the man couldn't let his son bear a name that was not similar to his own in some way. Initials were very important to Colonel Tapestry."

Galen nodded thoughtfully. Then he grinned at her. "My almost wife is a pretty sharp cookie."

"I'm glad it all got straightened out without me having to bother Lucy about DNA testing." Elizabeth got up and pulled a weed out of the patio garden and looked back toward the lawn and walled garden. "I love this place."

Galen rose from his chair and went over to take her in his arms. "And I love you."

After a minute, he pulled away. "Okay, Bits. Time to go."

They went through the house and out the front door, down the walkway and through the front gate.

Elizabeth stopped abruptly at the sight in front of her. Tables gaily decorated with bunches of helium balloons in festive colors, some laid out with food, some with gifts, and some with place settings lined the walk. The gift table had a sign on the front of it that said "Congratulations, Galen and Elizabeth!" And lining the walkway were their smiling neighbors.

Elizabeth swallowed a large lump that formed in her throat. Their neighbors! *Thank you, Lord.*

Chuck was bored. The food was okay, but watching Elizabeth and Galen open all that stuff was boring. Who cared about stuff like glasses and silver pitchers and junk?

Just as he was wondering if anybody would get mad at him if he slipped in the house to watch TV, Elizabeth caught his attention.

"Chuck! I forgot. I had something I meant to bring you when I thought we were coming to your house. Your Dad said it was okay for you to have it. Do you want to go get it? The front door is unlocked and the box is right inside the library."

Something for him? This party was looking up.

"Sure!" He walked down the path and through the gate at a slow pace, aware that everyone was watching him. As soon as he got behind the trees he ran to the door of the

Manor House. Letting himself in, he turned to the right and entered the library.

A box sat on the floor near the door. A newspaper covered the top but when he lifted the paper, the miniature ships he so loved were all there, nestled together, waiting for him to set them sailing again. In the place of his choice. *For me? Mine?*

Mine!

Chuck Tate grinned the biggest grin ever. The best day of his life was the day that Elizabeth Daily came to Tapestry Court.

About Amy Barkman

Amy Barkman has been writing professionally for many years but just recently got serious about book publication. She has written a newspaper humor column that ran for several years, radio programs, musical plays, short stories and poetry. In 2011 her first book, a non-fiction practical guide to victorious Christian living *Everyday Spiritual Warfare* was released, and the first in the Fun To Be One Club midgrade series *Which Witch?* was released in 2012 by Next Step Books. Amy has been a member of the American Association of Christian Counselors since 1989, is a prayer minister with Messiah Ministries, pastor of Mortonsville United Methodist Church, and Co-Director with her husband, Gary, of Voice of Joy Ministries.

Visit Amy on the Web: www.voiceofjoy.com